SNARK

William L. DeAndrea
SNARK

THE MYSTERIOUS PRESS • New York

Printed in the United States of America
First Printing: October 1985
10 9 8 7 6 5 4 3 2 1

Library of Congress Cataloging in Publication Data

DeAndrea, William L.
  Snark.

  I. Title.
PS3554.E174S6   1985   813'.54   85-15245
ISBN O-89296-142-2

For Ann and George Papazoglou

WARNING—the only thing real about this book is England, which is as real as this foreigner could make it after living there for close to a year. I mention this because, dictionaries to the contrary, the notion seems to have taken hold that the less in a book that is actually made up by the author, the better fiction it is. Despite this, honesty compels me to admit that practically all of this book is pure invention—all characters, events, and organizations (except the KGB) are fictitious, and everything else is used fictitiously. Minor details of history, geography, and architecture have been changed when the story demanded it.

There is no Agency in the American Intelligence community; the British have no Section like the one described here. As I explained in *Cronus*, the preceding volume in this series, there is a committee of the U.S. House of Representatives similar to the one described here, and it has a chairman, but the character called the Congressman is in no way intended to portray anyone who has ever held that position.

The central idea for *Snark* was given to me by my wife, Orania Papazoglou, and I want to thank her for it, and for everything else.

Thanks are also due to Marian Babson, a longtime London Yankee who helped me in too many ways to enumerate.

—W.L.D.

"The rest of my speech" (he explained to his men)
    "You shall hear when I've leisure to speak it,
But the Snark is at hand, let me tell you again!
    'Tis your glorious duty to seek it!

"To seek it with thimbles, to seek it with care;
    To pursue it with forks and hope;
To threaten its life with a railway share;
    To charm it with smiles and soap!

"For the Snark's a peculiar creature, that won't
    Be caught in a commonplace way.
Do all that you know, and try all that you don't:
    Not a chance must be wasted to-day!"

—LEWIS CARROLL
The Hunting of the Snark
An Agony in Eight Fits (1876)
Fit the Fourth

FIRST

"Just the place for a Snark!" the Bellman cried,
  As he landed his crew with care;
Supporting each one on the top of the tide,
  By a finger entwined in his hair.

"Just the place for a Snark! I have said it twice:
  That alone should encourage the crew.
Just the place for a Snark! I have said it thrice:
  What I tell you three times is true."

—The Hunting of the Snark
Fit the First

1

He felt better once they started trying to kill him.

It settled a lot of things he'd been wondering about. It told him they had a long reach and it told him they were efficient to have caught up with him so quickly. It told him they were very thorough, and very smart, because as far as the young man with the suitcase could tell, they had every reason to believe they'd already *killed* Jeffrey Bellman. Two weeks ago, on Christmas day, in a deserted parking lot outside a holiday-empty shopping mall in the State of Maryland, just outside Washington.

Which, in a way, they had.

He didn't know yet if the men with the guns thought they were after the old Bellman or the new one. He didn't know if they were the same men who'd done such a good job back in the States. He didn't know who they were, or who was behind them.

If he got out of this alive, he'd take some time to worry about it.

The new Jeffrey Bellman could have taken the Concorde from Washington—he was on an unlimited expense account, and the Congressman could have arranged a seat in minutes— but Bellman preferred to travel on a British Airways 747. It was less obtrusive, for one thing. When you stake yourself out as bait, it doesn't pay to be *too* obvious about it. Make them work, see how keen they are to find you, how smart they are at it. He also preferred the slower trip because he wanted time to think. He wanted to see if he could find any excuse for having put himself in this mess. He was here because a dying man croaked two words—"Leo Calvin." And there was no way he could afford to ignore that.

3

Less than eighteen months ago he'd been in a position to walk out on his father, walk out on the Agency for good, and make it stick. Now he was back in it, up to his neck. Jeffrey Bellman's neck. The replacement for the smashed throat of the man who'd been found in the parking lot. That neck.

Because he *wasn't* Jeffrey Bellman, any more than the agent who'd been wearing the name when he died. He wasn't Bellman, just as he hadn't been Harry Dekker, or Clifford Driscoll, or any of the two dozen or so other names people had known him by during the last thirteen years.

It occurred to him just after the plane took off that outside the Agency, he wasn't anybody. That had been enough thinking on *that* subject. He spent the rest of the trip looking out the window at the tops of clouds glowing in the wing lights. The plane had been hours delayed taking off—one of those sudden winter blizzards that sweep through Washington—and Bellman could have used the sleep, but he denied himself the luxury. He wouldn't sleep in the presence of another human being. Too dangerous. If they're going to take you, let them take you with your eyes open.

It was late when he landed in London, so late all the airport shops had closed. Aside from his fellow passengers, the only people around were airport staff—sweepers, customs officers, chars.

The red-faced man behind the desk at Passport Control seemed glad of the company. He took Bellman's passport, looked at it, decided it was genuine. It was arguable whether it was or not. It came from the United States Government, but the State Department didn't know anything about it, and wouldn't unless somebody got interested enough in Jeffrey Bellman to check back that far. The Congressman would hear about it in ample time, and take steps.

It shouldn't come to that, though, Bellman thought. The photo matches the printed description, and they both match my face—age 31, hair brown, eyes blue. The eyes were a legacy from the previous Jeffrey Bellman; in the interest of continuity the current one had been fitted with extended-wear blue lenses. He was supposed to take them out every two weeks to clean them. He hoped it would be less than two weeks before he could

4

finish this assignment (whatever it turned out to be), junk the lenses, and go back to his own horn-rims over his own feeble brown eyes.

The signature matched the one on the card he'd signed on the plane. The red-faced man gave the passport and the card a quick expert glance as he made small talk.

"How long do you plan to stay in the United Kingdom, Mr. Bellman?"

"Not entirely sure. About two weeks." Bellman risked a sheepish grin. "Want to be back in the States in time for the Super Bowl."

"It's on telly here, you know, if you can't get back in time."

"Live?" Bellman knew all about it. He supposed he was doing this for practice.

"Yes. On Channel Four. It'll be in the papers."

"Thanks," Bellman said. "Thanks a lot."

"My pleasure," the official said grandly. "Purpose of visit?"

"Business."

"I see. Terrible weather for a holiday, isn't it?"

"Better than what I left in Washington."

"All right, sir," he said. He stamped the passport and the card. "You've a visa for six months. Enjoy your stay."

Bellman smiled, nodded, moved on. He heard the red-faced man start his spiel to the lady who'd been behind him in line. He went downstairs, picked up his suitcase, got waved through Customs (they were only stopping Asians, apparently), and came out into the concourse of Terminal Three. He'd been told some-one would meet him, but there was no one there to meet anyone. Just sweepers and chars.

A mixup. They happened. British Intelligence probably had someone waiting for him to get off a British Caledonian flight down at Gatwick. He had a telephone number he could ring to check, but he could do that from his hotel.

He considered taking a cab, but decided against it. He was back in London after a long absence—he might as well reac-quaint himself with the public transportation. He had made a promise to himself long ago that the first thing he'd do whenever he got to a new town would be to learn all the different ways to leave if it became necessary.

5

Bellman looked at his watch. Twelve o'clock. If he hurried, he could make the tube into town before it closed down for the night. He picked up his suitcase, shrugged his shoulders more comfortably into his overcoat, and walked briskly to the escalator outside Terminal Two, where he could get the moving walkway to the entrance of the London Underground.

The in-flight magazine had called it Alphabet Way. It was a long corridor, not brightly lit, with a ceiling that looked low because the hallway was so wide. Along each wall was a moving strip of black rubber, about six feet wide. Only one of them was going at the moment, the one on the left. Bellman was grateful for the small break—it was the one he needed. The other was closed down for maintenance work, and two guys in overalls— one with a blond crew cut and an earring, and a dark-skinned fellow with a long beard and a turban—were working on it in the dim light.

Bellman hopped on the walkway, and added his own best speed to that of the strip. He compared alphabets as he went. To his left, the wall was decorated with the names of cities around the world (. . . Lisbon . . . Manila . . . New York . . .); across the corridor was an alphabetical list of cities in Britain (. . . Leeds . . . Manchester . . . Neasden). Bellman made a mental note to find out what British city with an airport in it began with X, but never followed through.

The first bullet dotted the "I" in Manila. The second hit the rim of the crater made by the first one. The silenced guns sounded like basenjis. They yipped twice more, but Bellman didn't see where they landed. His father hadn't spent all those years training him for nothing—with the first impact, he hit the deck.

Unfortunately, the deck was moving him along rapidly to the end of the walkway. Bellman could hear running footsteps. One of the maintenance men was running to meet him. Bellman was beginning to feel like a carcass on a slaughterhouse conveyor.

All right. He'd been waiting for them to try it. He just hadn't figured on their being so good.

Bellman had no gun. There are ways of getting guns past airport security, but none of them is foolproof except taking the weapons through under diplomatic seal. Bellman wasn't posing as a diplomat this trip, so that was out. His hosts were supposed to arm him on his arrival if they thought he needed it.

Well, by God, I need it, he thought. I just don't have it.

By now his brain was making it clear to him what he was up against. If he followed his first instinct, and got to his feet, his head was bound to pop up above the metal handrail like a duck in a shooting gallery. If he managed to avoid that, and stay in a crouch, he was still moving rapidly toward grief in the person of the man (his footsteps had passed Bellman now) running to head him off. Running the other way was out of the question. Running against the motion of the pedway, especially in a crouch, would put him in the same boat with Alice and the Red Queen—it would take all the running he could do to stay in the same place. All attempting it would gain him would be the privilege of being shot in the back instead of in the belly.

He could, of course, get up and jump clean over the barrier, but that was worse than useless. He'd be naked to their guns, and dead in ten seconds. Or less.

Bellman wasted a split-second being angry at himself for not sleeping on the plane. If he'd gotten a little rest, he might have been more alert.

Above him the alphabet sped by. Paris . . . Quito . . . Last stop, hell, thank you for flying British Airways.

Bellman shook it off and forced himself to think. He almost laughed when he realized he had a chance. Not much of a chance. Just enough to keep him scrambling, to pass his last few moments in action rather than in resignation and fear.

Bellman threw out his arms and legs like a starfish, pressing against the wall and the barrier, trying to stop himself. He was slowing down a little, but he was still sliding. . . . Rio de Janeiro . . . Singapore . . . Bellman was beginning to wish he *was* a starfish, with suckers to stick him in place. A seam in the smooth metal of the barrier tore most of the nail off the ring finger of his right hand as he went by. It hurt like mad, but it gave him an idea.

He'd been doing this the wrong way. He pulled arms and legs in, then rolled and twisted until his body was alongside the barrier. When he came to the next seam he got as good a grip as he could with his fingernails and pressed the toes of his shoes against the next one. It brought him to a precarious stop under the "E" of Singapore, caused as much by tension and balance of forces as any actual grip he had on the metal.

He could feel heat building up on his right shoulder and hip from friction with the walkway. He felt a thump on his back that almost jarred him loose. His suitcase had finally caught up with him—he'd thrown it backward when he dropped.

Bellman didn't want to risk changing his position, but he had to. Carefully, he took the toe of his left shoe away from the crack, then raised and drew back his left leg and kicked the barrier.

Too soft. He'd hardly made any noise at all. The idea was to kick the metal with his top leg hard enough to advertise his presence without jarring his right leg loose from its nearly nonexistent toehold.

He tried again, producing a fairly respectable thump, then again, a little harder, then over and over, rhythmically. He was trying to make it sound as if he'd gotten tangled in the machinery.

Now he needed luck. A lot of it. The only thing he had going for him was the fact that his playmates couldn't know he wasn't armed. Otherwise, the man at the end of the walkway could simply step around the barrier and shoot Bellman at leisure. Bellman hoped he'd remain prudent, and wait at the end in ambush.

He also hoped the other one would get curious at the thumping and come peek over the barrier to see what was what. He might do that anyway when Bellman failed to appear anytime soon after his suitcase, but the thumping was to tell the man where to look. He had to be where Bellman could grab him, smash his throat, take his gun, and deal with the one at the end, or all this effort, to say nothing of blisters and broken nails, would be for nothing.

It eventually worked. Unfortunately, the wrong one got curious. Looking down the pedway past his feet, Bellman saw one of his playmates appear. It was the Sikh. A beautiful white grin appeared in the middle of his beard. Bellman saw the gun go up.

Then a strange thing happened. The smile disappeared, and

the gun kept rising, as though the man were taking aim at something past Bellman, something unexpected.

A witness, Bellman thought. Some poor slob has wandered by, and he dies first.

Bellman winced as he heard the shot. He waited for the next one, the one he'd never hear.

Then he realized he shouldn't have heard the first one. At least not as a sharp crack. These guys were using silencers.

He looked again to the end of the pedway. The bearded man was down, his turban caught in the meshes of the moving sidewalk, twisting his head around at painful-looking angles. His gun kept bumping into his outstretched fingers, then bouncing away.

Bellman got to his feet. An angry voice said, "Stay down!" A woman's voice. Bellman crouched and looked back up the walkway to the source of the sound.

What appeared to be a Typical Young British Housewife was crouched below the barrier back at about Djakarta. She wore a plaid skirt, a light-colored wool sweater, a short coat, boots, and a dark scarf over shiny hair. Colors were hard to make out in the dim light. She had an American-made Colt .38 calibre shortnosed police special in her hand.

Bellman reached Zanzibar. He scooped up the Sikh's gun just before the pedway dumped him off, jumped over the body, and hid where the barrier ended. He looked around.

The crew cut was coming to check out the strange happenings behind the barrier. Better late than never, Bellman thought.

"Over here," Bellman said. He stepped out from behind the barrier. The crew cut whirled on him. He snapped off a shot that missed.

Bellman smiled. He didn't know he did that when he aimed a gun. In back of his target, though, the woman rose up from behind the barrier. She held the gun in two hands, like a professional. She fired it that way too. The maintenance man pitched forward on his nose. Blood oozed out from under his face, and a second later from under his chest.

The woman was clambering over the barrier, and having a little trouble because of her high boots. Bellman decided it would only be gallant to help her.

He took her by the arm and got her over the barrier. Even through coat and sweater he could feel strong muscles.

"Thank you," she said, safe on a floor that didn't move.

"Thank *you*," Bellman said.

"Are they dead?"

"They will be soon. If we want to clean up anything here, we'd better start moving."

"That won't be necessary. This gun is traceable to the IRA."

She had a West Country accent, the kind Long John Silver had in the movies. In her low, sweet voice, it was charming. "If you'd come along with me . . . ?"

"Sure," Bellman said. "Who are you?"

"Felicity Grace."

Right, Bellman thought, and mine's Bond. James Bond.

"And you are Mr. Bellman," she said. He gave her the password for the week and proved it. She not only gave him the countersign ("green lilacs"), she showed him credentials that would have embarrassed British Intelligence if the maintainence men had won that particular scrum.

But then, saving some important BI people from embarrassment was what his trip was all about.

"Let's go," he said.

"Just a second," Felicity Grace said. She picked up the other gun. "You can keep the one you've got if you like," she said, then led the way out to her car.

2

"Hungry?" she asked.

"As a matter of fact, yes. But it's too late to do anything about it, isn't it? I was hoping there'd be vending machines in the hotel." They'd been instructed to book him into the Kennedy

Hotel near Euston Station, an American-style place with a vengeance. The idea was to blend in with the businessmen and off-season package-tourists.

"I don't think it would be a good idea for you to keep your reservation."

"Tonight would probably be safe. Whoever sent our friends to the airport will probably wait till morning to see what happened before trying again."

"Mmm-hmm," she said. She was watching for the turn onto the Hammersmith Bridge; wherever she was taking him was either on the south side of the Thames, or was best approached that way.

Bellman could also tell she didn't come this way too frequently, and had to concentrate on intersections. He didn't want to distract her—just being on the road in Britain made him nervous enough. It wasn't so much driving on the wrong side, and it wasn't even the powerless feeling of being in the left front seat with no controls in front of him. It was seeing the other cars coming with no apparent drivers. It was irrational, and after a few days it didn't bother him, but tonight it was there, and it was strong. So he was delighted to let her concentrate.

He used the lull to study her. Not pretty, not really. Her nose was a little long and her chin was a little short, and there was something about her eyes that suggested sorrow and anger without really being either.

Her coloring, what he could tell from streetlamps and the headlights of oncoming lorries, was something special. The sad/angry eyes were bright blue, the color of a postcard sky, and the hair under the kerchief was a smooth helmet of copper. The fringe over her forehead accentuated the forlorn look of her face—it was as though she were looking up at the world, not expecting anything especially pleasant.

She was tall. Standing beside her at the airport, Bellman had noted that the top of her head was level with his eyes. Allow two inches for heels, and that still made her five-nine or better. She was slender, but she had what an old English associate of his father's—Bellman's father didn't have friends—would have been pleased to call "a fine chest for medals."

She had clear, smooth skin, which was common among British

11

women, and once, when she smiled, Bellman could see she had a set of white, even teeth, which was not.

They were on a narrow road of houses and stores now. There was a lot of traffic, more, really, than would be allowed to travel at this speed in the States. He wondered idly where it all was going to or coming from—it was after eleven o'clock, and he *knew* nothing in London was open.

"I think we can do better for you than a vending machine," she said, the tricky maneuver successfully completed.

"Somebody's opened a twenty-four-hour IHOP in London?"

"I know what that is," she said. "International House of Pancakes. I went to university in the United States."

"Oh? Where?"

"Syracuse University. I have given up trying to teach people here not to say the University of Syracuse."

Bellman, of course, was free to believe as much of this as he liked. Still, he played along. She had a pleasant voice, and it passed the time.

"What did you study?" he asked.

"Computer design."

"Hardware or software?"

"Software. Electronics defeats me completely."

"I'm surprised they let you do fieldwork," he said.

He could feel the temperature drop about half a degree. Perhaps he had been Questioning Her Competence. This was the famous English Reserve sliding into place.

Bellman could fix it easily enough—all he had to do was decide if he thought it was worth the effort. He supposed it was—before he was done he was going to stir up a lot of friction with his British colleagues, and their competence or lack thereof was the issue. No need to rush into it. Besides, she had been better than competent back at the pedway.

Bellman kept talking. "You're too valuable. Someday agents will be obsolete. Intelligence will be all satellites and computers." And, Bellman thought, that day won't come a second too soon for me.

"Thank you," she said. "My Section Head—acting head of the whole business at the moment, actually—keeps telling me the same thing. I prefer fieldwork."

"That's Mr. Tipton, correct?"

"Yes, he'll be briefing you tomorrow. I'm to ask you if three o'clock will be all right."

"It will be fine, as long as you're taking me someplace I can get some sleep."

"Well, I will, of course. I thought you were hungry."

"Yes. Food. Sleep. We Americans have very basic urges."

She laughed at that, a low, knowing laugh that made Bellman look again. The sexiest women were not always the prettiest women. Hardly ever, in fact. He filed the laugh away for further study.

"Well, there's an all-night restaurant in Fulham—the only one I know in London, actually, if you feel like crossing the river again. . . ."

"Or?"

"Or we'll stop at my flat, and I'll make you some real English pancakes."

"Where do I sleep? On the couch?"

"No, Mr. Bellman, you sleep in Bloomsbury in a guest flat my Section keeps vacant for just such situations as these."

"Ah. Does it have central heating? Television?"

"I thought you Americans had only basic urges."

"I didn't say only. Don't tell me. A shilling meter and a tube radio."

"No. Heating, telly, *and* an American-style shower stall. All mod cons."

"I'll take it."

"Good. Now Fulham, or homemade pancakes?"

"Pancakes," Bellman said.

They were driving up a wide road now, with one each of all the chain stores in Britain—Marks and Spencer, Pizzaland, Presto, McDonald's. The neighborhood High Street. It sloped gently toward a major intersection, then the stores stopped, but the hill continued.

Felicity Grace made a sharp right turn across four empty traffic lanes and into a driveway. "Good," she said, "we're here."

He had forgotten about English pancakes. He looked down at a plate of what appeared to be half-sautéed plastic doilies, doused them with lemon juice and sugar, and cut himself a wedge. It was good, egg-smooth and butter-rich, and it fit very nicely into the empty places in his stomach.

"Coffee?" Felicity Grace asked.

"No thanks. I hope to get some sleep before I see your guvnor."

She smiled again. He'd been hoping to see it. "My boss. You've been here before, I see. It isn't in your file."

"Good pancakes," he said, taking another wedge.

"I'll make you some tea," she said.

"That would be nice."

She put a kettle on to boil, went to the sink, and began warming a porcelain teapot decorated with blue flowers.

"You don't have to go to all that trouble," Bellman told her. "You didn't have to go to all *this* trouble." He tapped his fork on the plate.

"No trouble. I want some tea as well, and I don't like tea bags."

Bellman watched her as he ate. She looked so ordinary and domestic in her scarf and fringe and flat shoes (no heels—make her five-ten), spooning tea, and pouring gold-top Channel Islands milk into a creamer, all the while humming a little hum to herself like Winnie-the-Pooh, it was hard to believe that she was really *in* it, that she played the game professionally and full-time.

She was even good at it. He knew that not just from the way she'd saved him from their friends at the airport—there were plenty of women who could shoot straight, and some who could be relied upon to drop the hammer even when the target was meat instead of paper.

It was that little business about his *file*. It was dropped so casually, and in such a matter-of-fact tone of voice, that Bellman came damned close to responding. Which would have been a mistake.

There was no way any information about any previous trips made by "Jeffrey Bellman" (no matter who he was at the moment) should have made its way into BI files. His predecessor had been assigned, but had never had a chance to report to his hosts. And when the man eating pancakes at Felicity Grace's

14

woodgrain Formica kitchen table had been in England before, his name hadn't been Jeffrey Bellman or anything like it.

No, the file business had been an attempt at learning something about him, so simple and so blatant it had almost worked. Bellman decided he had to keep an eye on this woman.

"One lump or two?" Felicity Grace wanted to know. She put the tray down on the table and sat opposite him. Her eyes were darker blue seen straight on.

"Two," Bellman said. She put them in his cup with tongs, gave herself one, and poured out.

There was a cold mist outside softening the few lights that could be seen outside the window. Most of them surrounded a low modern rectangle of a building set back from the ridge of the road. He asked her what it was.

"South Thames College," she said. "Putney campus. I used to teach there sometimes."

Bellman raised a brow. "Pistol shooting, no doubt."

She shook her head. "Programming. It was a cover job, basically, but I liked the work. Some of the students—when they see what's possible, and how big the field is going to be, it's like the world changes for them overnight. I taught one boy whose family have been on the dole since the early nineteen-fifties. Found him a job. She poured a little more hot tea into her cup and took a sip. "It's not much, but it's something."

"Mmm," Bellman said. "Well, I'm glad you weren't teaching a class tonight."

"No fear of that," she said. "I have—how did we say it at university?—my priorities on straight. The teaching was just so the estate agent wouldn't think I earn the rent money as a tart. I work for the main cover company now. It's the Section first, last, and always, for me."

Bellman looked at her. That last sentence was grim enough, and sincere enough, to be true.

"How did you come to be following me, though?" he asked. "I thought you were supposed to be meeting the plane."

"I was. I even came in fancy dress as a housewife to make it look good. But then I saw our two friends. Maintenance men have too strong a union to work on that sort of non-emergency repair that late at night, for a start. And they don't show so much interest in the arriving flights announcements. After the third time one of them came out to check, I began to get an itch, if you'll pardon me."

"I know exactly what you mean."

"There was something I remembered about a Sikh heavy from the briefing book. So I rang the Section and described them, and got back the information that they often worked together. And they weren't particular for whom.

"I decided to wait near the information booth, to meet you when you came to have them page the person who was supposed to meet you. I though we'd just leave another way, and not use the pedway at all."

"I never thought of paging you," Bellman admitted. "I just thought there'd been a mess-up somewhere. I went for the tube."

"I decided eventually you must have done, and took out after you." She leaned over the table close to him. "Have I developed any gray hairs?"

"None visible."

"Surprising. Especially after the way I felt after I heard the silenced guns."

"So you came and delivered some gunfire of your own. And eliminated two problems for Scotland Yard."

"Yes," she said, finishing her tea. "I hope they never get the chance to thank me. The bloody Provos can have all the credit." She covered a yawn with a ladylike pat of her hand.

"I *beg* your pardon," she said.

"Don't mention it. I feel the same way. Maybe you'd better take me to where I'm supposed to sleep."

She looked at her watch. It was a man's watch, but the strap was shiny leather, blue with red and white trim. "Yes, we'd better, if you're the type who needs it dark outside when he goes to sleep."

She brought him to a white row house on a small square in Bloomsbury, not far from the British Museum. He had the whole top floor. It was all she had promised, and more—all mod cons *plus* a huge remote-controlled color TV and a video cassette recorder, identical, in fact, to the kind of equipment Felicity Grace had crowding the sitting room of her flat in Putney. The only thing she had that his hosts hadn't provided him had been an Apple III personal computer.

It also had three hidden microphones and two hidden cameras, but that was to be expected. Another test. Bellman found them all within twelve minutes of his chauffeur's leaving.

"What time shall I knock you up?" she'd asked.

Bellman forebore to make the obvious (to an American) joke. "About two?" he suggested.

"Let's make it two-thirty," Felicity Grace said. "The Acting Director likes a long lunch."

"Even better," Bellman said. They shook hands (hers was very warm), she left. He found the mikes and the cameras, said hello into each of them, took a shower, went to bed. He spent thirty seconds fighting off a sudden wave of why-am-I-doing-this panic before, with an exercise of will, he cleared his mind and went to sleep.

3

"Quite a single-minded young man then," the Acting Section Chief said.

"I certainly wasn't able to distract him," Felicity Grace said. "I gave him every opportunity short of stripping off or grabbing him by the w—"

"Don't be vulgar," the ASC said, but he smiled all the same. His name (at least within these walls) was Robert Tipton. He was a medium-sized man, with a large wave of gray hair splashing over a smooth brow. He always wore a dark pinstripe suit and a flower in his buttonhole. He talked posh; no one knew whether that was natural or acquired. The Americans, particularly the Congressman, the boss of the young man who was waiting to be shown in, considered him tough, competent, and, more important—*most* important—trustable. The Congressman's word, that. Trustable. Not trustworthy.

"Hell," the American chief had drawled over the scrambled phone last week. "My cleaning lady is trustworthy. She's worthy of it, but would she know what to do with it, that's the question, ain't it?"

The implication being, of course, that this Section (and this Section alone, for all Tipton knew), and by extension Tipton himself, and his missing predecessor, *did* know what to do with it.

It bothered Tipton enormously that he should be flattered by all that.

Flattered, perhaps, but not happy. Because there was a balls-up in progress, a colossal one, and the Americans had deigned to send someone to put things to rights. Which, of course, he might well be able to do. Tipton had his doubts. There was a factor involved that the Americans didn't know about. And never *would* know about, if Tipton had his way.

It was galling. During the '39–'45 war, British Intelligence had been the wonder workers, the can-do men of the hour. They had broken Enigma. They had conceived and executed the Man-Who-Never-Was gambit. But since. Philby. MacLean. Burgess. Blount. The others. The young fool who'd walked to the door of the Russian Embassy just a short time ago, offering himself to the Russians, hurt because they hadn't approached him yet.

And now the labor problems. Problems for the whole Kingdom, of course, but special problems for the Section. The need for permission from the Americans before they could lower their zips to piss. The imposition of a single-minded young American wet nurse for them.

"Felicity," Robert Tipton said. He looked carefully at her face for the flicker of resentment that used to cross it whenever he called her by that ridiculous name. It was no longer there—the flicker, that is, not the resentment. Tipton was sure she still hadn't forgiven him for welcoming her back to the Section by christening her with a name from a yellowback thriller. But it had been important, considering her departure, and the reason for her return two years later, to test her discipline, quickly and continuously.

Besides, Tipton thought, he was tired of an entire agency peopled with individuals named James Hampstead, or Emma Lewis, or Robert Tipton, for that matter. When it fell to him to assign new names, he decided to let his spies *sound* like spies.

It was whimsical, yes. He'd been warned against it, but had argued successfully that it was a potent psychological defense. A Russian would not believe a British agent would *have* a name like Felicity Grace, and would hesitate to accept indications to the contrary. He did promise not to name anyone Sexton Blake.

"Yes, sir?" Felicity said.

Tipton looked over pictures of the young American. Bellman yawning. Bellman stepping into the shower. Bellman sleeping. Bellman giving the camera a rude, one-finger salute upon arriving.

"He's quite tasty, isn't he?" the director inquired.

"If you like the type," Felicity said.

Tipton smiled. He did indeed like the type, that was no secret. After university, when he'd joined this section, he had taken measures, many of them unsettling and some of them positively humiliating, to see to it no one learned of his homosexuality. It affected his work—no one can function efficiently alternating between fear and resentment.

So young Mr. Tipton had come to terms with himself. Being a spy was not as important as being himself. He would take no extraordinary steps to hide his "shame." At the same time, he would do nothing to endanger his country's interests. He was not, after all, a fool. He was not promiscuous, wasn't hopping into bed with some blond thing off an East German freighter at any opportunity. He had a small circle of friends who thought he worked for a publisher of art and photography books. His sexual partners came from that circle.

The Cambridge mess, all the messes that grew from it, really, changed his approach. Within a week after the story broke, Tipton had walked into the old man's office and offered his resignation.

"What the bloody hell is this?" Sir Lewis had demanded. As usual when he was excited, his bald pate glowed red, and the

Cockney accent he'd grown up speaking grew thick enough to be perceptible. "The world is coming down around our bloody heads, Arabs and Russians and all laughing at us, and you're handing in your bloody resignation!"

"I thought it best," Tipton said. "Especially now."

"Now? Oh, that's bloody champion. First, we find out we've been done by a couple of Cambridge queers—"

"Sir, I am a Cambridge queer."

"Oh," Sir Lewis had said. His jowls bubbled with repressed comments. Finally, he said, "You're not queer for any Russians, are you?"

Tipton had smiled in spite of himself. "No, sir. One hundred percent British made, as it were."

His chief sat back and looked at him. "Would you mind giving us their names? Submitting to a check? Tests? Polygraph? Pentathol?"

"If you like."

"I don't like. I bloody hate it. But if I'm going to keep you, it's got to be done, hasn't it? I am bloody well not going to lose you at this stage."

"Yes, sir."

"And Robert, don't seduce any of the help. Things are complicated enough."

Felicity Grace said, "Sir?"

"Oh, yes, Felicity, I'm sorry. What is it?"

"Mr. Bellman. Shall I show him in now? Or is there anything else you'd like me to tell you?"

"No, send him in, by all means."

"Yes, sir," she said. "Shall I stay?"

"That won't be necessary. Arrange a visitor's badge for him. You can show him around when I'm done."

"Very well, sir."

Tipton watched her go. Remarkable young woman. She'd even remembered to pull the door to when she left, something none of his other subordinates ever seemed to grasp.

Tipton was treading a very narrow path for this operation—if an operation was what it could be called. He had to have Mr. Bellman's assistance—the Americans called the tune here, and they said he had to have it. On the other hand, there was

20

altogether too much Mr. Bellman might find out. Things that
would work—what was the phrase they'd used during the
War—to "the detriment of the Alliance."

He would need to keep Mr. Bellman distracted. Miss Grace
would be better able to distract him for not knowing she was
supposed to.

Felicity Grace was still wearing the flat-heeled high boots, and
the hair was still the same—copper-colored, straight, and
smooth, long fringe—but in between, she might have been a
different woman. She wore a severe dark gray suit and a white
blouse. The only touch of color was a light green scarf at the
neck.

Her whole posture and attitude were different—she was more
aggressive; she seemed to have a sharper edge. The Rising
Woman Executive.

Bellman wanted to smile. It was the nature of the work; one
chameleon rarely got a chance to see another before and after
the transformation. Without anything like a disguise, Felicity
Grace had become a different woman.

It was even apparent in her voice when she told him Mr.
Tipton would like to see him now. The accent was still West
Country—dropped h's, round i's, strong, almost nasal r's—but it
was a BBC, West Country accent, Londonized, with the edge
taken off.

She told him to have the secretary ring for her when he was
through, and showed him into Tipton's office.

"Ah, Mr. Bellman," Tipton said. "How nice to have you
here."

"My pleasure," Bellman said, and Tipton started to laugh.

The Congressman had told Bellman that Tipton was famous
for throwing people off their guard. So he was careful. "It's nice
to find you in such a good mood," he said.

"Yes, I suppose I am, now." Tipton came out from behind his
desk and offered a hand. The grip was dry, firm, and friendly.
Bellman had been especially briefed about that handshake, by
his father. The Congressman was one of the most un-naive men
in the world, but he had his blind spots, and an inability to avoid

being amazed by homosexuals who were not effeminate was one of them.

Bellman turned down cigarettes, cigars, brandy, and accepted a chair. It wasn't especially comfortable—this office, it seemed, had been designed to discourage long conferences.

"I'll tell you frankly, Mr. Bellman, that I have been in a wretched mood since this business started. But then, it's always a relief to have the lies out of the way, isn't it?

"It is *not* nice to have you here, and I doubt sincerely that it is any sort of pleasure for you to be here. This whole mess, and your part in it, can only be a reminder that you—and by you, I mean the Congressman, and the American Intelligence community in general—consider British Intelligence to be a collection of overeducated upper-class twits who will leap at any opportunity to betray you—and ourselves, if it comes to that—to the other side. We make a balls-up of everything we touch, and if it weren't for your needing Scotland to put atomic missiles in, you'd cut us loose altogether." He stopped to take a breath. "Isn't that the way the talk runs in Washington?"

"It's pretty accurate," Bellman conceded. "We make exceptions. This Section, for instance."

"Thank you," Tipton said sardonically.

Bellman ignored it. "Also, the Congressman applauds your efforts—specifically Sir Lewis's efforts—to straighten out the pipeline-to-Russia problem once and for all. The Congressman has the highest regard for Sir Lewis and for you. May I see his file?"

"I have it ready for you. After you look at it, Miss Grace will show you around the building. We've arranged your cover—you represent an American company that is thinking of obtaining an interest in Tournament Press. That will explain your coming and going, and any meetings we might have."

"Fine with me," Bellman said. "Since Sir Lewis is also on the books as a director, it will give me a legitimate reason to ask questions about him."

"Of course," Tipton said. "If you like, I have a rough draft of his report to the Cabinet for you."

"Good. When was the final report supposed to be ready?"

"The PM was expecting it in a month's time. Ten February."

"Good. Maybe we can find Sir Lewis, and get him back alive in time to deliver it."

4

Tipton leaned forward over his desk. "That is the object of the exercise, isn't it? The safe return of Sir Lewis Alfot."

The object of the exercise, Bellman thought, is Sir Lewis's report, and that won't be worth the trouble if it doesn't work. Tipton knew that. Bellman just said, "Of course."

The Acting Section Chief seemed to appreciate it. He picked up a blue folder and handed it across the desk, then went to the window to look out at Bloomsbury while Bellman read.

It opened, as they always did, with relevant photos. Sir Lewis Alfot. Bald, gray fringe. Gray eyes. Five feet ten inches (1.79 m.) tall, thirteen stone (83 kg.) in weight, stocky build. Born, 1920. Good health. Scar along back from German shrapnel during WWII. Movement of right shoulder and arm limited as a result.

Except for the exact location of the scar (right trapezius muscle, then along back), Bellman learned nothing from the file his father hadn't told him before he left Washington. This meant one of two things—either the Congressman's files were as good as he always bragged they were, or Tipton and company were keeping things from him.

The file had all the facts—Sir Lewis had been born in poverty in South London, but when he was about ten years old his father (Sidney Alfot, died under a buzz bomb in December, 1944) had opened a printing shop, got a lot of Labour Party business, parlayed that into a chain of shops, and made a whole lot of money.

Lewis had ridden the money to public school and to university—none of the best, of course, but enough to see him into World War II as a second lieutenant in the army.

The young Alfot had been a natural soldier. Just how natural could be seen from his rapid rise through the ranks. In those days, class told many times more loudly than it did today, but the printer's son overcame the lingering prejudice against anyone who was "in trade" and advanced through the ranks. A battlefield commission made him a first lieutenant. An exploit in 1940 led to a decoration and another promotion. Lieutenant Alfot had taken command of his outfit when the last officer above him had been killed, and led his men through miles of German-held France in time to make the last boat from Dunkirk. Questions were asked in Parliament about why Alfot had not been awarded the Victoria Cross. There was a transcript in the file. The MP pushing for the award quoted one of Alfot's men as saying, "We never would have made it without him—the senior officers didn't have a ruddy clue."

That, Bellman thought, probably did in the whole project right there. It was not politic to criticize dead officers, no matter how few clues they had. Alfot himself disowned the effort, and went on with his work.

His work until May, 1944 was Intelligence. His Labour contacts helped him coordinate with (and keep an eye on) Russian Intelligence efforts. It also brought him into contact with American Intelligence agents, among them, Bellman's father. There was a note next to the Congressman's name and a file number. It occurred to Bellman it might be interesting to have a look at that file.

He gave his mind back to Sir Lewis. Alfot was a colonel by the time he parachuted back into France to coordinate Resistance efforts for the D-Day invasion. He won more medals before an artillery shell ended the war for him just around the time the Battle of the Bulge was getting hot. They sent him back to London in time to bury his father.

He stayed in the army after the war, working mostly in Berlin, until retiring in 1950, a thirty-year-old brigadier, whose pension was paid to veterans charities.

After that the story split off. To the public Sir Lewis (knighted in 1960, ostensibly for his charitable works) was the kind of figure the press in Britain takes very little time to start calling "beloved." He ran his father's business benevolently, but efficiently—his was the only large printing firm in Britain never to have been hurt by a strike. He endowed scholarships for working class youngsters of promise. He sponsored America's Cup challengers. He saved bankrupt football clubs, earning the undying gratitude of local supporters. He stayed resolutely aloof from party politics, and so was the ideal man to serve on commissions.

Sir Lewis Alfot served on commissions on who got the third broadcast channel. He served on commissions on working conditions, and who got to live where. His voice was sought out whenever there was a question that divided along class lines, which was practically everything in postwar Britain. He always responded with what the people (who loved him and trusted him) perceived as "plain common sense," and what the government felt it could live with.

Sir Lewis never married. He lived quietly and simply, first in London, now in retirement in Sussex.

"Keeping bees, no doubt," Bellman muttered.

Tipton begged his pardon, but Bellman waved it off and kept reading.

So the public face of Sir Lewis Alfot was an open book. In fact, there had been a book about him called *The Uncommon Common Man* ("not a Section project—see file 9704-A") that recorded it for the world to see.

The other half of his life had been the Section. The Section had been his own idea, and he'd fought to get it put through. It was to be a small, largely independent, wide-ranging group that would work avenues not usually worked by the Intelligence establishment in Britain (the upper-class Oxbridge twits Tipton had referred to). He would draw his operatives from wherever he could find them, and he would use his own wide personal acquaintance and experience to make things work.

He muscled approval through, but hardly any budget. He subsidized the Section for years out of his own pocket. But he had one thing going for him that became more important as the years went by and the scandals mounted—the Americans found him "trustable." It was a reality of the postwar world that there was damn little Britain could do without at least the tacit support of the Americans.

So the section had grown, in power more than in size, and prospered in effectiveness as the rest of Britain faltered. Then, the first PM since Churchill whom Sir Lewis (despite his past ties to Labour) truly approved of took office and started turning things around.

Which made Sir Lewis so happy, he decided to retire.

Bellman frowned. That was the way the file would have you read it, but Bellman wanted a closer look before he bought it.

Then last week, in the midst of his latest and farthest-reaching undercover operation (and in the midst of a charity drive to aid relatives of the victims of a killer the popular press was calling the "Sussex Cyclops"), Sir Lewis had disappeared.

The file ended with the words TO BE APPENDED . . . TO BE APPENDED . . .

"To be appended," Bellman said, closing the file and flipping it back to Tipton's desk. "I'll say. What's the most popular theory?"

Tipton begged his pardon again. It was getting on Bellman's nerves. We were all supposed to be professionals around here.

"Sir Lewis disappeared off a sizable estate. He had security men watching him. Discreetly, of course. So *somebody* professional did this. Was he kidnapped by the Russians, do you think? Or somebody working for them? Or did he defect? Or decide to slip down to Brighton for a short holiday?"

"It's anybody's guess, Mr. Bellman."

"Yes, I suppose it is. I'd like to see the police reports, your people's preliminaries, all that, after Miss Grace shows me around." Bellman rose to his feet. "So, if you'll just have your secretary ring for her—"

"We're keeping this quiet, Mr. Bellman. Please keep that in mind when you make your inquiries."

"I'm not clumsy, Mr. Tipton. It will be completely hush-hush. Until the time comes to make his report public. Then we make a lot of noise."

Tipton nodded, but his face said he didn't like it. "I'm not clumsy either, Mr. Bellman. After that, we say he was taken by the Russians in a desperate attempt to stop his report from getting out."

"Exactly." It was nice to know that Tipton had had experience with this kind of thing. The trophy they were playing for was public opinion. Get the British public outraged enough at the Russians, and Sir Lewis would achieve his objective even without delivering his report.

"And for maximum outrage," Tipton offered, "Sir Lewis should be found dead at the hands of the Russians." It wasn't a question.

"At the hands of the Russians," Bellman said. "Yes." He let some silence accumulate, a good ten seconds of it. The Acting Section Chief was getting a good taste of responsibility, and Bellman wanted to give him enough time to get it swallowed.

Finally, he said, "So the only thing to do is find him before the deadline, right, Mr. Tipton?"

"Is that what Washington wants?"

"It's what everybody wants."

5

Leo Calvin stood at the sink doing the washing up. Margaret would be pleased. Not to say surprised. It would be the first time since he'd tied up with her that he'd done anything like housework, in any of the houses they'd been in since early last fall, when he'd arrived in England under the name "Tyrone Slothrop" and gone to ground.

Leo squirted green Fairy Liquid (*Fairy*, for God's sake) over cheap Marks and Spencer china and scrubbed at hardened pieces of egg and Weetabix and dried ketchup with a long-handled brush.

It occurred to him that this was perhaps the second time in his life he was washing dishes—the first had been to butter up his mother when he was eight years old. His mother never found out about it—instead, he got reamed out by the maid, accused of trying to take her job. An early lesson in the politics of labor.

He was doing the work now only in the desperation of boredom. A sinkful of suds was a change from daytime British television, at least. He was tired of looking out the window.

It might have been different if they'd found a flat near the ocean. Brighton rose on hills from where the Atlantic lapped Britain's ass in constant heavy waves. The waterfront was all hotels and guest houses, or places too expensive for Leo's limited resources. Margaret had signed up for the dole, of course, but that was risky. Leo no longer had a valid visa or anything resembling one. And, in his current status ("pariah dog," Leo thought) he had no real prospect of getting one.

No. That was wrong. He could get one, really, anytime he wanted to.

He could hop the train to London and spend 10p on a call to Bulanin at the Soviet Embassy. Bulanin was the Agricultural Attaché. Usually, KGB men are Cultural Attachés, but the Russians knew that most of the militarily important places in Britain—British, NATO, and American—are surrounded by farmland, and it never hurt to have an excuse to get close. Bulanin would be delighted to make the trade any time Leo wanted to.

Not yet, Leo thought.

Bulanin was one of the main reasons Leo had chosen England as a refuge when the Cronus operation had fallen apart back in the States, and it became known that Leo had been operational chief of it. The late Chairman of the Communist Party of the Soviet Union had spent thirty years setting up and nurturing the Cronus Project before hiring Leo to put it into operation. When things went sour, the Chairman, old, sick, and desperate to hold on to his power for as long as possible, was not about to blame himself for the failure. Leo would have been put on a to-be-disposed-of list simply on the strength of his knowing too much about Cronus, much of which could still be made operational when the time came. Dead spies, as they say, tell no tales.

But it was much more than that. There was a vindictive

element to it—Cronus had failed; Leo Calvin had been in charge; Calvin betrayed us; Calvin must die. And die swift, and ugly. It made no difference that the Chairman was dead. Borzov, the cellar-dwelling gnome of the KGB, had been the other father of Cronus, and Borzov was very much alive.

It had not, Leo told himself, been his fault, but he wasn't naive enough to think it made any difference. Leo knew whose fault it was, and Leo could be vindictive, too. That's why, even though he could offer the Russians something to make them forget the embarrassment of Cronus, make them forgive Leo—hell, even make them want to build him a statue in Red Square—he wouldn't do it until he was ready.

Which brings us back to Bulanin, Leo thought.

Bulanin was ambitious. No surprise. He was also imaginative and flexible and willing to take a chance. Of all the Cultural or Agricultural Attachés Leo knew, Bulanin was least likely to shoot on sight.

So, when Leo had fled his native land with a fraction of the fortune he'd accumulated during years of arranging things for Russians and Cubans, with the Americans after him like hillbillies after a Revenooer, it was Bulanin he'd thought of. The plan had been at the fill-in-the-blanks stage then, just a vague outline, but Leo had known that sooner or later he'd need to talk to a Russian who might just listen for fifteen seconds. Maybe even help him a little, if Leo could convince him it could be done without much risk. Now the time had come, and Bulanin hadn't disappointed him. He had listened, and he had helped. He'd still kill Leo when he saw him, unless he saw him in order to complete the trade.

No. Not yet.

Leo reached through greasy water, found the chain, and let the water out of the sink. He washed away the last of the suds with the cold water tap, then pulled little particles of Mushy Peas from the trap. He rinsed his hands, turned off the tap, wiped them on the dishrag.

He went and looked out the window, wishing he could see the ocean, and looked out at Brighton instead. Britain's answer to Atlantic City, except the gambling casinos were older. Gray and deserted in the winter, probably loud with phony gaiety when summer brought the tourists.

From the window, Leo could see part of the train station, a low-rise concrete gambling club, and more buildings like this one. The building directly across the street had flats over a defunct newsagent. Leo and Margaret and their guest were living over a bankrupt chemist.

Leo wondered what Driscoll was looking at.

Bellman. Leo had to remember to think of him as Bellman.

He was in Britain now. He was within reach. That was probably why the itch was so bad. When he'd had the ocean between him and the man who'd ruined his cozy little life as a free-lance terrorist, it hadn't been so bad. Part of the project of reclaiming his life. A little footnote. Revenge was a luxury, true, but what was a reclaimed life without a little luxury in it?

It had taken most of his money and all of his remaining influence back in the States to maneuver Dris—Bellman into position. Setting up the British-American crisis (though that was an inevitable by-product of obtaining the trade bait); revealing just enough, through some remaining contacts back in the States, to let the right people in Washington know Leo Calvin was in Britain.

That part had been the biggest gamble. Leo got it passed along by way of a Washington newsman whose impartiality was as thin as the surface of a TV screen. Sympathetic or not, though, he had cost Leo a young fortune. Leo could understand, he supposed. Not even a network paid enough to support that sort of cocaine habit.

Leo had been sure that with the message passed, Driscoll—Bellman—would come looking for him sooner or later. Bellman wanted a showdown as badly as Leo did.

Bulanin was willing to help. The Agricultural Attaché contacted one of his counterparts in Washington. The CIA man assigned to the British situation, the original Bellman, was killed and dumped in a parking lot. Just to whet their appetites.

Two weeks later a new Bellman was booked for the flight to London. Leo had his own sources at the English end, so that part was easy. He spent more of his money arranging for the reception committee at the airport, but the party had been broken up by the tall redheaded woman.

On consideration, Leo was just as glad. It had been a mistake to send others to kill Driscoll. Bellman. Whoever. It would be much more satisfying to attend to it in person.

Because Bellman was something new, something Leo had not been aware America had. He was as ruthless and as skillful as Leo himself, as the best of the Russians. He had moved into the Cronus situation in Pennsylvania, grabbed it by the throat, twisted it, used it, exploited it, got people hurt, got people killed, and won in a rout. Americans didn't work that way. Oh, sometimes they did, like in Chile, or Greece, but their hearts weren't in it. If Bellman, on the other hand, the new one, the one who had nothing to do with the CIA, had wanted Castro dead, he wouldn't try to hire the Mafia to do it for him. And if he wanted to *embarrass* Castro, he'd think of something a lot better than some half-assed plan to put something in his shoes to make his beard fall out.

Bellman would take somebody of his own caliber to handle him. Leo, for instance. He *deserved* it. The last time they'd met, Leo hadn't been ready for him. Now he was. It was going to be a pleasure to attend to this personally.

A noise from the other room told him there was something else he had to attend to personally. He sighed, even though he was more than happy to have an excuse to leave the window.

There was another rustle from the bedroom, another muffled grunt. Leo wanted to yell hold your horses, for Christ's sake, but of course he didn't. There was no way to know how nosy the neighbors might be, or how sound-resistant the walls were. He didn't want anyone to hear him talking when he was supposed to be alone in the flat.

Leo went to the refrigerator and opened the door. The compressor started up a whine of protest, which Leo ignored. He took a cabbage from the vegetable bin, pulled aside the outer leaves, and removed a rubber-topped bottle from a hollowed-out space within. In the bathroom he got a disposable plastic syringe. He filled a light dose, put the vial back in the cabbage and the cabbage back in the fridge, and went to the bedroom just in time to be greeted by another muffled noise from the bound and gagged figure on the bed.

Leo smiled down at the eyes below the bald scalp. "Don't try to fool me, Sir Lewis," he said quietly, "I know you're awake. We're running low, and we've had to lighten your dose."

Angry noises came from behind the gag.

Leo wiped the inside of Sir Lewis's left arm with alcohol. "I gave it to you in the other arm last time, didn't I?"

No response. Anger and hatred flashed from the bald man's gray eyes.

"I must compliment you on your constitution, Sir Lewis. For a man your age, you throw off the effects of this drug very rapidly. The last person I gave it to was a strikebreaker up in Nottingham, and he died from it. Of course, he got a larger dose than I give you."

Leo wrapped a cloth noose around Sir Lewis's upper arm and pulled it tight. "You've got great veins, too, for a man your age. It makes this easy. Don't thrash around, you'll only hurt yourself, and I want—I *need* you in perfect shape."

Leo dug a thumb into the joint, and the vein popped up even larger. Leo gave another wipe with the alcohol, jabbed the needle into the vein, pulled on the plunger to see the color of the blood, was satisfied. Then he depressed the plunger and fed the drug into the old man's body.

Leo saw the eyelids start to flutter. "We'll feed you when this one wears off. Sweet dreams. Maybe I'll get you some Russian-language tapes to listen to in your sleep. You don't speak Russian, do you? It would make things so much more convenient when you're in your new home."

6

"What do you think?" Felicity Grace asked.

"Delicious," Bellman said when he finished chewing. "English lamb is as good as I remembered it. Much better than what we get in the States."

She had taken him to The Cut Above, a restaurant on the seventh level of the Barbican Centre, a convention and entertainment complex in London's Square Mile. The Barbican had been completed in the late 1970s, but the site had been cleared years before, courtesy of Hermann Goering's airborne demolition company. Bellman had his doubts about restaurants in big public buildings, but The Cut Above was a pleasant surprise. If they'd put it in a Victorian town house, it would be world famous.

"I wasn't talking about the lamb," Felicity said, "I was talking about business."

Bellman turned his head and looked out the window across London to the dome of St. Paul's Cathedral, and looked at it until the smile left his face.

"Have I said something funny?"

"No, not at all. Just a vagrant thought." He smiled again.

In a strange way, he really enjoyed being with her. Bellman had never, in all his life, under any of his names, had an honest relationship with a woman. Not that this was one, either, but it was refreshing not to have the pangs of conscience that usually troubled him when he was maneuvering some innocent into an impossible position.

Felicity Grace was no innocent, and she was the one who was doing all the maneuvering.

There was also the continuing kick of watching a fellow professional at work. Tonight, for instance, there was yet another version of Felicity Grace. She still had on the office uniform from this afternoon, but her voice and manner were different again. The West Country accent had been replaced by a London upper-middle accent that said one never travels north of Watford or west of Hounslow unless one is flying away for one's holiday.

It made sense. In the paranoid world they both inhabited, possible sources of trouble were everywhere, and the fact that a red-haired woman with a West Country accent had been to dinner with an American might sometime, somewhere, come back to haunt her. Much better to take no chances. Bellman was tempted to start talking Southern, like his Daddy, or put on a Down East Maine drawl (or even Liverpool scouse or a Scots burr—he'd been coached in all of them), but it was too late for it to do any good.

Then there was the question about business. Another test. It's easy enough for two spies to talk business in public, and not especially risky. The idea was to stick to one metaphor, and not to mention any names.

"All right," he said, "let's talk business. I read the chairman's report this afternoon."

"What did you think of it?"

"Seems to me he might want to tone it down some before he presents it."

"Of course. My boss mentioned it was only a first draft, didn't he?"

"Your guvnor," Bellman said, and they smiled. "Yes, he did. All right, allowing for the fact that it's still in raw form, I'd say it's a masterpiece of analysis for this particular business."

Felicity cut a piece of her Yorkshire pudding, pressed it down into the dripping from the slab of beef, and conveyed it to her mouth, remaining neat and ladylike throughout the operation.

When she had swallowed she patted her lips with her napkin and said, "I mean it seriously."

"I'm serious. If you want an outsider's opinion, that document sums up everything that's gone wrong with this company, and how the history relates to the current problem. What do you think of it?"

"I—I haven't read it," she said. "Yet."

"Oh. Well, when you do, you'll see what I mean. I enjoyed the tour of the operation."

"We're proud of it. In spite of the problems."

"Every operation has them. I'm sure you've heard of the screw-ups in my own corporation."

"Hasn't everyone?"

"Touché," Bellman said. This could get to be fun, he thought. "That boy in the computer room, the one with the five different color earrings in each ear and the two-tone hair . . ."

"Yes?"

"Is he the one you got the job for?"

"Yes, he is. How did you know?"

"A guess. The way he greeted you. Is he being groomed for bigger things?"

"I think so. He started doing typesetting. Now he makes most of our travel arrangements. He's just beginning to learn the full scope of the company, but we do promote from within."

Just don't use him for fieldwork, Bellman thought. Then he thought again. There were plenty of places Dave Hamilton could move unnoticed. It was the white shirt and tie that made him ridiculous when it was added to the black-on-the-sides platinum-on-top hairdo, the earrings, and the heavy, bulging bovver boots on his feet. Replace the slacks with black chinos and the shirt with a black leather jacket and chains, and not one Londoner out of a hundred could pick him out of a lineup, except maybe his mother or another punk.

"He's a brilliant boy," Felicity said.

"Polite, too," Bellman said.

Felicity nodded, as if she'd just come to the end of a paragraph. "There's something I've been meaning to ask you," she said.

"What's that?"

"About your arrival party . . ."

"Ah," Bellman said through a broad grin.

"Now I have said something funny."

"No. It's just that I've been wondering when that was going to come up. If something like that had happened to you or one of your colleagues arriving in New York, or Washington, you'd be in a room somewhere at this moment with two guys blowing smoke in your face and asking you if you were *sure* you didn't know anything about it."

"Do you?"

"Do I what?"

"Know anything about it?"

"Nothing but suspicions, and damned few of those."

"Do you think it might affect our . . . business project?"

"Don't know. I doubt it. I've notified the head office, and they're working on it from that end."

"Well, that's all right then," she said. "I hope."

A small blond waitress with a movie-cliché French accent came by and asked if zey were ready for zeir dessert. Bellman said they were, and the waitress went off to get the sweets trolley.

"There's just one problem," Bellman said. "How did they know I'd be on that plane? How did they know I was coming at all?"

"There was a leak," Felicity said. "From your people or from mine?"

"Mine, I hope," Bellman said. "If your people start to leak, who the hell are we going to trust over here?"

That pretty much stifled conversation for the rest of the meal. Dessert was something with cream poured over it. The cream was rich and sweet enough to be dessert by itself. Coffee came with little square chocolate mints and demarara sugar.

And a surprise. Bellman reached for a mint, and found one of Miss Grace's soft hands clasping his. He looked at her.

"You know, Mr. Bellman—"

"What the hell, we're holding hands, call me Jeff."

"Jeff. I—I've been more or less ordered to seduce you."

"They hand out some nasty jobs in this business."

"You're making fun of me."

"Possibly," Bellman conceded. "Is there a time limit on that part of your assignment?"

"I don't know what you mean."

"Just keep working on it, and you'll succeed before you know it. Not tonight, though, I have to work."

Felicity Grace laughed. It sounded like real humor, real warmth. "You *bastard*," she said.

"As a matter of fact . . . ," Bellman said. "But seriously. I haven't been oblivious. It might even be fun."

Felicity looked up from her coffee cup with her eyebrows raised. "For you or for me?" she asked innocently.

"We'll just have to find out."

"That's the idea," she conceded. "To find out. But that part of it's not going to work, is it?"

"Never can tell. Let's get the bill and get out of here. I want to go over that report again. Maybe by tomorrow I'll have some idea of what I want us to do."

The eyebrows went up another notch.

"On the project I mean."

Felicity Grace smiled and said nothing.

7

Bellman leaned back against the padded headboard and wondered what the hell it was with these guys. These brilliant and dedicated Hot and Cold Warriors like his father and Sir Lewis Alfot.

Sir Lewis had fought the Germans, the Russians, and the Establishment with equal fervor. He'd spent his own fortune to assure that there was at least one outfit in British Intelligence who would do things right—i.e., his way. He fought for his ideas; he fought for his autonomy. Reading between the lines, Sir Lewis had fought retirement like a tiger with a toothache, and still resented being sidelined.

The Congressman was much the same. Bellman's father had had no personal fortune to use to ensure his vision of a safe America, but for the most part he hadn't needed one. He'd built his unit during World War II, and postwar anticommunism had helped him make its autonomy damned near impregnable. Until

Watergate. Watergate-related muckraking and reforms were the only things Bellman could ever remember scaring his father.

As usual, the old man had taken steps. He'd found a safe district in his home state and got himself elected to Congress. Through a combination of favors, persuasion, and downright blackmail, he had gotten himself appointed Chairman of the House Intelligence Oversight Committee. He did a good job, too, riding herd on the FBI, the CIA, and everybody else he could think of—except his own people. This made the Congressman quite proud of himself. It enabled the reformers to have what they wanted, and it enabled the Congressman's own Agency to go about its work unimpeded.

Men like Bellman's father, and Sir Lewis—and Borzov in the Soviet Union, and others—guarded their visions more zealously than prophets, using any means (as Bellman knew too well) to keep them alive.

So, *why*? Patriotism? Paranoia? Egomania? Sheer bloody-mindedness? Probably, Bellman decided, it was a combination of all four.

Bellman sighed and said a rude word, which he didn't care if Robert Tipton heard a tape of or not. When he'd gotten back to the flat, he'd checked to see if Tipton had kept a promise he'd made to remove the cameras and microphones. When he didn't find any he decided to take it as a gesture of good faith and be encouraged. He also decided not to do any thinking out loud or talking in his sleep, good faith or no good faith. It would take tearing up the walls to make *sure* there was nothing else planted here, and Bellman was too good a guest to go in for that.

Bellman rolled over on the bed (too soft, but then they always were) and started Sir Lewis's report for the third time.

It occurred to Bellman that here in England, where it was customary for newspapers to pay for hot stories, he was probably holding a cool million pounds in his hands. In between the cross-outs and strikeovers was dynamite.

Sir Lewis's basic premise was that British Intelligence, for the most part, was a sieve. "The difference between telling something to London and telling something to Moscow," he wrote, "is the same as the difference between posting a letter second class and posting it first class. It may take a little longer, but it gets there all the same."

He had some good words for the Americans. "We are all aware of the fiascos of American Intelligence, their arrogance in Greece and Chile, their incompetence against Castro, especially the ill-fated Bay of Pigs invasion.

"But the American mistakes came while America was on the *offensive;* they erred by an excess of zeal. Compare that, please, with our own well-publicized failures—our lack of warning over the Argentines' invasion of the Falklands, or the shameful episode over the invasion of Afghanistan." There were a few lines angrily crossed out here. The document resumed. "These were *passive* mistakes, hence mistakes inherent in the defence of the Realm as we attempt to prosecute it. Indeed, the Afghanistan fiasco was a crime against the entire free world—a letting down of our allies, who were justifiably angry that we could for so long turn a blind eye to the situation that made this possible."

The situation that made that possible was the situation that prevailed at an installation called GCHQ in Cheltenham, just on the English side of the Welsh border. GCHQ stands for Government Communications Headquarters, and it is the main code and cipher department and emergency message relay center for the whole Western Alliance, but especially for the U.K. and the United States.

The employees at GCHQ fell under Civil Service, and as such belonged to the Civil Service union. And on the day in June, 1980 when Russian tanks rolled into Afghanistan, the workers in GCHQ were engaged in an Industrial Action. That meant they were showing no industry and taking no action. Emergency reports came in, but no one decoded them. No one passed them on. Even if Mrs. Thatcher or Mr. Carter had any ideas on what to do about the invasion, they never got the chance to use them.

That had been the last straw. The message from the United States had been to fix that situation or go it alone. That, Britain was not prepared to do, so the union had been banned at the GCHQ.

That was not the end of it. There was publicity. There was controversy. All the political might of the British Left came into play. Eventually, with direct payoffs to the workers, and relocation aid to anyone who wanted to stay in the union and still work in the Civil Service, the Thatcher government had finally done the job.

Until the union ban had been overturned in court last fall.

That had *really* been the last straw. Washington was inches away from serving notice of a pullout, when the idea of the Alfot report was offered. Sir Lewis was loved and respected, and absolutely safe. He would, as an ostensibly impartial observer, prepare a report to be shown, secretly, to important members of Parliament, selected judges, the saner union officials, etc.

The GCHQ situation itself was decided by the House of Lords in favor of the government but by that time the Congressman was so in love with the Sir Lewis idea as a way to cure all the ills of British Intelligence, he had insisted the project go on, despite great reluctance from the Brits.

The report, Bellman realized, would have to be considerably toned down before it would do more help than harm. This first draft had the sound of a man at the end of his tether blowing off steam. There would have to be a lot more hedging, a lot more consideration of the feelings of the unions, before anybody outside his own Section might be allowed to see Sir Lewis's work.

Still, it was remarkable, and useful, if for no other reason than to give Bellman some idea of what was going on in Sir Lewis's mind.

Sir Lewis found the deep causes of the current troubles of British Intelligence in the Second World War. It gave Bellman a remarkable feeling of déjà vu—it might have been a cleaned-up transcript of the background his father had given him just before he'd left.

The Congressman said the British approach to recruiting was wrong. "They recruited all these brilliant young men out of the great universities, see. And there's no denyin' they *were* brilliant. Did a great job against Hitler. Only trouble was, they were doin' it because Hitler was fightin' Russia. These boys had their hearts in—what do you want to call it? Socialism? A Just Society? A Workers' Paradise? They had their hearts in that stuff more than my mama had hers in the Antioch Baptist Church Choir.

"When Russia became the problem, their hearts and their

brilliant minds sort of dozed off, if you know what I mean. It made things tough on us, I'll tell you.

"Not all of them, of course, not even most of them. Hell, son, if people like Lew Alfot weren't there, they'd be singing God Save the Central Committee of the Workers by now.

"But there were a damn lot of them. Too many. Couldn't get rid of them—they were heroes from the war. Some got caught, yes. A lot of them just stayed in place, hiring people they were comfortable with. Establishing rules and procedures that made it tough to do anything about it. Retiring on pensions from a Grateful Nation.

"Thank God for Margaret Thatcher," the old man had said. "If old Denis ever cashes in his chips, I swear you're gonna have a stepmother. First person in charge over there with any balls turns out to be a woman."

Bellman did not smile.

"But then," the Congressman said, "maybe it takes a woman to clean house right."

A woman, Bellman thought, or a fanatic. Somebody like Sir Lewis Alfot, or the silver-haired man in Washington who shared so many of his opinions.

In a way, Bellman envied them their commitment. As it was, he had no opinions other than the one that said Leo Calvin was in Britain, and that he ought to be killed before he could exact his promised revenge on Bellman.

And that, Bellman realized to his surprise, presupposed the opinion that he thought it was a good idea to go on living. He hadn't always felt that way. He was trapped in the world of espionage, born into it, and had no way out.

The stepmother joke hadn't been funny because Bellman had never known a mother. His mother had been a captured Russian spy his father had impregnated when he'd realized he'd never be able to make her talk. Bellman had been born by cesarian section when his mother had beaten her brains out against a metal bedstead rather than carry the pregnancy to term.

Bellman had been raised by his father and a succession of tutors. He'd been taught espionage the way a circus child is trained to the trapeze. He'd begun to do analysis at fifteen. By seventeen he was in the field.

After the Cronus operation, after years of trying to get away, he had enlisted the help of an FBI man named Fenton Rines to get his father off his back. He was independent now, but not free. Not as long as Leo Calvin was out there. So Bellman was back in harness. Doing the job and listening for footsteps coming up behind him.

It was really beginning to look as if it was always going to be that way. Fate.

He wondered about volunteers. His dead colleague, Miles. Felicity Grace.

Felicity Grace. What was a nice girl like that doing in a dirty business like this? If she was a nice girl. Still, she must have been once. A family, even an orphanage to grow up in. Comic books and cartoons, dolls, something. Boyfriends. Ambition to be a nurse or a business executive or a mommy or Commissioner of Scotland Yard. Options.

A normal life.

More than Bellman had ever had. More than he ever would have.

Why in the name of God would anyone give it up?

Bellman sighed again, rolled over, and drifted into a troubled sleep.

8

This, Margaret decided, was no time to break the news to Leo. He wasn't going to like it no matter when he heard it, but today he might get nasty. Even violent.

She'd seen him this way once before, shortly after they met. She was up in Yorkshire, organizing support for the striking miners, trying to get local shopkeepers, the postmen, rubbish collectors, from servicing the working miners in any way. She stressed class loyalty, and the need to keep the pits open no matter what the cost to the bourgeois ratepayers in the rest of the country. Margaret was very persuasive in a reasoned argument—all the instructors at her university had told her so.

With all her skill, though, Margaret was nowhere near as successful as Leo had been. After the first shop caught fire, the rest fell into line.

Margaret had not, at first, approved. Violence was sometimes necessary, but only as a last resort. Besides, any strenuous action was twisted and distorted in the capitalist press until it was something quite unsavory.

She tried to tell this to Leo when she met him. He didn't get angry—at least not outwardly. He slipped into a calm more frightening than any rage, a calm that hinted at deliberations that barred no action, and considered no one. Margaret had hastily changed the subject. It wasn't only fear. There was something fascinating about this American.

It wasn't surprising that he should be in the midst of this particular skirmish of the class struggle—there were many of these American brothers and sisters helping in the fight.

It wasn't his looks—that particular concept was hopelessly sexist. Leo was tall, fair, and bony, all planes and angles and bumps. In a rare lighthearted moment, he once told her someone had said he resembled an albino Abe Lincoln.

Margaret herself, of course, was no one's dream. She was short and plump, and at twenty-six, still fighting spots. Not that that mattered either. She had had her share of lovers, male and female, since her schooldays, and no one had ever complained.

It might have been, Margaret decided, that despite the difference of nationalities, their backgrounds were really quite similar—the bourgeois suburban life, the feelings of emptiness engendered by the realization that so many had so much less, the guilt, the desire to help the People. The feeling of fulfillment that came from being a part of something so much bigger than oneself. The thrill of defying corrupt authority.

They had, over the months, talked about these things, but when the defiance of corrupt authority came up, Leo became electric. He talked of justifications and plans—

He talked about this plan. That night, in a cot in the back of a storefront office, he had told her he needed her help to bring about the victory that the miners and all the trade unionists (the ones who weren't traitors, at any rate) had worked for for so long. It was dangerous, but it was essential.

Margaret didn't hesitate. Leo was offering to escort her through the first steps down the path he'd traveled, the path she knew she had always wanted to walk. Leo had told her she'd never regret it, and they had made love again.

Margaret was sure that was the night she had become pregnant. She'd got the results of the test today—that was why she was late getting home with the marketing. The news had been in her throat as she'd come through the door, but it froze there in the blast of Leo's calm.

"What took you so long?" he demanded.

She'd save the news for another time. She still felt frightened of him when he was like this.

"I—I had some trouble finding our friend at the clinic."

"Did you get the tranquilizer?"

"Of course. I just had to wait until he returned from his tea break. There was one problem."

"Oh?"

"He couldn't give me as much this time. He says—he says unless we're reselling it, we're using too much."

"I washed the dishes," Leo said.

Margaret tried to make some hidden sense out of this remark, when a glance into the kitchen showed her he had indeed washed the dishes. "Thank you, Leo, that was very ki—"

"He wants more money," Leo said.

"Sorry?"

"Our friend at the clinic. The greedy bastard thinks we're a steady market, so he's setting us up to raise the price. Or he thinks we're selling it, and he wants a cut."

Margaret said, "Yes, Leo," and went to the kitchen to put the marketing away. She felt a great relief—the deadly calm was gone, replaced with an intense concentration. This could go on for hours. When he was working on a way to sneak Alfot past all the extra police who had flooded Sussex to hunt for the Cyclops killer, it had taken a day and more. Leo was not to be interrupted at times like these, but he was no longer frightening. She might even tell him about their child before dinner tonight.

"Margaret," he said.

She poked her head out of the kitchen. "Our friend at the clinic is in for a surprise," Leo said.

"What are you going to do?" She tried to keep the apprehension out of her voice.

"To him? Nothing. He's not worth the effort. I think we'll stop needing it before we run out. Things are coming to a head. I need to work out a few details. I want to go walk by the ocean. Do you think you can handle our guest if he wakes up before I return? You'll have to feed him and reinject him."

"Certainly." It had been Margaret, after all, who had been instrumental in keeping Sir Lewis quiet in the back of the borrowed sound truck as they drove past a cordon of the filth. She injected him and hid him, while at the same time giving an excellent speech in support of the miners over the loudspeaker. Leo just drove. And, of course, bundled the old man out to the truck in the first place. But Margaret was sure she could handle one bound old man just coming out of the effects of tranquilization.

"That's a good girl," he said. "I won't be too long." He put on his anorak, and left without kissing her.

Margaret struck a match and lit the grill and put two chops on, one for herself and one for her guest. She'd cook for Leo when he got home.

9

Sir Lewis Alfot would have been ready to escape days ago if he could trust an old man's body. There was no way, apparently, to stop himself from groaning when coming back to himself as the drug wore off. Not that it happened all the time, of course. It hadn't happened this time. But when it did it gave them a much better idea of the efficacy of the drug.

The plan, since the moment he found himself a captive and felt that first needle sliding into his arm, had been to stay motionless, to *act* drugged as long as possible after he woke up, trying to get them to decrease the dose, and give him that much more precious consciousness. He hadn't counted on their running low, but since they had, so much the better.

And if he'd heard right, the American was going out. Perfect. Sir Lewis used his tongue and lips to force his gag down around his chin, then began to work on his bonds.

He'd done a lot of eavesdropping on those two in the week they'd held him captive. They would be contemptible if they weren't so ridiculous. This was what he'd fought all his life to protect. He swallowed bile.

His instinct was to cough to clear the clog, but he fought it down. He mustn't give any sign of being awake until he was ready to.

The ropes had been expertly tied, immobilizing Sir Lewis's thumbs as well as spreading him out on the bed. It took an effort of will to force aging muscles to twist himself so that he could bring his teeth (all his own, thank God) to bear on the rope that held his right wrist. The pain and tension were excruciating, but he was damned if he'd be beaten by this pair.

He distracted himself with bitter thoughts. Sodding little bastards, refugees from some damnfool Marxist fiasco of a strike, hoping to sell him to the Russians. Never knowing how much the Russians would like to have him. How was the kidnapping of jovial, public-spirited Sir Lewis, though, supposed to help the bloody miners? There was no answer to that. There was never any answer to them. Except a bloody good kick in the arse, which Britain, it grieved him to say, grew more and more reluctant to administer. They just kept turning a blind eye—

Sir Lewis bit heavily on the rope to stifle a scream as a spasm sliced down his back alongside his old shrapnel scar. Sir Lewis fought to keep his position—if he relaxed now, he'd never be able to go back to work. Eventually, the pain abated a bit. He turned again to the rope.

He'd show them. He'd show them all. The bastards who retired him. The bastards who kidnapped him. The bloody Russians. The government, whose only idea on how to use him was to throw him as a sop to the Americans. He'd show them, too. There was still one Briton who remembered how it should be done.

About the only group of people he could think of he didn't resent was the group of neighbors who'd asked him to look into the Cyclops case. At least someone wanted him for something. He had half a mind to take them up on it. Yes, dammit. When he'd dealt with this lot, that was exactly what he would do.

Sir Lewis smiled at the thought, and at that moment the knot gave way. He pulled his right hand free, then fell back on the bed, panting, trying to get his tormented muscles to relax.

Get a move on, you bloody fool, he told himself. She'd be in to check on him in a minute. She might even bring the tray, and try to wake him. They'd done it before. The man had, at least.

He didn't have much time. The rattle of pots and pans had been replaced by the rattle of china.

Working like a mole in the dark, Sir Lewis tore frantically with teeth and fingers to free his other hand before going to his feet.

The door creaked.

Too late. Sir Lewis got his left hand free, lay back down, and wrapped the now loose ends haphazardly around his wrists just before she switched on the light.

"Come on, then," she said. "I know you're awake. Dinner."

Sir Lewis groaned.

The woman pulled a table and chair close to the bed and put down the tray. "You're eating better than a lot of people in this country are," she told the old man. "Chop. Broccoli. Potato. Tea."

Hypodermic needle. She didn't mention that, Sir Lewis thought. He said nothing. He never spoke to either of them.

He kept waiting for her to notice the ropes, how they were different against his skin, but amazingly, she didn't. Something on her mind, he supposed.

He wasn't complaining. Just let her offer him that first forkful, just let her get close enough—

47

SECOND

"What's the good of Mercator's North Poles and
    Equators,
  Tropics, Zones, and Meridian Lines?"
So the Bellman would cry, and the crew would
reply,
  "They are merely conventional signs!

"Other maps are such shapes with their islands
    and capes!
  But we've got our brave Captain to thank"
(So the crew would protest) "that he's brought
    us the best—
  A perfect and absolute blank!"

> —*The Hunting of the Snark*
> Fit the Second

1

When the phone woke her, Felicity Grace was irritated to see that she had gravitated away from the center of the bed. Toward Derek's side. Not that Derek had ever seen this particular bed, or this flat, or known anybody calling herself Felicity Grace. Everything that made up her life now had come A.D. After Derek. After Death.

"Hell," she said aloud, but the phone wouldn't give her the leisure to feel properly sorry for herself. She reached for it as she squinted at the clock. Not seven yet, good God, we must be at war.

"Yes?" she said. Anybody who wanted anything more civil would have to wait a while.

"Good morning, Miss Grace."

"Bellman?"

"I thought you were going to call me Jeff."

"How did you get this number?"

"A fine agent I'd be if I couldn't get hold of a phone number."

"I cannot deal with an American being coy at quarter to seven in the morning."

"I read it off your telephone the other night."

"No you didn't. You were never near the bedroom, and that's where the phone is."

"My mistake," Bellman said. He left it open whether he was talking about his little lie, or about not having got near the bedroom. "Seriously," he went on, "I don't have your number. I prevailed upon the night man here at the Tournament Press to ring you for me."

"You're at the office?"

"Why not? It's a short walk. I need you to take me somewhere, and I want to get an early start."

"Where are we going?"

"To the horse's mouth," he said cryptically. "How soon can
you be here?"

"Thirty minutes' time." My body will be there, she thought.
My brain might not show up until sometime later.

"Fine. I just want to catch up with my friend before he takes
off." She heard Bellman say something away from the telephone, then, "Oh, okay. My friend here says you should report
to room thirty as soon as you arrive."

For one brief phone call, it had certainly given Felicity a lot
to puzzle over as she drove to the office. What in the world was
Bellman up to? And how had he got hold of Section phone code
so quickly? "The night man" was Mr. Tipton, speaking from his
flat through the desk watcher's phone at the office. The phrase
"my friend" in that context meant that the speaker was armed
with the delegated authority of the Section chief.

But room thirty was the most puzzling thing of all. Ostensibly,
room thirty was the private studio of the art director of Tournament Press's catalogue department. In reality, Tournament Press
had its catalogues done by anonymous free-lancers, and room
thirty was given over to craftsmen of a different sort—makeup
and disguise people.

What in the world was Bellman doing in room thirty? What
sort of disguise would he need, on top of that cover story of his?

"Disguise?" he said when she put the question to him in room
thirty twenty minutes later. "No disguise at all, in the proper
meaning of the word."

"Then what—oh, good morning, Natalie."

"Good morning, Miss Grace," Natalie said. She was a plump,
pretty black woman of about forty or so. She had come to Sir
Lewis's attention in the mid seventies, when more and more of
the refugees from the madness of Idi Amin told of how they
were able to elude capture and flee the country because of the
skill of a woman member of an underground group. Asians,
Europeans, Africans, all were given simple, natural-looking disguises that had saved their lives.

Inevitably, it was Natalie's own life that had been on the

line—her son had betrayed her, after having held out against torture for a month. She used her skill to save herself, and got to Kenya, where one of Sir Lewis's men found her. They brought her to London, and put her to work for the Section, where she'd been ever since. Perhaps literally. Felicity knew that any hour of the day or night she was needed, Natalie was in room thirty ready and waiting.

Felicity turned back to Bellman. "Then what are we doing here? Why are we bothering Natalie at this hour of the morning?"

"No bother," Natalie said. "Mr. Bellman and I have been having a nice chat." Natalie's voice was always mellow and musical, but this morning there was an extra riff of amusement that Felicity found herself resenting.

"What we're doing here," Bellman said, "is getting ready to pay a call on the Russian Embassy."

"The Russian Embassy," Felicity echoed.

"Right. The one in Kensington Palace Gardens."

Felicity decided not to ask the obvious question just this second. Instead, she said, "That still doesn't explain the makeup section being called in. Especially since you tell me there's not going to be a disguise."

"Properly understood. Do you have those pictures, Natalie?"

"I do, Mr. Bellman. Mr. Tipton rang me and told me to have them ready." Natalie wiped her hands on her smock and picked up two color glossies, eight by ten, full face and profile showing a woman with curly brown hair and too much makeup. The jewelry was just slightly overdone, as well, and the picture went down far enough to show that the woman was displaying just one button too much chest. The whole effect was rather tarty, but not offensive to anyone short of Mrs. Whitehouse.

Felicity recognized the photos. "That's me," she said.

"I know. You looked like that in Sweden, when you were working liaison on the captured submarine thing."

"You want me to look like that today?"

"That's the idea."

"But we can't. They already know me that way. They—"

"Exactly. They know the woman in that picture is a British agent. When I spoke to Tipton on the scrambler this morning, I asked him if he had someone who'd been made by the Russians that he could loan me for the morning. Imagine my surprise when it turned out to be you."

"I'm ready for you, Miss Grace," Natalie said. She bowed Felicity into a padded, adjustable chair, then covered her to the chin with a sheet. She covered the red hair with a cap of fine mesh, and started smearing things on Felicity's face.

When Natalie had finished for the moment with her mouth, Felicity said, "All right. You appear to have taken complete command of the Section—" Natalie chuckled. "—complete command of the Section," Felicity repeated. "Am I to be allowed to know what we're about?"

"Of course. We want to know what's happened to Sir Lewis, don't we?"

"Of course." It occurred to Felicity that along with all the other things he'd learned about the Section, he also knew that Natalie had a class A security clearance, or he wouldn't be talking so freely in front of her.

"And we suspect that the Russians had something to do with his disappearance, right? Or that at least they know *something* about who's behind it."

"That's our best guess at the moment," Felicity conceded.

"All right, then. What we're going to do is pay a call on the Agricultural Attaché at the Russian Embassy."

"Bulanin?" If Felicity hadn't been so well trained she would have gasped.

Bellman nodded. "Grigori Illyich Bulanin. We've never met but I know of him from his days in Washington."

"But he's KGB!"

"*I* know he's KGB. Why the hell should I want to talk to an Agricultural Attaché if he *weren't* KGB?"

"But what's the *point?*"

Natalie chuckled again. Felicity wanted to glare at her, but the black woman grabbed her by the chin, turned her head around, and started applying crimson to her lips with a brush.

"The point is, we show up on Bulanin's doorstep, readily identifiable as an American spy and a British spy, and demand to know what the fuck is going on with Sir Lewis Alfot."

Natalie was fitting the brown wig over the hairnet. She gave it a few pokes with the end of a rattail comb, surveyed it, poked again, and pronounced herself satisfied. She whipped the sheet off Felicity's body rather like a magician completing a trick.

"So we just walk up to the Russians' chief KGB man and start causing trouble, is that it?"

"That's it."

Natalie said, "Undo another button on your blouse, Miss Grace. Put on the baubles. And you better change into some tarty shoes. I've got some high heels with ankle straps for you."

"Thank you, Natalie. Jeff—I am still calling you Jeff—I don't know what to say. Your plan is—"

"Unorthodox? Foolhardy, perhaps? Not by the book?"

"Not by the book!"

"Don't you say that here? It means—"

"I know what 'not by the book' means."

"Good," Bellman said. The banter was gone; he was practically grim. "Then you know the Russians have a copy of the book, too. You go by one chapter, they go by the next. Things get done, but they take time."

"Yes, but—"

"But nothing. We *have* no time. Look. This is the only way I can work. I tear pages out of the book and use them to light fires. What are the Russians going to think when I walk up to their KGB man and start kicking ass?"

"How am I supposed to know what they're going to think?" Felicity was having more than a little difficulty deciding what *she* thought.

"They'll think I'm insane. Then they'll wonder, if I'm so crazy, why I'm running around loose. Why a known British agent is giving me aid, and for all they know, comfort.

"It will make them nervous. They won't want to make a move until they *know what the hell this American maniac is up to.* They'll—Bulanin, I mean—will start making moves in the dark."

Bellman turned to Natalie. "She looks great to me. How about those shoes?"

"Right here," Natalie said. She handed them to Felicity.

Felicity pulled off her boots. Before she handed them over to Natalie, she pulled a .32 automatic from a holster in the top of her right boot and put it in her purse. Then she fixed the straps of the high heels, and noted with angry satisfaction that Mr. Bellman was enjoying the exhibition of her legs.

"I'm ready," she said, and stood up to go.

"Good," Bellman said. "We'll still be there plenty early enough."

"We're really going through with this."

"Oh, yes. Because you see, Felicity, once you get someone moving around in the dark, it's a lot easier to make him stumble."

2

The American said, "What the fuck is going on with Sir Lewis Alfot?"

Grigori Illyich Bulanin put a bemused smile on his face while he lit a cigarette. It was an American brand, Merit, a low-tar filter cigarette. The ones obtainable in Britain were made in Belgium, but Bulanin was still careful to put them in a cigarette case so that no one could see the pack, and to crush them to shreds when he was done to make it less likely that anyone would take note of the brand printed on the paper. One could never tell what went into one's dossier, and that made a difference, if a man had ambition.

Bulanin had enough ambition for three men, and it frequently occurred to him it might be less trouble if he would smoke Russian cigarettes. He even tried to switch from time to time, but the Russian cigarettes made him gag.

He did not like to smoke. He did not like the taste of tobacco. He had a positive horror of prospective lung cancer. But he needed to smoke. Or rather, he needed cigarettes to light. Bulanin had a tendency to be impulsive, to speak before he had considered all the ramifications of what he might say. The tendency had cost him dearly in his youth (not that he was old now, barely forty—it would be another fifth of a century before he would be in a realistic position to fulfill his ambition), and experience had shown him that lighting a cigarette was a man's only method of temporizing without appearing weak.

Bulanin lit his cigarette and thought. What were the American and the silent Englishwoman doing here? Yes, asking indiscreet questions in vulgar language, but *why*?

Bulanin took a deep drag on his cigarette, ignoring the stinging even this mild American smoke brought to his throat. He blew a gray stream toward the ceiling. "Mr. Bellman," he said. "I'm sure you know more about it than I do."

"I doubt it sincerely," Bellman said.

Bellman, Bulanin thought. Jeffrey Bellman. The name had been the reason Bulanin had let them in. Now, as they sat in the special visitors room, performing for the microphones and cameras, Bulanin looked at the man who (one of his Washington counterparts had assured him) had been killed a few weeks before. At the time, Bulanin had no reason to doubt the report; a Bulgarian hit team had been dispatched, and the Bulgars had no equals as killers.

It had to be an impostor. This visit had to be a clumsy attempt to see how Bulanin reacted to a brash young man wearing the name of the agent he had ordered killed at the request of Leo Calvin.

"I have read about Sir Lewis's disappearance, of course," Bulanin said. His English was impeccable, his voice suave. He had worked long and hard to get them that way. Books, and records, and live tutors, and sleep tapes, to help him master the language. Voice coaches and singing lessons and exercises to remove the harshness Westerners thought they heard in the throat of a Russian.

It was all part of his first job for the KGB, the time when his ambition changed from wish to plan, a plan that was still in progress. He remembered Borzov, the legendary Borzov, condescending to explain things to him.

"Grigori Illyich," the old man had said. "You have been given a great gift, to use for the good of the State. First, though, you must hone it, sharpen it. Your voice and manner must be as beautiful as your face and body. And your brain must be more perfect than either."

Borzov had laughed then, and Bulanin knew that the whispers were true, that people had died with that laugh in their ears.

"When you are ready," Borzov had said, "we will send you, literally naked, into the West. You will learn the contents of minds through the weaknesses of bodies. You will exploit their weakness, their decadence. And you will be a hero for it."

Bulanin didn't know if what he had done had made him a hero. He supposed so—it had earned him promotions sufficient to let him stop degrading himself for Borzov and the Motherland.

Bulanin had not asked to be handsome. He had not asked for the cool gray eyes or the clean straight jaw, the jet-black hair, the broad shoulders, the narrow waist. He had not asked to be looked on by women as a challenge, as a trophy.

It was, as Borzov said, a gift. And like most gifts, it had its price. The price was loneliness. Grigori Illyich Bulanin had made love to hundreds in the fifteen years he spent as a Raven. A Raven. A small black bird that steals shiny baubles and eats carrion. Borzov had a sense of humor when he chose the term. A woman who did what Bulanin had done was called a Swallow.

As a Raven, Bulanin had nested with women, men, groups. He felt no love for any. He felt hatred for some, indifference for others, pity for the rest. And guilt over all.

It wasn't right to garner secrets by wringing them from a lonely heart. Torture was better. *Murder* was better. They, at least, left the subject some dignity; they spared the agent the necessity of hypocrisy.

The bill for his gift was still being paid. After fifteen years as a hypocrite, Bulanin had learned to trust no one. After so much time spent inviting lonely people to his bed and betraying them, it pained to see even a flicker of interest in a woman's eye or a man's.

Like the flicker he saw in the eye of the silent Englishwoman. She was undoubtedly a trained agent. From the look of her, she might well have more than once been the bait in what the

Americans called a Honey Trap herself. But the flicker was there, and she couldn't hide it.

Bulanin thought with envy about men who were bald by the time they reached his age. Or fat or toothless or wrinkled. Every wrinkle Bulanin accumulated added "character." A gift could be a curse. How was he to fulfill his ambition if he still looked like a movie star in his old age? That might be all right in the West, but to get where he was going, Bulanin would have to impress not a shallow, fickle-minded electorate, but the tough old buzzards of the Supreme Soviet and the elders of the Party.

"I beg your pardon," Bulanin said. Bad. Bellman had been talking, and he had missed it with his woolgathering.

"I asked you what you thought."

"Of what?"

"What you read about Sir Lewis's disappearance."

"Most disturbing. Of course, I've never met Sir Lewis—my brief is exclusively agricultural matters."

"Naturally. And Sir Lewis is a capitalist and philanthropist. Somebody of whom the Soviet Union has no need."

"The State fills the functions of both," Bulanin said. He took one more puff on his cigarette, then crushed the long stub to shreds in the ashtray.

"Still," Bellman said, "if you should happen to hear anything, his company and his American friends would be delighted to hear about it."

"Of course. But it's unlikely in the extreme. I really don't know why you came to me at all, Mr. Bellman."

"Let's just say in times of trouble it's comforting to take the counsel of a man of intelligence. If you know what I mean."

Bulanin gave him the smile again. "Not precisely, Mr. Bellman. But I shall keep my ear to the ground. Now, if you'll excuse me, I have matters to attend to."

"Agricultural matters," Bellman said.

"Of course. Good day."

He shook the hand Bellman offered, kissed the woman's, just to see how she'd react. She reacted as he'd expected—by pretending not to be pleased. He had the attendant show them out.

"Damn you," Bulanin said to his aide, an impossibly eager

young man who undoubtedly was nourishing an ambition of his own. "What can you tell me?"

"Nothing on the man, sir. He is *not* the Bellman who was touched in Washington."

"I know that, who *is* he?"

"He is not CIA, sir. That's all we can say for sure. The woman, however—"

"Yes?"

"She matches description and photograph of a British agent who was in liaison with the Swedes over the submarine affair in 1978. She hasn't been seen since."

"Not looking that way, at least."

"No sir. It does look like the same woman, though, see for yourself." He handed Bulanin the pictures taken today and a still-damp photo wired from Moscow. "Of course," the young man went on, "a voiceprint might have clinched it—"

"But she barely said a word. I know. All right, get back to your regular duties."

When he was gone Bulanin went to work, but not on agricultural matters. It was going too far; he was leaving too wide a trail. The agenda of his life required that risks be taken. Bulanin had let Leo Calvin live—at least temporarily—and had pulled strings and juggled documents to make the touching of a minor CIA man seem justifiable to Moscow—as a gesture of good will to Leo Calvin, in order to have a chance to present Borzov with Sir Lewis Alfot, the most valuable man in Britain. As a potential captive, that is. At large, he was probably the most dangerous.

Either way, delivering him to Moscow would be the kind of coup legendary careers were built upon.

But now, it seemed, the kind of noise was brewing that led to legendary silences.

What *were* they up to? The Americans? The British? Why were they so open, so belligerent? Why were they so contemptuous of the polite fiction that Bulanin was interested in fields and cows? Were they—could they be serving notice that they were willing to go to *war* over this old man? Was he *that* important?

Bulanin wanted to tremble with anticipation over what Sir Lewis Alfot might reveal under the proper stimulus back in

Moscow. And he wanted to shiver with fear at the thought of what a failure in this project could bring.

He did neither. Instead, he decided to arrange for a little conference with Mr. Leo Calvin.

3

Spies are perfectly capable of genuine orgasm. Professionally speaking, it's better for them if they are. When a woman is out to ensnare a man, he is much more likely to be convinced by a woman who is left sweating, shuddering, skin-flushed, and nipple erect by his embraces. A man feels tenderly toward a woman who responds to his technique as a lover.

Bellman knew all this, knew it before he brought Felicity Grace back to his apartment after lunch (Lancashire Hot Pot and apple pie with custard at a wood-beamed pub) to talk over what they'd accomplished at Kensington Palace Gardens this morning, if anything.

He knew it when he let her use the bedroom mirror to get rid of the wig and the makeup, and told her when she emerged, "I like you better this way."

She'd smiled shyly, a proper little West Country miss. "I wasn't sure you liked me at all."

He knew it when he came to her and kissed her and led her back to the bedroom. He thought about it as they stripped each other and learned each other. And when she straddled him and shook her hair back like flame, sighed, and said, "Mission accomplished," it was on his mind behind his happy laughter.

Then for a long time he thought about nothing but the woman.

The knowledge was back now, but in spite of it, Bellman felt closer to Felicity Grace than he had to anyone in years. He wondered how long he could allow himself to enjoy it—a week? The rest of the day? Till they got out of bed?

Felicity was snoring softly beside him, close but not touching. That flattered him more than the orgasm had. To sleep in the presence of someone else—especially to sleep *naked*—was an act of trust Bellman had never been capable of.

He leaned over and bit her softly on the earlobe.

"What time is it?" she said, instantly awake.

"Why? Are you one of those people who keep a double-entry ledger on how many minutes of sleep they get?"

"No, I just try to catch the news on television when I can."

"Excellent timing then. It's about three minutes to six."

Felicity was up and doing a little dance to get into Bellman's bathrobe. "I want to be sure there's nothing new on Sir Lewis," she explained.

"Sure," Bellman said. She disappeared into the other room to turn on the television. Bellman slipped into a pair of jeans and padded out to join her.

He got there just in time for the announcer to tell him he was watching BBC 1. There was a sting of music, then a black woman began reading the news. She had the best diction Bellman had ever heard. Right now she was using it on the lead story—the Sussex Cyclops had struck again, the fourth such killing in the past year.

The scene switched to a grimy street in Brighton, where an immaculately groomed man held a microphone just the right distance from his mouth. "Sussex CID say there are several differences between this and the previous murders—one, the victim was tied up; two, the weapon used was a hypodermic needle; and three—" dramatic pause, then breathless, all at once—"this time there is a suspect."

Bellman saw Felicity bite her lip.

"*And*," the reporter added, "there is reason to believe he might be an *American*."

Felicity turned to him.

"Not me," Bellman said, "honest." It failed to get a laugh. Felicity turned back to the screen.

The reporter went on to interview a few neighbors. They said the dead woman (whose name was Margaret Hepwood) and her husband had lived there only a few weeks, and kept mostly to themselves. But they were sure the husband, who gave his name as Thomas Hepwood, was a Yank. At least two of them actually said "Yank."

Bellman was going to make a comment, but the words never made it as far as the front of his mouth. He was looking at the screen with eyes wide, but that wasn't enough. He sprang from his chair and knelt on the floor three feet from the screen.

"Son of a bitch," he said.

"What's wrong?" Felicity demanded. She seemed put out that anything might be.

Bellman gestured for silence. Not that he was hearing anything special. The announcer was saying that the husband had not been seen by anyone since a few hours before the time of death as fixed by the coroner. The police were seeking him to, in the fine old British phrase, assist them in their inquiries. A police artist had drawn this composite sketch of the man. Police believed him to be an American (or perhaps a Canadian) over six feet tall, very fair hair, pale complexion, blue eyes. . . .

Bellman tuned out. He didn't need the description. He knew what he looked like.

"What's the fastest way to get to Brighton?"

Even through his excitement Bellman noticed how quick she was with the information. "It's forty-five minutes from Victoria," she said, "but we might have to wait a little while for a train. We can drive down, if I can beat the traffic as far as the A-23."

"Get a police escort, if necessary."

"We'll see," she said. "We may not need it." She was running to the bedroom. The robe flapped behind her, then came loose like a shed skin in her haste to dress.

Almost as if, Bellman thought, she'd been trying to figure out how she was going to get *him* to Brighton.

Which was ridiculous. He tabled it for now, sprinted for his own clothes. This kind of plum needed to be picked while it was fresh.

4

"Are you absolutely sure this was a Sussex Cyclops murder?" the red-haired woman asked.

"No," said Detective Inspector Maurice Stingley. "She was born with a goddam hypo*dermi*c needle sticking out of her left eyeball." DI Stingley's mouth worked, the result of perfectly balanced impulses to laugh sardonically, curse, or spit.

He did none of them. Instead, he hastened to apologize. That really made him want to spit, but he was under orders. Stingley was a burly, balding man of forty. He had a wife, a teenage daughter, an overdraft, and an incipient ulcer. He also had university-trained, public-relations-minded superiors.

A lot of big things had happened in Sussex lately. Last fall, the IRA had just missed killing Mrs. Thatcher and the entire British Government with a bomb at the Grand Hotel in Brighton, where the Tories had been having their annual conference. They'd come up with a suspect on that one—and Scotland Yard called them naughty when they released the composite picture to the papers. Not in private either. The Big Boys of the Yard had gone openly, embarrassingly public with their criticism. Relations between the Sussex Constabulary CID and the Yard were still somewhat cool over that one.

Then, a little less than a month ago, Sir Lewis Alfot had disappeared from his estate. There was no evidence—not the slightest bit—that it was a crime of any sort. The old man might have turned senile and wandered off. He could be living under a bridge like a troll, for all anybody knew, or on a ship at sea under a new identity.

But try telling the public that. They loved the old fart. Stingley was rather fond of him, too, but you had to be realistic.

The public, though, were having none of being realistic. The beloved Sir Lewis is gone, the beloved Sir Lewis has obviously met with Foul Play, and I ask you, what are the police doing about it?

Thank you, sir, glad you asked. The police are busting their bloody arses over it. They are giving it every spare moment, every moment not spent chasing leads to the Provos, or examining another corpse left by this Cyclops madman.

The Cyclops. Damn his eye, Stingley thought, and fought another impulse to grin. A grin wouldn't do—he was still being abject, and he didn't want to give the wrong impression.

The Cyclops. The Yard were in on this one, but were keeping a low profile. Cool relations. The Cyclops was Stingley's main responsibility, had been since the second murder back in May. The first one had been in February, then May, then a long layoff until November, now again in January. The first three had been in the suburbs and towns outside Brighton, the fourth had been right here in town. The public weren't too pleased with the police over this one either.

It was something about the *eyes*. Something chilling about having something other than light, or nerve impulses, or whatever the hell it was normally, pass from eye to brain. It caught the imagination and held it in a tight if somewhat clammy grip. What did it *feel* like to push a pointed instrument into someone else's eye? What did it feel like to have it happen? What did it *look* like, inside that mutilated head, before the lights finally and irrevocably went out?

Stingley had lived months with those questions, plus one other—what kind of madman would run around doing it to people? He had plenty of clues, but no answers, and neither the public nor the press were too pleased over that. There had been talk of asking Sir Lewis to form one of his famous commissions to look into the matter. Stingley was almost willing to bet that was why he'd left town.

So. After all the excitement, the police in Sussex found themselves decidedly short of friends. And Stingley was under orders not to reduce the number any further, especially when the friends in this case were a woman from Whitehall (or something) and the American was someone she kept looking to for approval.

Stingley apologized again. "You know, press on your back all day, one more question gets me leaping for a throat.,"

Miss Grace smiled at him. Quite pretty when she smiled, actually. "Not at all, DI Stingley. I phrased the question awkwardly. What I meant was, aside from the MO, is there anything that tells you that this murder was committed by the same person who did the others?"

Stingley tightened his lips. Then he thought, all right, the brass have laid down the law. Cooperation it shall be. He got up, walked to the door of the CID office, which fortunately they had to themselves for the moment, looked about the corridor, closed the door tight, came back, and sat on the edge of his desk.

He leaned forward before he spoke. "Fingerprints," he said.

"Fingerprints," the American said. It was the first time he'd spoken since "good evening."

"Fingerprints," Stingley said. His voice was bitter. "Our friend the Cyclops has left fingerprints around like Easter eggs. This is the fourth murder—the third time he's left his dabs on the weapon. We always get the thumbprint, sometimes the index finger as well."

"This hasn't been released," Miss Grace said.

"No," Stingley said. "Nor leaked, either, which is bloody surprising, these days. We've kept it in for two reasons."

Stingley paused, took a breath, looked at his audience. Cooperate, he told himself. Orders. From above.

Still, he hesitated. "This is strictly confidential, you understand."

"Of course," Miss Grace said. "Naturally," said Bellman, the American.

"Well, the first reason is that the distribution of the prints gives us the way our man strikes. Righthanded, but not overhand, or even a little bit to the side. You see, on the screwdriver—he killed the postman with that, we got only a smudged partial print, no good for identification, because of the grooves on the handle; the icepick—that's the one where he did the tart over in Hove; and now this hypodermic needle, all the thumbprints have been at exactly twelve o'clock. Pointing toward the top of the head, I mean, as it stuck from the victim's eye."

It occurred to Stingley that might be a little strong for the average stomach, but his listeners were taking it as if it were *Jackanory*.

"There were no prints on the switchknife—he killed the one and only skinhead in a village of about a hundred and fifty on that trick, used the victim's own knife—because, we think, his thumb was over the gap where the blade was when the knife was folded. Which is consistent with what we think he does. You've got it, there, Mr. Bellman."

The American was drawing his right arm straight back, then pistoning it forward. There was a puzzled look on his face.

"We've felt the same way," Stingley said. "Why the hell would he strike that way, like the power portion of a snooker shot? It doesn't seem exactly natural, does it?"

Stingley sighed, remembering the theories that little bit of deduction had inspired. The best one was the Sussex Cyclops was a top snooker player, and all they had to do now was go out and clap the irons on Steve Davis or Terry Griffiths or Ray "Dracula" Reardon.

"Anyway, you know why we've kept it back. It's our litmus paper for false confessions, which we get by the dozen."

"You mentioned two reasons," Miss Grace said.

"Oh, yes, the other reason. The other reason, miss, is that we don't want to look bigger charlies than we already do look."

"What do you mean?"

"I mean the prints haven't done us a damn bit of good, aside from letting us know the killer's stroke. We've run them through the Yard, through Interpol, through the army, Civil Service, the Home Office, Social Security, every damned thing we could think of, and sod all. After eleven months."

"Well," Miss Grace said, "thank you for cooperation—"

That was when DI Stingley decided he could use a little cooperation back. "Don't mention it, don't mention it at all. I am curious, you know, just what your interest is in all this."

Miss Grace looked a question at Bellman. If Stingley were any good at reading faces, she'd like to know the answer to that question as well. But that was ridiculous. They were working together, weren't they?

Still, it was the American who did the talking. "Your composite picture." He gestured to a photocopy of it on Stingley's desk. "How good are your witnesses?"

"Better than average. They all gave descriptions that could be the same human being. And they all agreed he was an American. They all like the drawing, too. Interviewed them separately about it, of course."

"An American," Bellman said. "All right. I think the man in your picture is an international terrorist. The one I'm here looking for. His real name is Leo Calvin, and he's been working for the Russians for years."

Stingley fought a grin and lost. "Come on," he said. "Pull the other one, why don't you. Isn't this sort of thing small beer for an international terrorist?"

"If I knew what he was up to," the American said, "I would be in place first and capture him."

Stingley was still grinning until he looked straight into Bellman's eyes. "Uh—well. I guess you really mean it, don't you?"

"I didn't travel from the United States to London to Brighton to jerk you off, okay?"

"But we don't even think he's the killer!"

Miss Grace seemed a little concerned over that one. "But the news said—"

"The news can say what they like," Stingley said. "They don't know everything, and we don't tell them everything."

"Why don't you think he's the Cyclops?" Bellman said. He didn't seem nearly as displeased by the idea as the woman had been.

"Fingerprints."

"Again?" Miss Grace said.

"Again," Stingley said.

"Distribution?" Bellman asked.

Stingley nodded. "There are prints of three people in the flat. The victim, the killer, and a third person. The prints of the victim and the third person—who, we guess, is the husband, or what have you—are just everywhere. Plates, tables, the flush handle on the WC, all the places you put your fingers when you live somewhere. The killer left his dabs on the weapon, and a few wild prints about the flat, but nowhere near the number of the other two. He may have been there longer than a few minutes, but he wasn't *living* there.

"The only reason we put the picture out is that we want to talk to him. It *looked* like being a case where he came home, found the body, and buggered off in a panic. Now, of course, if he's an international terrorist, that could explain why he wanted no part of a police inquiry."

"If you find him, I want to know about it. Miss Grace will give you a telephone number." She did so. They thanked him for his time and trouble and rose to go.

The phone rang as they were on their way out. Stingley picked it up, listened, then told his caller to wait a second. "Miss Grace," he called. "Mr. Bellman, I don't know if this makes a difference to you, but the coroner says that Margaret Hepwood was pregnant. About three months gone."

Bellman took the news deadpan, nodded his thanks. They left. Through the door he could hear Miss Grace say, "Now, what the hell was *that* in aid of?" but he didn't hear Bellman make an answer.

THIRD

"I engage with the Snark—every night after dark—
  In a dreamy delirious fight:
I serve it with greens in those shadowy scenes,
  And I use it for striking a light;

"But if ever I meet with a Boojum, that day,
  In a moment (of this I am sure),
I shall softly and suddenly vanish away—
  And this notion I cannot endure!"

> —*The Hunting of the Snark*
> Fit the Third

1

Young Dave Hamilton stood in Robert Tipton's office like a boy summoned to the headmaster. Respectful, so far. Polite. Hoping nothing would happen to the fragile pride he kept within him to make him obliged to act otherwise.

Tipton hastened to reassure him. "Sit down, Mr. Hamilton," he said. The boy sat, feet together, back not touching the upholstery. His heavy lace-up boots looked incongruous against the plush blue carpet.

"First of all, I wanted to thank you for working the extra hours."

Young Hamilton smiled. "Yeah," he said, running a finger against the colored plastic in his ear. "When Miss Grace told me about the job, she said we wouldn't be working union hours, and all."

"Where have you put up Miss Grace and Mr. Bellman?"

"At the Bellingham, sir. It's a good respectable place on the shingle some way west of the marina. Private baths, lifts. I got them separate rooms, I hope that's all right, sir."

"You had no instructions to the contrary, Hamilton. Quite all right."

"The rooms do adjoin, sir." Hamilton raised his eyebrows in query.

This time Tipton smiled. "Good. I like to see my people have that kind of initiative. But I didn't call you in here just to check on your work."

"Before we go on, sir, speaking of initiative, and all, I'd like to ask you for your permission to update the accommodation program for Brighton. When I punched in the requirements this evening, the machine was all set to put through a call to the

Grand Hotel down there. We couldn't have that, now, could we?"

Tipton told him they certainly could not. He should get together with Research and update the entire accommodation program.

"But the reason I called you in here was to tell you that you've been awarded a rise in salary. This reflects not only the growing importance of the computer to the Section, but your continued good work with the computer. I was going to send you a notice tomorrow—I still will, in fact—but since we were both working late, I thought I'd tell you in person."

"Thank you, Mr. Tipton. Me mum will be tickled. Will that be all? I've got some expense accounts to process."

"That's all, Hamilton, keep up the good work."

"Yes, sir. Cheers."

One of the phones on Tipton's desk rang while the young man was still rising from his chair. Tipton picked it up and heard a voice say, "Robert?"

Tipton tried to keep his voice calm. "Yes?" he said, then he put his hand over the mouthpiece and hissed, "*Hamilton!*"

The young man stopped and looked at him eagerly. His coxcomb of hair seemed to vibrate with anticipation. Spy fever, Tipton thought. It gets us all in our younger days.

And apparently, he reflected, in our second childhood, too, because this was Sir Lewis Alfot on the line, the Secure Line, checked daily, a line to which only the Prime Minister and the Minister of Defence and the man who sat at the desk it rested on were supposed to have the number.

"It's me, Robert. Free, and only a little the worse. Listen to me. Your phone is secure, but not mine. Don't mention any names. . . ." He went on with similar shilling-shocker nonsense. Tipton took the time to whisper to Hamilton to rush down to Communications and get them to work on tracing this call.

"Where are you?" Tipton demanded. "We've been worried sick about you, the PM is after heads, and the Americans have been treating us like buffoons. Tell me where you are, and we'll send someone for you immediately."

"No."

"*No?*"

"Not yet. You put me out to pasture, but you were wrong. I have work to do."

"You have a bloody *report* to deliver, or the Americans will leave us with a totally bare bottom."

"Bugger the Americans. We can clean up our own bloody messes."

The idea now was to keep the old man talking. "Listen," Tipton began.

"You listen, Robert. There is something wrong."

"I had a feeling there might be," Tipton said. *"Where the bloody hell are you?"*

"Something wrong in the Section," Sir Lewis went on. "In the whole apparatus of our business. In the Kingdom."

Tipton squeezed the bridge of his nose, as if he were trying to pinch off the words forming in his brain from reaching his mouth.

"I've seen it, Robert. And I am bloody well going to do something about it! I always have done, haven't I?"

"Yes," Tipton said wearily, "you alw—"

The click told him the old man had hung up. He replaced the handset. A few seconds later the telephone next to it buzzed. Communications. No trace. Naturally. But they did have a recording of most of the conversation.

"Splendid," Tipton said wearily. He had to hope for a miracle if he wanted to keep the Americans from learning the truth now. He rubbed his eyes. He was beginning to see how sitting in this chair had sent Sir Lewis mad.

2

She didn't come to him during the night. Bellman had had no expectations one way or the other, so he wasn't disappointed. When they met the next morning for breakfast (bangers, eggs, fried potatoes, toast, jam, and tea), Felicity was impatient and irritable. Maybe I was supposed to go to her, Bellman thought.

"Do we have any plans today?" she asked.

Bellman looked at her. From the bag she'd grabbed from her office before they started down to Brighton last night, she had managed to put together the perfect "off-season holiday outfit," a bulky black sweater over a white turtleneck, black slacks, black silk scarf holding back her hair. She had also managed to retrieve her boots, and was therefore probably armed.

"Well," he said. "First I'm going to work on finishing this breakfast; that will take a while. Then I'd like to get up to Sir Lewis's place and look around there a little."

"People have been over it and over it," she said.

"I know, I'd just like to see it."

"All right, it's a twenty-minute drive, we can do it any time. Anything else?"

"It might be a good idea to get me a gun. I didn't like the ones we confiscated at the airport."

It bothered him that Felicity took a casual but thorough glance around the room before answering. She might have known he would have checked before bringing the topic up.

"I've an extra in my bag. Thirty-two automatic all right?"

"Perfect. I've even got a holster for one somewhere."

"Anything else?"

"Why? You want some time off? Doctor? Beauty parlor? Can't stand the sight of me anymore?"

"I can stand it," she said grimly. "I want to show you something. Maybe tell you something."

"Such as what?"

"I said maybe. I'll see how I feel." She looked at him long and hard; her eyes were like bright blue searchlights. Bellman got the feeling that his answer would have a lot to do with the future of their working relationship. And for professional reasons (and reasons more personal than he wanted to admit), their working relationship was something he wanted to take good care of.

"All right," he said softly. "We'll see how you feel."

She drove him down the beach to the Grand Hotel, parking illegally across the road from it. She gestured him out of the car, leaned against a wing, and pointed.

Bellman had read about what had happened here, had seen some of the reports that had made their way into the Congressman's files. The explosion had ripped upward through the middle of the building that October night. It missed wiping out the entire Thatcher government. It had succeeded in killing a few, crippling several, and wounding dozens.

The IRA insisted it was war. The photos had certainly looked like it, the great V-shaped wound in the middle of the building might have been caused by a blockbuster dropped from an airplane rather than a hand-carried device wrapped in a garbage bag to thwart the noses of explosives-sniffing dogs.

It didn't look that way now. They'd been working on the building, clearing away the rubble, squaring off the ragged edges, getting it ready for repair. It now resembled nothing so much as a tooth the dentist was about ready to fill.

Against the morning sky, one of the shocking electric-blue kind Britain will offer about once a month in contrast to the usual gray, it seemed even more benign. Under construction, routine repairs.

"That's what we're up against," Felicity said, and Bellman knew she was still seeing it as the orgy of confusion and destruction and pain it had been immediately after the blast.

"That's the symbol of all of it, Jeffrey, that building."

Bellman maintained an encouraging silence. It occurred to him that lately he had been taking a lot more of what Felicity Grace said at face value. That ole debbil sex, he thought, then pushed the notion away. Let the woman talk. There was plenty of time to be skeptical.

"I love this country, you know," she said. "That's not quite back in fashion here the way it is in America, but I do. I wouldn't do this work if I didn't."

To look at them, you would have thought they were just another couple of tourists, come to rubberneck at the scene of some particularly dramatic human misery.

"They're out to destroy us, you know. Britain is the target right now. They're trying to break us."

"They're trying to break all of us," Bellman said.

"They are concentrating on Britain," Felicity said. "The IRA gets training and money, and probably the very bomb that blew up this lovely old building, from the Libyans. Who are backed by the Russians. Who, along with the Libyans, are funneling in money to the NUM, with their bloody eternal coal strike."

"Which is dividing the country, and hurting the economy, and victimizing the poor stupid innocent bastards in the union itself, and screwing over the economy and ruining life in a lot of villages probably forever," Bellman said. "I know. Every country goes through something like that from time to time. We had ours in the late sixties and early seventies—"

"Don't teach me history, dammit. You Americans are very little better, anyway."

"Are you done looking at the building?" Bellman said.

"What if I'm not?"

"Then let's sit in the car before we get loud enough to draw a crowd."

She glared at him for a second, then got in and started the motor. Bellman had to step lively to get around to the left side of the car before she drove off without him.

"All right," he said, "tell me about Americans."

"What good will it do?"

"You never know."

"You're so bloody smug. You make me sick."

"Who? Americans in general? American spies? Or just me?"

"Take your pick." Felicity turned the car away from the ocean. "Here you are, with all this *thunderous* backing, the White House and the rest, to come and show us how to do it. You have no conception of the problems we're up against, what Tipton and Sir Lewis before him had to put up with."

"I do now," Bellman said. "You just explained it."

"You are not funny. If you just let us hold up our end—"

"The Russians march into Afghanistan, while the union takes a tea break. Who next, Canada?"

"We can do our job!"

"And *we* can't take any chances over it. The work *has* to be done, all right? Whether it's you or us doesn't matter—if it isn't, your country and my country are in deep shit, if I may use an Americanism. Slow down if you don't want to crack us up or get us arrested."

"We've got a friend on the Sussex police," she said grimly. "Why worry?" But she eased up on the accelerator.

"I happen to have," Bellman said, "an overriding affection for Britain. This is the country that invented capitalism. And sportsmanship. And trial by jury, and freedom of speech. Most of the things that make America most worth fighting for are direct bequests from Britain. You people built an empire, stood out alone against Hitler, led the world in science and technology."

"And everything you've mentioned is in the past tense," she said.

"I know. And it doesn't make sense, does it? There's just too much greatness in the gene pool here for this country to have gotten as screwed up as it is."

"People write great fat books about the reasons. The Class Structure is a big one. The war. Treachery from Within. The Cruel System of Capitalism. The Welfare State. Which do you fancy?"

"Take your pick," Bellman said. "They all contribute, but at the bottom they're nothing. The only thing that could really yank the curtain down on you is the attitude I see that says nobody can do anything about it."

" 'The only thing we have to fear is fear itself?' " Felicity said.

Bellman grinned. "How about this one? 'Some chicken; some neck.' "

"Beautiful words, Mr. Bellman. But why is it that I feel my country, my Section and me are being a bit *used*?"

"Beats me," Bellman said.

"How much do you really care about Sir Lewis Alfot? And how much of your visit is concerned with this international terrorist of yours? One glimpse of him on the telly, and you drop everything to come down here."

Bellman tightened his lips and nodded. "Ive been wondering if you were going to bring this up. I don't suppose you'd believe me if I told you I made it all up to have a story for Stingley."

"I would not. Why the mad rush down here then? We could have just as well stayed in London. You could have watched *Doctor Who*. We could have made love again. Not that I'm giving you any news, but you're quite good at it."

"When I have the proper inspiration."

"More lies."

"Not that one. All right. I'm going to tell you the truth."

Felicity made a noise. "I don't expect the truth. Just a little respect. As a colleague. A professional."

"Sure. I'll give you both. I tell the truth sometimes just to hear what my voice sounds like when I'm doing it. Helps me give more verisimilitude to my lies. Are you ready?"

Felicity nodded.

Bellman told her the truth. Not all of it. Nothing about the Cronus operation, or his dubious past and his love/hate relationship with his father. He did tell her that he wasn't the original Jeffrey Bellman, that he replaced the agent who'd had that name and who'd been assigned to help in the hunt for Sir Lewis. He told her that Leo Calvin, the international terrorist in question, had a personal grudge against him, and that Calvin had had *something* to do with the death of Bellman's namesake.

"So yes," he concluded, "I have a personal ax to grind. I want Calvin off my case so I can sleep in peace."

"He's probably in Russia, drinking tea with Kim Philby."

"He is not. He's here, and he's running for his life. The Russians are angry. But he's still working on having me killed. It's long past time for a showdown.

"But it's all tied in. Calvin and the Russians and Sir Lewis— the death of the previous agent tells us that. And that composite drawing ties him in with the Sussex Cyclops, though God knows how."

"There's no proof of that."

"Proof? Of course not. Police work on proof. We have to work on possibilities. Do you really think it's a coincidence that the Cyclops, with fifty-five million people in the Kingdom to choose from, wound up killing the girlfriend of my own personal playmate?"

Felicity said nothing.

Bellman piled on questions. "After the way I inherited the case? After Sir Lewis had been approached by a local deputation to look into the killings and Sir Lewis disappeared?"

"No," she said at last. "I suppose I don't believe it's coincidence."

"Feel respected now?"

She kept her eyes on the road and drove. Bellman took the opportunity to look at the scenery. Fields mostly, dormant under a crust of old snow, sloping gently away from the sea. This would be beautiful in the summer, he thought. It's not so bad now.

"I think I will tell you," Felicity said.

"Tell me what?"

"What I was considering telling you this morning. I want you to understand me. I know it's dreadfully unprofessional, maybe even dangerous, but that's what I want."

"I can't promise to understand you," Bellman said.

"Just listen," Felicity said. She didn't look at him while she talked, just kept her eyes straight ahead, on the road. As if she were in a psychiatrist's office, or a confessional.

"The first thing I want you to know," she said, "is that I'm going to file a report with Mr. Tipton at my earliest opportunity and tell him what you've told me today."

"Of course," Bellman said. "I never thought you weren't professional."

She ignored it. "This is my second time round with the Section," she said. "I was out of it for over a year and a half. Out of the Civil Service altogether."

"Voluntarily?"

"In a manner of speaking. I did the worst thing an agent can do—I loved someone. His name was Derek. He was with the Special Branch. We met during an operation. He was brave and strong and deliciously ugly, and he loved me, too. It was the first thing we'd ever had outside our jobs. I resigned; we got married. Derek was going to leave, too, but he was in the middle of an important investigation. He was going to leave as soon as he was through. It dragged on and on.

"It wasn't supposed to happen until Derek was safe and dry in a normal job, but I got pregnant, something," she said, "that will never happen again. The investigation was drawing to a close—"

"IRA?"

"Yes."

"There's something extra in your voice when you talk about them."

"Something extra, indeed. One night, he disappeared. Someone had leaked something, and Derek disappeared. Two weeks later, he was found. Dead. Naked. I will not speak of what had been done to him before they killed him. I'll just tell you that the operation eventually came off without a hitch, proof that whatever they'd done, they hadn't been able to get him to talk.

"I went mad when I got the news. They tried to keep me from seeing his body, but I insisted, and I went mad. I also went into labor, and it's just as well, because I think I might have destroyed the baby if I hadn't.

"I never saw the baby—they tell me it was a boy—I didn't want to. The sight of him would remind me too much of his father. I let him be adopted.

"I was mad all winter. I wanted to kill. Myself; the people who gave Derek such dangerous assignments; Irishmen at random. I knew I'd never be able to find the specific ones who'd hurt and killed him.

"I decided at last that the only thing to do was to go back to work for Sir Lewis. If I couldn't fight them in particular, I'd fight them in general. As I said today, it's all connected, anyway.

"It took time, months, but I persuaded Sir Lewis to take me back, and Mr. Tipton gave me this ridiculous name and put me back to work. Every time I frustrate another plan to destroy my country, or at least help; every time I kill a thug or a terrorist, I feel like I've done a little something for Derek. And maybe for his son. His greatness is in the gene pool, Jeffrey. I feel good about that.

"So the work is important to me in a special way. I may still be mad. Do you understand? You may be working with and bedding a madwoman."

For the first time, she looked at him. Her eyes were clear and frank and showed no trace of madness.

"Does that bother you?" she said.

"No," Bellman said softly a few seconds later. "I think I can handle it."

3

With the universal instinct of futility that Bellman's father called the Barn Door Response, the powers that be had doubled the guard (unobtrusively, of course) at Sir Lewis's home, and made them be extra careful. Even Felicity's magic little document, the one that had so impressed DI Stingley the night before, wasn't good enough, and they had to wait while a fresh-faced young man (who was pouring a new driveway with his partners while they kept an eye on the place) went to his truck and radioed London for approval.

Bellman spent the interval looking at the place. Sir Lewis hadn't gone in for ostentation. It was a four-room cottage, painted white, gray roof. A couple of rosebushes. The only tip-off to the educated eye that there might be something special about the man who lived here was the slightly over-elaborate TV antenna buckled prosaically to the chimney, a remnant from the days when Sir Lewis had to be kept In Constant Touch.

The name of the place was Advance, Tipton had said, because Sir Lewis Alfot would be damned if he ever needed a retreat. A nice little place, Bellman supposed, but hard to guard without disrupting the whole area and blowing the cover to bits. Sir Lewis might step into the back garden to smell the roses, get pulled over the fence, and disappear. That, in fact, was the best theory anybody had so far. The only lead Tipton's men had on it was the sound truck that had been heard in the neighborhood the day Sir Lewis disappeared. They were trying to follow up. Bellman wished them luck. If Leo Calvin had had anything to do with that truck, anybody who might be either willing or able to tell the authorities anything about it would be long gone from Britain, dead, or both.

The young man came back from the van, pulled off a tar-smeared glove, shook hands with Bellman and Felicity, unlocked the door, and let them in. It was colder inside than it had been outside, since no sunlight had reached the place in weeks.

Bellman followed his breath around the room, looking at everything, but nothing in particular.

"I don't know what you expect to find," Felicity said. She had an anorak over the sweater now, and looked like she'd just come in off a ski run. "All the official things and the radio equipment and the like were removed as soon as Sir Lewis went missing."

"You've met the man."

"And?"

"And I haven't. This is the next best thing, not that it's any too great. Still, I want to get *some* kind of handle on his personality."

"Sir Lewis's personality was too big to be lifted by just one handle, I'm afraid."

"We'll do the best we can. This is the trophy room, I take it."

Felicity didn't bother to answer. The walls were lined with plaques, scrolls, certificates, swords, silver and gold cups, and plates and bowls, all engraved with glowing testimonials to the goodness of Sir Lewis Alfot.

"Well," Bellman said. "I know something about him already. He was proud but not vain. He kept all this stuff where a visitor could see it, but he didn't spend much time looking at it himself."

"How do you know that?"

"No furniture. Most men with collections like this make a study out of the room they keep it in, to have an excuse to sit with it for a long time and make sure it's still there."

"You didn't say 'elementary,' " Felicity said. "Would you like to see the study next?"

Bellman told her to lead on. The study was cozy and book-lined. There was a television and a stereo system tucked unob-trusively away. Bellman took a closer look at the shelves. The books were histories and thrillers, indiscriminately mixed among British and foreign authors. The records were resolutely easy listening—probably everything Mantovani ever recorded.

"The hottest music here is Petula Clark," Bellman said.

"He came here to relax," Felicity said.

"Okay, no value-judgment implied. I wanted to learn about the man, and I'm making progress."

There was one shelf that was practically empty. It was at eye-level for Felicity, who was (Bellman remembered) about the same height as Sir Lewis. The shelf held a silver-framed photo-graph of a bunch of ragged-looking soldiers, with signatures on the bottom. The faces were haggard, but game, the kind of face seen in every unposed photo taken in Britain from 1939 to 1945.

Next to it was a silver loving cup about the size of a demitasse. The inscription, which had obviously been hammered in letter by laborious letter, filled up nearly all of the available surface. It read:

TO LIEUTENANT LEWIS ALFOT
IN GRATITUDE
FROM THE MEN HE LED
OUT OF THE JAWS OF DEATH
FRANCE, 1940

The other side had "If you can keep your head when all about you are losing theirs," and the designation of the outfit Alfot had taken command of during the flight from France.

Bellman held it gently, as though afraid he might bend it, read both sides, then placed it back precisely in the circle it had left in the dust.

Felicity had been reading over his shoulder. "You think this was the one he was proudest of, then."

"Unless he was a fanatic for Kipling or Tennyson." He turned away from the shelf and put his hands in his pockets. "It makes sense. It was the first of his citations, from men he'd been through hell with. I'm sure that made it special."

The rest of the cottage showed him nothing you wouldn't expect to see in the home of any elderly bachelor with money and simple tastes. Bellman took it in, then went back out into the bright, cold sunshine.

"What now?" Felicity wanted to know. "Back to London? I can have our things sent up."

"No, back to Brighton."

"Your man is long gone from there by now."

Bellman shrugged. "This is a small island. When I find out where he is, I can get to him. What I want in Brighton is for you to join me for a seafood dinner."

"Am I ever going to understand you?" she said. It was possible that the twist of her lips was a smile.

"You can try," Bellman said. He *was* smiling. "No one ever has yet."

4

Leo Calvin had been involved with pistols, rifles, carbines, bombs. Knives, drugs, poisons, and homicidal maniacs. He had never felt so close to death as he did now.

Grigori Illyich Bulanin's handsome face was pinched in a movie-star scowl. It was nonetheless deadly for that. Bulanin wanted explanations, and he wanted them rapidly.

Leo would provide them. Or he would provide something. He would have to trust to luck that the Russian had no knowledge that would ruin the story Leo had been polishing so carefully on his way back to London.

Leo was uncomfortable, quite literally not himself. He was in disguise, and he hated it. It had been a matter of pride with him that he had always managed his affairs in such a way that he could flaunt his individuality, his unusual appearance. Now, hiding it, he felt diminished, less able to control people and events at a time when it was essential that he do so.

But the hair that fell in front of his eyes was a muddy brown instead of the customary platinum. That was the color a whole bottle of Grecian 2000 had made it. It had also made his hair oily, and his scalp seemed to want to crawl away from it.

The round frames of the eyeglasses he now affected rimmed the world for him—he couldn't stop seeing them. And he could feel the weight of the false moustache on his lip. It seemed to get in the way when he wanted to speak, muffling his words, hampering his mouth. It was also impossible to forget that the moustache was not the same color as his slicked-down hair. He kept reminding himself that this was the case with many men with natural moustaches, but the fact failed to comfort him.

Leo was also upset with himself. He had made his plan, and kidnapped an important Englishman to use as a pawn. The pawn had ideas of his own. Margaret was no great loss—her time would have come soon in any case, especially now, with the child she had been foolish enough to allow to be conceived. But he wished he had Sir Lewis back. What capital Leo could have made of him, if only he'd seen the truth. Now, he didn't dare use it.

It hadn't been a mistake, Leo reflected, to agree to meet Bulanin here, in the Tombs. Just a necessity.

The Tombs was a collection of dank chambers tucked away in the storage space under the South-Bank side of one of the multitudinous bridges across the Thames. Like the London Dungeon not far away, the Tombs was a wax museum for those who found the Chamber of Horrors at Madame Tussaud's insufficiently horrible. The Tombs boasted loving reproduction of every method of torture ever used in the British Isles, as well as working models of methods of execution, and depictions of famous crimes, certified for accuracy by eminent historians. There was a notice posted at intervals stating that every skeleton and partial skeleton, every mummified hand or head, were Genuine Human Remains, and another notice informing the reader that the building was open every day except Christmas and Good Friday, from 10.00 to 19.00.

Leo walked with Bulanin down a cobblestone walk in the middle of a reproduction of Jack the Ripper's Whitechapel, breathing an eye-searing concoction that purported to be authentic-formula 1870s smog.

"It's good you rang me," Bulanin said. "I've been looking for you."

"Everybody has been looking for me," Leo said.

"More than you know." Bulanin coughed. "This is worse than cigarettes. Let's find a more wholesome area to walk."

They turned a corner into a torture dungeon, watching some poor wax bastard being torn apart by red-hot pincers. He looked at the dummy's face. That was the way they looked, all right. Leo wondered how the artisan had found out.

"What do you mean, more than I know?"

"I mean I am not the only member of my organization with access to BBC news. Nor the only one who knows your face."

Bulanin paused to let that sink in, a move wasted on Leo, since it had sunk in quite thoroughly already. The police were the least of his worries. As far as that went, he might turn himself in to the next bobby he ran across and let British Justice take its course.

"I am being pressed," Bulanin continued ominously, "for results."

"There's a lot at stake here," Leo said.

"I know what is at stake. *My* career. *My* life. I must have delivery of the goods you promised."

"You will, but you have to accept that it can't be done just like that."

"It could have been done just like that weeks ago. Instead, you had some private project in mind, using the one thing that could save your life as bait. I was foolish to let you."

"This can make it better."

"What can make it better? Your being a fugitive? American agents making threats—" A group of noisy, shouting schoolboys came by, testing macho by ditching class to look at the gruesome reproductions. Bulanin waited for them to go by, then said in a lower voice, "Making threats in *my own building*. Oblivious to surveillance. Accompanied by an Englishwoman we know to be a spy. Unheard of behavior for the CIA."

"He isn't CIA."

"No? What, then?"

"I don't know. He's not the original Bellman. He's not the one you had your friends get in touch with for me."

"I didn't think so. Who is he?"

"When I knew him before, his name was Driscoll. He claimed to be working for the Defense Department, but that wasn't true either."

"I ask you again—who *does* he work for?"

"I don't know exactly, but he's something new. Follows no rules. Takes incredible risks."

Bulanin grinned. Leo didn't join him. It wasn't appropriate, and he still wasn't sure of his moustache.

"He works like us, then," Bulanin said. "You and I."

"Exactly. That's why—"

"I am done taking risks in this instance. There is a death order on you which I have ignored. I have even helped you. Because you promised me the old man. I must deliver the old man, or I *will* deliver you."

Leo acted more concerned than he felt. If Bulanin had been absolutely determined to pull the plug on their little joint venture, he wouldn't be here breathing smog and talking. He would have set up the meet, and had it kept by a couple of trained Bulgarians. And Leo would have been delivered, with Bulanin getting credit for a job well done.

But Leo had a hunch that Alfot meant even more to the Russians than Bulanin was letting on. His KGB friend wasn't going to give up while there was still the slightest chance that Leo might succeed. Leo noted with an almost academic interest that he could now feel fairly confident he would continue living for the time being. That had been in some doubt.

"I don't think you're going to touch me," Leo said. "You're too smart."

"It isn't my wisdom that keeps you alive," Bulanin said. "It's my ambition. My instinct for survival is stronger than either, and that wants you dead. I suggest you use this last opportunity to persuade me otherwise."

"Leaving aside the old man," Leo began, "I have something your people have wanted for years, and you know it—a way into Alfot's section."

"Revealed to you, no doubt by the old man himself, under drugs or torture. His security checks are too good for you to have learned any other way."

Leo let him think so. It was vital that Bulanin never know Leo no longer had Sir Lewis in custody.

"Test me if you want," Leo said. "Give me two days to find out who the woman is."

"I don't care who she is."

"Never mind, then, it's beside my point."

"Yes. Your point. Get to it, please, I have work to do."

"The point is Bellman. *He's* behind all this. He's framed me in this murder business—"

"What do you mean, he framed you?"

"I mean he killed the woman I'd been hiding out with, using the technique of this Sussex Cyclops maniac in order to get the British police after me."

"That is extreme for an American," Bulanin said.

"I told you that." Leo watched the Russian carefully. This was the lie that had to go across. He watched as Bulanin ran the story over in his mind, waited for him to speak.

"If he knew where the woman was, and knew you'd been with her, he did not *need* to get the British after you. He could have gone to your flat, killed the woman, and disposed of you when you returned home." For the first time in many minutes, Bulanin turned to look Leo in the eye. "I would have expected a more skillful lie."

"He doesn't want to *kill* me. He wants to *turn* me. He *wants* publicity. He wants to make a mess. It's a good thing I had the old man in a safe place." Vital Lie Number 2.

"Why would he want this?"

"My friend, he works for the American government. What do you think he's after?"

It was a suspenseful ten seconds before Bulanin nodded. "It makes sense," he said. "This Sussex Cyclops has his horrible fascination. . . ."

"More horrible and more fascinating if he can pin it on someone he could make say the Kremlin was behind it."

"The public would believe it. They think all spies are monsters."

"And you're an expert, as I am. You know anybody could be made to say anything under the right circumstances."

"You are giving me," Bulanin said, "more reason to kill you."

Trap sprung. "It doesn't have to be that way," Leo told him.

"I was sure you'd be able to suggest an alternative." Bulanin didn't smile, just looked at Leo expectantly.

"Kill Bellman," Leo said.

"Again? I think not."

"I can find out exactly where he is for you by late this afternoon. If you have him taken care of, it will be safer for me to retrieve the old man. You get what you want—your ambition, wisdom, and survival instinct are all happy—"

"And you live."

Moustache or no moustache, Leo decided to risk a smile. "And I live," he said.

"You would still have the police to deal with. And you'd be at my mercy."

"I'm at your mercy now. And I'm not worried about the police. I told you from the beginning, what I'm hoping to buy with the old man is a welcome in Moscow. I am not ambitious—I like the game. I could be very useful to a man with ambition."

"Let's go outside," Bulanin said. "I would like a cigarette, I think."

Leo suppressed the sigh of relief he felt building. Home free. It was a shame to have to forego (again) his personal revenge on Driscoll. Bellman. But as Bulanin had said, this was a matter of survival. Let the Russians take care of Bellman.

All Leo had to do was to find Sir Lewis Alfot by the time they did.

5

The hardest part after the escape itself had been getting to the storage company in Hove. Sir Lewis had walked along the Kingsway through the night, cursing the cold wind and the age that made him feel it. He shivered, but he shouldn't have shivered. It had been cold in Europe, too, and the Germans had been shooting at him on sight.

No one here was going to shoot him. Only his friends were looking for him. Except, of course, for one young American kidnapper, perhaps. Sir Lewis wasn't all that worried about him—if there was any justice at all, that young man would have other things on his mind. Sir Lewis smiled, but the wind got him cursing again. He pulled the hood up over his head and shrank back deeper into the anorak.

It was foolish to worry about the cold. Bad tactics, demoralizing. If he wanted to be warm, all he had to do was stop at a phone box and dial 999, or ask a stranger to take him to the police. His face was well enough known. He had no doubt it had appeared in the newspapers and on telly frequently enough since they'd grabbed him. He'd find somebody to take him in. He could be welcomed with everything short of a fatted calf. If that was what he wanted.

Which it was not. He was cold (don't think about it, he told himself angrily) and he was tired, but he was alive, he was free, he was back in the hunt. He was the *master* of the hunt. The years behind the desk hadn't dulled his enthusiasm for it, and he was pleased with himself to know that. If he went back now, he wouldn't even have the desk, just chores to do for the Americans.

The Americans. They were all right, couldn't have staved off the Russians this long without them, but they had the annoying habit of wanting to teach their grandmother.

Not that Sir Lewis wasn't willing to learn. For example, the plan he was walking through the wind to execute had been inspired by the cinema comedian W.C. Fields. Sir Lewis would take a good idea where he found it.

He had read it years ago in a magazine while waiting for a train. This Fields, it seemed, had a pathological fear of losing his money, being wiped out by another Depression, or by a lawsuit, or whatever. To hedge against that, he opened bank accounts all over America under feigned names, figuring they couldn't all be wiped out.

It had struck Sir Lewis as a natural precaution for an agent to take at the beginning of a risky operation, not just money, but clothes, gun, new papers, whatever he might need if he were forced to run. Prepared fall-back position, as it were. It worked for the military.

So thirteen months before, when he first decided (reluctantly) that the Cyclops operation had become inevitable he had placed caches of supplies all around Sussex. Not anticipating failure, mind you—it was a poor planner who launched an operation without confidence—but in recognition of the fact that no one can anticipate everything.

It was well he had. He certainly hadn't anticipated some crazy lefties coming along to kidnap him. And even if he had done, he wouldn't have dreamed that once having escaped from them, he'd decide to remain at large with no interference whatever.

But Sir Lewis had spent most of the waking moments of his captivity thinking, and he didn't like the pictures his mind showed him. The kidnappers had known his schedule too well— Sir Lewis hadn't expected to be home that day, and the next day he was going to leave for his villa in Malta to tone down some of the language in his report. They'd grabbed him at the one opportunity they had.

That might have been a coincidence. And it might have been a coincidence that the kidnappers had worked so well around his (unasked for) bodyguard's schedule of patrol.

Sir Lewis didn't think so, as much as he wanted to. He wanted to because the alternative hurt too much. A leak in the Section. He felt as if his own child had betrayed him.

Thinking of that made him so angry, he forgot about the wind.

Within six hours of his escape from the kidnappers, he had money, a new suit, a suitcase, a toupee, a small revolver and ammunition, materials for disguise or demolition, and soft dental-appliance pads to wear in his cheeks to change the shape of his face. He had eaten two sausage rolls and a bag of crisps purchased at an all-night petrol station. When the sun came up, he had a proper breakfast, checked into a hotel, and slept the day through.

That evening, he went out to a phone box and placed a call to Robert at the Section. Sir Lewis still was planning to solve this problem (*all* their problems) by himself, but he had to let Robert know that something was rotten in the Section. *Robert* hadn't been the one who'd sent him packing. Queer or no, Robert was a good man, and deserved that much of a briefing.

He spent the rest of the night making plans. The next day, he rented a car—he had a vehicle operator's license in his new name with the rest of the stuff—and drove to the Advance. He wanted to watch it for a while, and see what Tipton had his men up to there.

What he'd seen was Felicity Grace and some young man leaving the cottage.

They got into a car he knew was Felicity's and drove south, back toward Brighton. Sir Lewis followed.

He thought of many reasons for following Miss Grace over the next several hours. Who was that she was with? Could she be the traitor? Sir Lewis doubted it, but then he would have doubted *anyone* could be. On the other hand, sooner or later, he might need some help, and Felicity was a good agent. He'd have to go home sometime, and she was as good a person to approach as any. It might also help him in his own work to know what she was up to, she and this young man he didn't recognize.

All rationalizations. Sir Lewis knew that, didn't worry about it. He had a hunch, and he taught his people never to ignore a hunch.

Now he sat in a hotel room across the hall from his former employee and her friend, listening, waiting for them to make a move. The hotel was nearly deserted. If there was any noise to hear, it was the wind, or it was the two of them.

About eight o'clock he heard the door open across the way. Voices. A man saying, "How far is the marina? Should I have them call us a cab?" Felicity replying, "No, we'll take the bus. We could almost walk if it weren't so cold."

Sir Lewis thanked God they weren't going to make him walk the oceanfront again. He heard the door close, and a key turn in a lock. He waited a few moments, then followed them.

6

"Next time," Bellman said, "we take a cab."

"We must have taken a wrong turn somewhere."

"Just one?"

"I'm sorry."

"Don't worry about it," Bellman said. "It's fascinating. The place advertises in the newspaper. They answer the phone, and take our reservation. They just neglect to tell anybody that the restaurant is somewhere that's inaccessible at night."

"I've been here only in the daytime," Felicity said. "It will be a damn long time before I come here again, too."

They were good-natured, which each considered to be something of an achievement. It was cold now, much colder than it had been during the day, and clouds rolled in, bringing with them a thin, misty drizzle, just on the point of freezing.

The bus had let them off on a ridge above the ocean. Crossing the road and looking down, they could see the marina, a graceful fantasy of looping concrete quays, over- and underpasses for cars and pedestrians, and boat lights reflected in the still water of the harbor. They could even see the sign proclaiming the name of the seafood restaurant they wanted to get to.

What they couldn't do was get to it. They found a likely entrance to the marina, a ramp that took off from the ridge and soared over the water like a gray rainbow. Several ramps peeled off it. They chose the one on the left, since the quay the restaurant sat on seemed to be in that direction.

Wrong choice—the way was blocked by a huge pile of sand which filled up the space between bridge supports. It had been left there no doubt to be used as construction material for new complications to the marina.

They doubled back to where the roads converged, and tried again, this time coming to a tall wire fence on a wood frame, whose gate was uncompromisingly locked.

"There's the restaurant," Bellman said. "Want to climb over?"

"I could, you know."

"Never doubted it. I asked you if you wanted to."

"Let's save it for a last resort."

They went back to the divergence. There were two approaches remaining. "Let's take the one on the far right," Felicity said.

"That one looks like it goes to Hove, for God's sake. Cornwall, maybe. The opposite direction entirely."

"Have you read *Through the Looking Glass?*"

"Right. Let's try it." The path led them on an interesting walk to several locked gates, past large construction equipment, and through unlit tunnels that resembled nothing so much as drainage pipes.

Bellman's good nature was giving way to impatience, to say nothing of hunger. But there was more. The seeming irrationality of the layout, the dark, the quiet. The impression that someone was watching, enjoying their frustration.

"If I didn't think it would give you doubts about my manhood, I'd tell you how spooky this place was."

"There's nothing wrong with your manhood. It *is* spooky down here."

They smiled at each other, amused by the idea of two highly trained intelligence agents afraid of walking around in the dark.

"The old man who got off the bus when we did is probably at the restaurant by now. We should have asked him the way," Felicity said.

"If he was heading for the restaurant, he's probably on dessert by now. Oh, no!" He pointed and started to laugh. Looming ahead of them again was the sand pile.

"What's that?" Felicity said.

"It's the sand pile that stopped us the first time we tried to get down here."

"I mean that noise."

Bellman listened to a faint tapping noise, regular but rapid, that soon sorted itself out into the footfalls of several joggers. Only a jogger, he thought, would want to run through a freezing drizzle through southeast England's answer to a gigantic outdoor Laff-in-the-Dark, but if they were confident enough to *run* through here, they probably knew their way around.

It was impolite, he knew, to ask a jogger to stop, but he could shout out a question, and perhaps get an answer yelled back over a shoulder, if any of them had enough breath.

They came out from one of the pipe-tunnels, three of them, middle-aged, but golden-haired and obviously glowing with health. No problem with breath shortage. They were probably Finnish marathoners or something, tuning up for a race.

"I'll ask these guys," he told Felicity.

"Might as well do," she said.

"How do we get from here to the restaurant?"

At which point somebody fired a gun. One shot. Bellman saw the little explosion on the side of the sand pile.

The front runner of the joggers looked angry. He cursed in a foreign language (somewhere in Bellman's brain a circuit connected—Russian) and then asked who fired the shot. At the same time, he reached under his sweatshirt and came up with a .357 Magnum. Bellman ran two steps toward the sand pile and dove for cover, wondering as he did so how far a Magnum would penetrate through sand. Felicity, he was glad to see, was already there, scrambling through the seam where the sand rested up against the concrete abutment of the overpass.

A geyser of sand shot up a foot from Bellman's head. He wished he was an armadillo, or a mole. The man was making dire predictions about the fate of the idiot who fired that first shot.

Bellman was becoming one with the cold, wet sand, burrowing, climbing, trying to get around to the other side. Sand was in his shoes, his hair, his ears, his mouth, his eyes.

He felt a hand on his wrist and fought free. Then he saw it had been Felicity, trying to pull him over to safety. And making an unnecessary target of herself.

"Get your head *down!*" he told her.

She did, but she reappeared a few seconds later. She had disappeared just long enough to go to her boot and come up with her gun. Now, as she had at the airport, she was taking careful aim and squeezing off shots.

She winged one of them, which gave the other two something to think about, and gave Bellman time enough to make it to reasonable safety. He crouched beside her, hugging the sand, listening. Felicity pulled his sleeve and pointed to the restaurant about two hundred yards down an unobstructed quay. She mouthed the words *phone* and *help*.

Bellman shook his head angrily. They couldn't make it to safety before the joggers could get over the pile. They'd be naked to two, possibly three guns. Besides, what was to say they'd be safe if they made it to the restaurant? Who knew how many people these bastards would be willing to kill in order to get the two of them?

They had to meet them here, and take them. Bellman tried to close his eyes to picture what was happening on the other side of the mound, but sand at the edges of his contact lenses made that agony. He could feel his eyes start to tear, and welcomed it. He'd just have to picture what they were doing with his eyes open.

They'd come around the sides, one to the right and one to the left. Slowly, carefully, guns drawn. The wounded man, if he were able, would back them up from a distance, in case Felicity and he tried to come over the top, or if they somehow handled one of the Magnums and tried an end run.

Okay. That's what they were doing. Now, what the hell was *he* going to do?

A preemptive strike. Bellman made some gestures to Felicity, but if she understood what he was going to do, she had gotten it entirely through telepathy. She did the right thing, though, stationed herself about two-thirds of the way toward the right wall, to give her gun hand a better advantage against the man coming over that side.

Bellman wished he could wink at her. Instead, he drew the gun Felicity had given him, and nodded. He started climbing up the mound.

As long as he was making wishes, he wished the damned sand pile could have been less flat on top. As it was, he was going to have to show altogether too much of his body before he could get a shot off.

What couldn't be changed had to be dealt with. He crouched as close to the top as he could, got the best purchase the sand would allow, then threw himself forward in a dive that plowed a furrow through the sand. As soon as he landed he reached out with both hands around the gun, raised himself on his chest, and snapped off two shots at the wounded man, who had been standing with his gun dangling nonchalantly from his good arm. Not smart. Bellman's first bullet took him in the base of the throat, the second between the eyes as he fell. He never did let go of the gun.

Bellman couldn't take the time to admire his work. He pulled his feet up under him, and with a yell, launched himself feetfirst down the left side of the sand pile. A shot roared past his ear, but that was all the man (the lead jogger, Bellman saw) had time to do before Bellman landed on him.

The impact knocked both guns loose, and they fought hand-to-hand in the treacherous footing. The Russian pushed off the abutment and sent Bellman sprawling. Bellman shook his head to clear his vision just in time to see a kick aimed for his face. He twisted and took the sneakered foot on his shoulder, where it did no harm. Bellman grabbed for the other foot, the planted one, caught it in both hands, pulled, and twisted.

The Russian was thrown violently off balance and went down. His head smacked against the concrete on the way. Bellman was on him before the sand settled. He had his right arm around his throat and his knee in the small of his back. He pulled above and pushed below and waited for the crack.

When it came it sounded like a gunshot. It took a full second before Bellman realized that what he had heard *was* a gunshot, simultaneous with the cracking of the spine.

Bellman froze. A lorry went by on the road above. He wanted to call for Felicity, but he didn't dare. If she'd been the one shot, he still had someone to deal with.

He waited. Silence. He thought about the noise he'd heard, decided at last that it hadn't been loud enough to be a Magnum.

Finally, he said, "Felicity?" then scrambled sideways to spoil the angle of a possible attack.

"Jeff? Thank *God*."

He scrambled over the sand to her. It was unprofessional, but he took her in his arms and gave her a quick but thorough kiss.

The body of the third man was sprawled prone, head downward on the sand. The blood soaking into the sand was black in the mercury vapor light.

"What do we do with them?" Bellman asked. His voice was rapid with unburned adrenaline. "Bury them in the sand pile?"

Felicity said, "Jeffrey," but Bellman cut her off.

"No, I know better. Let's just find *my* gun—here it is—and leave them here. I'm still hungry, aren't you?"

"Jeffrey—"

"We'll call the police from the restaurant. You do that—I'll be in the gents trying to get the sand out of my eyes. Talk to Stingley and no one else. He was impressed with the little blue paper you showed him. Tell him this is wrapped up in the official secrets act, but that we'll have a story for him by tomorrow. Which we will. Tell him—"

"*Jeffrey!*"

Bellman stopped short. "Sorry. What is it? I'm always like this. I don't like to kill, I don't like the way I feel high afterward. I get so—and here I am running my mouth again. At least we got out of it alive. Nice work you did on this one."

"I didn't."

"Sure you did. One shot, thirty-two automatic against a Magnum."

"I didn't shoot him."

"Don't be ridiculous."

"Look at him, damn you. He was shot in the *back* of the head."

Bellman took a closer look. "So he was."

"I was ready for him. I heard him scraping the concrete and I had my gun up, but as soon as he appeared he pitched forward the way you see him now. I thought you'd shot him somehow."

"Not me. I was busy."

"Then *who was it?*"

"Excellent question. Let's go eat."

"Jeffrey, this is important."

"I know. I'll think better about it with a fish inside me and the sand out of my goddam eyes."

"Who *could* it have been?"

"I don't know," Bellman said. "Have you been to church lately?"

"No. Why?"

"Maybe it was your guardian angel."

7

"Jeffrey?" Felicity said.

"Mmm?" He reached under the covers and stroked along her back.

"What have we accomplished down here?"

"I don't know. We got *somebody* stirred up. Somebody who hires people who speak Russian when they're angry."

She pulled herself up on one elbow so she could see his face. His eyes were strange—red around the rims, clear near the blue part in the center, where the contact lenses had guarded them from the sand.

They'd made a strange picture in the restaurant, disheveled and sweaty on such a cold night, gritty with sand. When they walked they made a noise like a soft-shoe music-hall turn. Fortunately, the restaurant was nearly deserted (Brighton was a summer town), the lights were dim, and the lone waiter too bored to notice.

DI Stingley had taken the news with less than equanimity, but a promise to call on him early tomorrow was at last reluctantly accepted. They'd eaten, come home, taken showers. Gone to Felicity's room to make love.

It had been remarkable, Felicity thought, truly remarkable. The best since Derek, and she had been in love with him. She was romantic enough to believe that that made a lot of difference. Maybe all the difference.

She was not in love with Jeffrey Bellman. Intrigued, yes. Attracted to him. Irritated by him. That wasn't much of a combination. But if it wasn't the man who had reached her, what was it? The situation? Was it escaping death, was it the *act of killing* that had brought her body and mind fully awake again?

The thought bothered her. It was good to be alive, yes, and enjoying a man was an important part of living, at least as far as she was concerned. But it bothered her.

And the conversation always came back to death.

"Bulanin sent them, then," she said.

"I hope so," Bellman said.

Of course he would, Felicity thought. Jeffrey had spoken to Bulanin about Sir Lewis, and not much else. If Bulanin had sent the joggers, it meant something about Sir Lewis bothered him. That was progress. It was an area to work in.

"And," Bellman added, "I got some great Dover sole."

"No luck on Leo Calvin, though," Felicity said.

"No. I was stupid. I'm not cut out to chase people. I've got to make him come to me."

Felicity couldn't help a smile. "How do you propose to do that?"

"I'll think of something. Who killed the third Russian?"

She kept smiling. "I'll come up with the answer as soon as you think of what to do about your terrorist. *And* think of some way to find proof that he's tied in with Sir Lewis's disappearance."

The false-blue eyes narrowed at her. "You know something," he said.

"I know a lot of things," she said. She bent her head and bit him gently on the chest. "For instance, girls with long noses make the best lovers."

102

"Mmm," he said. He stroked her back again. "You know more than that."

Felicity was studiously not paying attention. She bit him again, a littler harder, began kissing his neck. Pressed the whole of her long, warm body against him.

She heard him sigh, and looked up at him.

"What the hell," he said. "We're not under orders to trust each other, are we?" There was a surprising tinge of sadness in his voice. It could, Felicity thought, almost be genuine.

"No," she said softly. "We aren't."

"No," Bellman echoed. "All we have to do together is kill Russians and screw. Come here."

He pulled her close and took her with a fierceness that was almost suicidal. In total silence; Felicity stifled her own cries against his shoulder.

It took a long time. When it was done, he kissed her softly and went back to his own room. Felicity lay awake and tried to decide what she was going to do about him.

8

If she'd been asleep, she wouldn't have noticed it at all. Even awake, she didn't hear it at first, or at least it didn't register. It just blended in with the winter sounds of the ocean outside, the wind, the thumping of the waves on the shingle, the hissing as the water filtered through the stones to rejoin the ocean.

But this particular sound was out of rhythm with nature. Syncopated. Now that she concentrated on it, she realized it came from the other direction. Not the window, but the door. Someone was scratching on her door.

At first she thought it might be Jeffrey playing the fool, but she dismissed it. He could walk right in, if he wanted. He could certainly knock. And if he *did* scratch, he would scratch on the connecting door between rooms, not the one that opened to the corridor.

Then she caught the rhythm. One. Pause. Three. Pause. Two. Long pause. Then it started over. A simple agency code. In her earliest days with the Section, she had equated code knocks and passwords with secret handshakes and decoder rings and similar rubbish, but she'd learned the usefulness of being able to make the acquaintance of a fellow agent with no one else noticing, and the comfort of knowing that the person on the other side of the door was a friend.

She was slipping into her robe when it struck her just who this friend might be. If she was right, then this was a happy occasion. Success for the Section, achieved *by* the Section, with the American present only to witness their competence.

She had to decide what to do. She couldn't call Jeffrey (not that she especially wanted to) without her visitor becoming aware of it. There was no telling what he might do if that happened. Mr. Tipton would not be pleased to hear that she'd come this close and then frightened her man away.

If, of course, it *was* Sir Lewis Alfot on the other side of the door.

This was not the time to take chances. Of any sort. Just in case someone unfriendly had learned the code knock, Felicity got her automatic and jerked a round into the chamber. The click could be a key turning, she decided. It wouldn't send him running.

It didn't. When Felicity opened the door and peeked, it was Sir Lewis she saw. He was disguised, but not enough to fool someone who knew him well and was expecting to see him.

Especially when he grinned. Felicity saw that grin and could almost think that the old man was in complete charge, as usual. That he was his old sane self.

Sir Lewis put a finger to his lips for silence, then gestured for her to come with him.

"I'm not dressed," she whispered.

"No matter," Sir Lewis said. "I'm just down the hall."

Felicity took one apprehensive look at the door to Jeffrey's room, then took a tighter grip on her gun and followed Sir Lewis to a room five doors down and across the hall. It looked like an afterthought, or a converted closet. The walls all met at acute angles, and triangles of concrete jutted into what little floor space there was. One of them held a WC. The sink was visible just past the head (or foot) of a rumpled single bed. The window looked out at a small slice of the hilly street that ran alongside the hotel.

"I'm conserving my money," Sir Lewis said. "Haven't much. Fortunately, the rates are much lower without the ocean view."

"It's . . . it's good to see you again, Sir Lewis," she said. She nearly winced at the inanity of it. The next thing would be for him to offer her a cup of tea.

"Good to see you, too. Of course, I saw you earlier. I've been following you from the Advance, in fact, trying to decide if I ought to talk to you. Who's the American? The way you two were occupying each other, I was afraid I was going to have to give it up for the night. Must have listened at the door five separate occasions. Didn't hear much, but enough. I could hardly believe it when I heard him go back to his own room. Who is he?"

Felicity hoped to God she wasn't blushing. That *would* have been inane. "He's called Bellman. Washington sent him over to help."

Sir Lewis made a noise. "You mean take charge."

Felicity let it go. "Was that you this evening?" she asked. "At the marina?"

Sir Lewis laughed. "I almost spoke to you on the bus. Then I saw you taking those wrong turns, and I didn't know *what* the two of you were about. I was tempted to give you directions. Of course, I eat there fairly often, now that I live in Sussex. Don't expect to get there this visit to Brighton though."

He laughed again. "Then I saw the Russians, though I didn't know they were Russians at the time. I didn't like the look of the bulges under their sweat suits when they ran by me, so I fired a shot past them into the sand pile to warn the two of you. I wanted to see the American in action."

He made a face. "I'm sorry, Felicity, I'm forgetting my manners." He pointed to the bed. "Sit down, please. I'll stay here by the door. Nothing improper, I assure you."

Felicity sat. She didn't trust herself to say anything. She had known that Sir Lewis was . . . different, but she hadn't expected him to be like this. All the moves were there, all the words and mannerisms. He still carried authority like a coat of mail, and she could feel the strength of his regard and concern for her. For the Section. For the Nation.

But something was wrong (well, naturally, she thought, something is dreadfully wrong), something it would be difficult to put her finger on. Sir Lewis's personality had always been . . . well, incandescent, but now he was burning too brightly, the way a light bulb that's had air let inside it will flare into a new brilliance. Before it burns out. Felicity kept a firm grip on her gun.

"Where was I?" Sir Lewis asked. "Oh. The American. Yes. I bloody well got my money's worth on him. Formulated a plan in seconds, carried it out perfectly under less than ideal circumstances. Neat job he did on the leader's back as well. Did you see that? No, I guess not. You were waiting for the one I shot. My apologies, dear. I just wanted to see if an old man who can't use his right arm too well could still shoot. I know you would have handled him perfectly well."

"Where have you been all this time?" Felicity said.

"Here in Brighton, mostly, I gather," he said. "Some bloody American—not your fellow—kidnapped me and kept spouting nonsense about giving me to the Russians. He never got around to doing it, though. Had some other project in mind first, apparently. Anyway, they kept me drugged most of the time. I bided my time until I was able to escape."

He took a biro and some folded sheets of paper from his pocket. "I've been making some notes on it for Tipton. You can take them to him. I'm sure he'll be interested. Maybe he'll know what to make of this American. The one who kidnapped me, I mean."

He clicked the button of the ballpoint against his chest as he talked. "It was the Russians tonight that made me decide I wanted to talk to you. I thought at first the one who took me— the woman with him called him Leo—this Leo was just an amateur who struck it lucky, but if real Russian killers turn up in his wake, I just don't know."

Click. Click. "So you show these papers to Tipton." He held

them up. "Don't let the American—what is it, Bellman? Don't let him know about them until Robert's had a chance to think it over."

"Why—" Felicity began. Her voice sounded strange to her. She tried again. "Why don't you just give them to Mr. Tipton yourself?"

"I want him to have them as soon as possible. I assume you'll be going back to London tomorrow, won't you?"

"Tonight, if you come with me."

Click. "That's not on, I'm afraid. I've got things to do. Projects I've been working on, things that can't be interrupted. Things I mustn't tell even you about."

"Sir Lewis . . . "

"If it's the bloody labor report you're worried about, don't. I'll get a copy delivered in time, revised and polite, if that's what Tipton wants."

Felicity didn't point out that the report was no good to anyone if it purported to come from someone universally believed to be dead, kidnapped, or a fugitive. Instead, she said, "Sir Lewis, we know."

"I beg your pardon."

"We know about your project."

Click. Click. Click.

"Nonsense. You . . . you couldn't."

"Since just after the third one, Sir Lewis. The prostitute in Hove."

"Just before I was forced out, then." The old man's voice was bitter. "I should have guessed. You think I'm an old fool, don't you?"

"Of course not," she said. "You're just tired. You need some . . . " Felicity's voice dribbled away when she realized she had no idea what Sir Lewis needed.

"How did you find out?"

Click. Click.

"You left your fingerprint on the ice pick. It came to us as part of the blanket bulletin, and someone in Identifications matched it up and brought the matter to Tipton. It checked with the partial print the police had from the first—the first one. At least it wasn't inconsistent. Mr. Tipton made sure the identification never got through to the Yard or to Sussex."

"I see. Then he went over my head to force me to retire." Click. "I knew he wouldn't understand. Nobody would understand. I see. The bodyguard at the cottage was to keep me *in*, not to keep kidnappers out. No wonder it was so easy for them. I knew he wouldn't understand."

"He might, Sir Lewis. Come back to London with me, and we'll explain it to him."

"I'll explain it to you! Can't you see it? The country is going to hell. Strikes. Shoddy work. Violence! My God, violence! Decent people can't even go to a bloody football match without having to fight for their lives, damned yobs making the name of England stink all over Europe, the world, bloody Libyans, Irish, make this country a battleground, Russians circling like vultures, all gone, no pride left, no pride . . ."

Felicity looked at him. The thought of shooting him crossed her mind. It would put the old man out of his misery; it would make things less complicated all around. His death might even be blamed on the Russians they'd (with Sir Lewis's help) taken care of tonight.

But she couldn't do it. She gave herself no airs of transcendent humanity, she just couldn't bring herself, at this time and in this place, to end the old man's life.

"And everyone turns a blind eye!"

Felicity jumped. The light bulb burned even hotter. It was sad to watch a great man burning himself up.

"A *blind eye*," the old man said again. "No one can face it that if this country is going to survive, we need *pride*. In our work, and ourselves. And the nation. Nobody wants to see.

"It was up to me to show them. My duty, you can see that, can't you, Felicity? The message was plain as day—*a blind eye can kill you!* Kill all of us, dammit! Kill all . . . of . . . "

He crouched down against the wall and started to sob. He pushed the heels of his hands so hard into his eyes that his fingers knocked his toupee awry. Felicity got off the bed and moved toward him. "Sir Lewis?" She took another step and said his name again.

For the rest of her life she would curse her stupidity. Because

Sir Lewis Alfot was a cunning and dangerous man, and she had forgotten that. Sir Lewis came out of his crouch like a tiger. His first blow knocked her gun away, the second was a left to the jaw that stunned her and sent her reeling.

She tried to gather herself to fight back, but he was on her again, choking her, hitting her. He was strong in spite of his age, hideously strong. Strong as a madman. She clawed at his hands on her throat. She went for his eyes, his groin. But Sir Lewis had been the brain behind all her training, and he knew how to counter every move.

As she was pulled from consciousness, her mind raced. *I respected him, I felt sorry for him, I'm going to die because I like this old man, and he went mad, and I forgot everything he taught me and now he's going to kill me. . . .*

She heard a sound through the red haze. A click.

"No," she said, and tried to get away, but she was too weak, and he had her throat in a strong left hand. She was on the floor with her back against the bed, and when she forced her eyes open she could see Sir Lewis standing over her and she could see the biro in his hand. There was a look of genuine sadness on his face.

"I am sorry," the old man said, and tightened his grip so she couldn't scream.

She remembered DI Stingley saying, the *eyes*, there's something about the *eyes*, what does it *feel* like, what does it *feel* like . . .

Felicity learned. Fortunately, she would never remember.

9

Bellman got tired of looking out the window at the storm; he decided to peek in on Felicity and apologize to her if she was awake. Not, he thought, that he had endangered the State of the Alliance—if you wanted people to refrain from holding things back, you shouldn't deal with spies. He was more worried about what he'd done to his working relationship with Felicity Grace.

Bellman's problem was (and always had been, if you asked the Congressman) that he had an ornery streak of idealism, or optimism, or *some* kind of positive expectation of life that no amount of experience had been able to expunge. He was also just too damned emotional to be a spy. He'd been trained to hide it, but he didn't *like* to hide it. He, in fact, hated it, hated the whole life.

Which was why, he reminded himself as some strange sense of propriety made him pull on a pair of pants, you got the hell out. There was no one to blame for putting him back in but himself and Leo Calvin.

He knocked on the connecting door and said Felicity's name. No answer. He turned the knob and opened the door. He stood well clear of the opening. Felicity might be a nervous sleeper—he already knew she was a good shot. It would not be funny if he opened the door to apologize and got a bullet in the forehead for his trouble.

She wasn't there.

Bellman stepped into Felicity's room with the idea that maybe the Alliance was shakier than he'd thought. She wasn't in the toilet. Had she run out on him? If so, why?

Another look showed him the question was academic. She hadn't taken anything with her. Maybe her robe.

It didn't make sense. She was a pro, she had a gun, she knew he was next door, how could anyone have gotten her out of there without her cooperation? Bellman decided he could figure it out later. He stepped out into the hall, he wasn't sure why. To check for muddy footprints from Polish-made shoes, smell a Russian cigarette, something.

He heard a commotion a short way down the hall. Thumps. Grunts. Moans. A man's voice and a woman's. There weren't enough people in the hotel for the woman to be anybody but Felicity. He ran to the door and tried the knob, cursing himself for wasting time as he did it. Of course it was locked.

A bare shoulder isn't the best way to tackle a locked door, but it beats a bare foot. Bellman threw himself against the white-painted wood four times before it gave way, and he found himself staggering across the room. The stagger kept his body low enough for the bullet to miss him. The man who had fired the shot followed up by clipping Bellman along the side of the head with the gun, then running for it.

Bellman blinked a red curtain from his vision and went to the door. The man was out of sight, in a lift or down the stairs by now. Bellman went back to the room.

Felicity was on the floor, sitting very still. Her head was thrown back on the bed. He felt weak when he looked at her face, at the obscenity of the blue plastic pen sticking out from her eye. His shoulder began to throb and then his head, and he looked around for a sink to be sick in.

Then she moaned. And moved her head.

Bellman leaped across the room and clamped her head in his hands. He didn't know what he could do to help her, but he was sure moving her head around with that *thing* in her could only make things worse.

She moaned again.

"It's all right, honey," he told her. "It's all right."

God, he couldn't stand to look at her. He wanted to grab the pen and pull it out. Whatever damage had been done, it couldn't be worse than this . . . this *violation*. And if he pulled it out, he would probably kill her.

What he needed was to get someone here who knew what the hell to do. He looked around for the telephone. He might just be able to reach it.

Carefully, trying not to alter the position of Felicity's head, he stood up. He pressed his left knee against the back of his left hand, then gently eased the hand free, leaving Felicity's head clamped between his right hand and the inside of his left knee. He stood with his right leg well back—he didn't want to hit the pen accidentally and drive it the rest of the way into her brain. His interruption had probably stopped the Cyclops from doing it—he had no intention of finishing the job for him.

Bellman reached across his body with his left hand, stretching as far as he could without jostling Felicity. He cursed English phones for having no handle under the breaker buttons the way American phones did. Finally, he pressed his fingers against the bottom and his thumb against the dial, and got the phone down from the bedside table to the mattress, where he was able to get a new hold and bring the phone to where he could use it.

He clamped the receiver between left shoulder and ear and, still holding the woman steady, dialed 999.

Nothing happened. Random phone static, perhaps the hint of a distant conversation.

Bellman fought panic. *Goddammit!* If the phones are defective, if they cost her her life, I'll tear this goddam place down brick by brick, starting with the hotel management, I'll—

Hotel.

This was a hotel phone. He needed an outside line before he could do anything. He dialed another line. There was a click, and the quick double whirrs that told him the phone was ringing.

Two minutes later, an ambulance was on the way.

FOURTH

The Bellman looked uffish, and wrinkled his brow,
  "If only you'd spoken before!
It's excessively awkward to mention it now,
  With the Snark, so to speak, at the door!

"We should all of us grieve, as you well may believe
  If you never were met with again—
But surely, my man, when the voyage began,
  You might have suggested it then?"

                    —*The Hunting of the Snark*
                    Fit the Fourth

1

Bellman winced as he lowered himself into the black leather chair in Tipton's office.

"Are you all right?" the Acting Section Chief asked.

"A bruise," Bellman told him. "It's nothing. About the third day the numbness wears off."

A two-day wait, Bellman reflected, had probably been good for Tipton's health, too. Because as Bellman waited the other night to hear what would happen to Felicity Grace, his brain came back from vacation, he put the pieces together, and figured out just what the hell had been going on around here. And he was angry.

He was still angry (too much emotion, he'd never be able to kick that), but he did not now intend to strangle Robert Tipton with his bare hands as he would have the other night if he'd been given the opportunity.

Instead, he'd taken the weekend to go back to what he knew best. He'd dug up some old contacts, found some specialists, and gotten things in place to work on his own. He preferred it that way. The one thing wrong with the Establishment was that it was established. Your enemy could find you if he looked hard enough. He could learn what you were up to. A pickup team could hit, run, and dissolve, and they couldn't be caught by trolling the usual channels.

They were also answerable to Bellman alone. You could not ask for the heartfelt loyalty of someone who did this kind of work free-lance for money, but you could pay them enough to make it unlikely they'd want to wander. And for insurance, there was fear. Cross me and die. It wasn't infallible, but it worked well enough. The Russians' whole system was based on it.

Not that he'd be cutting ties to Tipton and his Section. They could still be useful to him. That was why he was here. The idea was to react naturally without letting Tipton know that the game had been switched at halftime.

"You've seen Felicity?" Tipton asked.

"Every day," Bellman replied. She'd been moved to a hospital in Chelsea on Saturday afternoon.

"How is she?"

"Her eye didn't grow back. There's still a hole in her head."

Tipton made an expression of distaste. "I meant, how is she taking it?"

"Oh," Bellman said. He crossed his legs. "That's interesting, the way she's taking it. She's depressed, which you'd expect, and she's angry at herself. She says she was stupid to let the Cyclops take her. She thinks she's let you down."

Tipton's face showed concern, but it wasn't all necessarily about Felicity. "Mmmm," he said. "Could she tell you anything about this Cyclops?"

"Could she?" Bellman shrugged. "She didn't. Says she didn't remember anything about him."

"You sound as if you doubt her." Tipton was tapping a pencil on the desk, point, eraser, point.

Bellman let it go on for a long time before he spoke. "I think *you* ought to go visit her, Mr. Tipton."

"I intend to. I was waiting to be absolutely sure she was out of danger. And, of course, though we've tried to keep it to a minimum, there has inevitably been some publicity about the case. It wouldn't do for me to be seen in a newspaper photo."

"She'll recover. They'll start fitting her for a glass eye as soon as the swelling goes down. They might have a tough time matching the color, but they'll get there. But I do think you ought to go. Have Natalie whip up a disguise for you. Get out to the hospital. Reassure her."

"We take care of our people," Tipton said. "There's no need for me to reassure her."

"I don't mean medically or financially, I mean professionally. Tell her she shouldn't feel stupid."

"Mr. Bellman, I hardly think—"

"Tell her," Bellman went on, "that she has no reason to feel concerned about her stupidity compared to the stupidity of *the asshole who put the fate of the entire Anglo-American Intelligence communications network in the hands of a fucking homicidal maniac.*"

"So you know," Tipton said.

Bellman wanted to laugh. Tell Tipton, no, it was an inspired guess. Instead, he said, "I know. I should have known days ago. It wasn't going to take forever, Tipton. I'm only allowed so many stupid days a year, and I've used them all up through June on this."

"Did Felicity tell you?"

"She told me nothing. That is a brave and loyal woman. She's lying on a gurney being wheeled into an operating room with a pen sticking out of her head, and she's worried about the honor of the Section."

"How did you know?"

"You mean, will Stingley or any of the police down there be able to figure it out? Relax, you've got nothing to worry about."

"Stingley is a good man," Tipton said.

"Sure he is, but you've got him stifled. That fingerprint business, for instance. That's your doing, isn't it?"

"It's down to me. As is everything else in this fiasco. I'd still like to know how you learned Sir Lewis was doing these murders."

"The shoulder was what clinched it. After I beat the thing to a pulp trying to get the door open, it seized right up. Couldn't even brush my hair with it. It's still pretty sore.

"But it got me thinking about Sir Lewis, and his war wound, the scar tissue along his back and shoulder that kept him—how did the file have it—'from having full range of motion.'

"Then I thought of the Cyclops's style of attack, like the power portion of a snooker stroke. Just about the only way a man who can't raise his right arm can generate any power at all."

"I see," Tipton said. He was leaning back in his chair, holding a finger across his lower lip. The perfect picture, Bellman thought, of an executive being patient with an underling who's telling him where he's screwed up.

Bellman decided to oblige him. "Of course, that was just the clincher. The rest of it—Leo Calvin, the kidnapping, the Russians, the attempts on my life before and after I spoke to them, the timing of Sir Lewis's removal from that chair—the only way *any* of it made sense was if Sir Lewis was the Cyclops." Bellman raised his eyebrows. "A fact," he added, "that no one thought fit to tell us."

Tipton planted both fists on his desk blotter and shoved himself to his feet. "*What would you have us do, damn you?*"

Bellman looked at him. "Are you serious? I would have you not give one of your most delicate problems to a man who goes around poking people's eyes out, that's what I would have you do."

"Very droll, Mr. Bellman." Tipton's face was red with controlled anger; his lips were so tight, his voice seemed to be escaping through the pores in his skin. "We had no sooner seen that fingerprint when we—it's no use explaining. Go back to Washington and tell them we're hopeless. That's obviously what you intend to do. We'll muddle through."

"That's the spirit," Bellman told him. "Pecker up. Stiff upper lip."

For the first time since Bellman had met him, Tipton looked dangerous. "You go to hell, Mr. Bellman," he said.

"That's two places you've tried to send me. I'll go to both of them, no doubt, but not right away."

"Whyever not?" Tipton said venomously.

"Because, Mr. Tipton, there is still a goddam *job* to be done. It's more important than ever, don't you think, that Sir Lewis Alfot be found before some bobby catches him and talks to the *Mirror*? Take a few moments and think about what the Russians could do with this."

"I have thought about it."

"I'll bet you have. That was rhetorical. While I'm at it, I'll tell *you* why you sent Sir Lewis off to do that report."

"We sent him because your bloody Congressman wouldn't take no for an answer!" Tipton sat down again. He played a rhythm track behind his words on the desk with his fist. "The labor trouble had to cease! Sir Lewis's cover was unbroken! Sir Lewis had the people in his pocket! Sir Lewis was, God help us, 'trustable.' Sir Lewis would be chafing at his retirement! It was foolish of him to have retired! Sir Lewis would prepare and deliver the report! Or else the United States would have to rethink their entire Intelligence posture, and the U.K., to use the Congressman's quaint, charming phrase, would be *included out!*"

"Yeah," Bellman said. "That sounds like him. But I don't think, somehow, the Congressman would have insisted if you'd just let him know *why* Sir Lewis retired."

"Simple to say, Mr. Bellman. I was not shocked by Philby or Blount or the rest, but when that fingerprint came through here, I was shocked. This man had built the Section. Recruited me, damn near all of us personally. He represented *values*, Bellman. Don't smirk, damn you."

Bellman was injured innocence. "I always look like this. I read the file, and I read the report. I know what Sir Lewis meant to you here."

"You couldn't," Tipton said flatly. "The Congressman talked about how the people love Sir Lewis, and they do. It's a return of his love for them. But they don't know the half of it. He has been, Bellman," Tipton sat straight and solid in his chair, as if bracing himself for a gust of laughter, "a great man. A true Englishman."

Bellman nodded soberly. He laughed at no one's patriotism.

"If he's gone mad, it's because he's taken too much on himself—felt like a father to a rebellious family that he feels has let him down. God knows, I feel that way myself sometimes, and I haven't a tenth the justification Sir Lewis has.

"And I was not, Mr. Bellman, going to destroy what was left of the greatness of Sir Lewis Alfot. I cleared my actions at the highest levels. It was agreed to ease him out without letting him know we were aware of what he'd done. He was to be kept under guard so that he'd never do it again. His food was medicated, his contacts, and environment kept strictly regulated under the supervision of the Section psychiatric officer to make sure he never did these things again.

"He was, in short, under control.

"When the Congressman called, with his plan, his *ultimatum*, I was *not* going to tell him that Sir Lewis Alfot was no longer 'trustable' because he had decided for some dark reason to kill people at random. I would not do it!"

"No doubt this was backed up at the highest levels, too," Bellman said.

Tipton raised his chin. "I take full responsibility."

"Bully for you," Bellman said. "Now I am smirking. Not at your sentiment, or even your action. But don't underestimate the Congressman. I've regretted it every time I've done it. He's not my favorite person in the world, but when his interest runs with yours, he can be the most trustable man on earth. I've seen him swear the President of the United States to secrecy—never mind which one—and I can tell you right now, when he finds out about Sir Lewis—"

"Which he will, if he hasn't already," Tipton said. "Don't underestimate *me,* either, Bellman."

"Which he will," Bellman echoed. "I wanted to talk to you before I reported. You could always shoot me before I leave the room."

Tipton ignored him; Bellman went on. "When he finds out, no power on earth will be able to get the secret from him. He's got a lot invested in Sir Lewis, too."

Tipton folded his hands in front of his face and took several deep breaths. "Well," he said at last. "You haven't taken me over all these jumps for nothing. What is it you want?"

"I want you to tell Felicity to talk to me, to tell me everything. It might just help."

"Do you have an idea?" Bellman replied with a pointed silence. Tipton said, "I'll write her a note. She'll know it's from me. I'll tell her not to feel stupid, either."

"That's more like it," Bellman said.

2

Bulanin was frustrated.

There was so much to keep track of when one made great plans. And great plans required great risks. But the peril of a great risk should be a dramatic, even a heroic failure. It should not find him sitting in his office with a scrambled telephone to his ear, being scolded like a schoolboy.

Yet here he was, listening to Borzov speaking from his basement in Moscow. Lying to him to save his own neck.

Did Bulanin realize that the supply of trained operatives was limited? That he could not divert them from their more important and legitimate function in Britain to satisfy some whim? Just what did he think he was *doing?*

"Yes, Comrade Borzov," Bulanin said. "I diverted them from their activities in the coal fields—"

"Do not be specific!" Borzov said. The KGB chief's voice was always high and somewhat nasal; when he was angry, he sounded like a kitten snarling.

"This is a secure line, Comrade," Bulanin assured him.

"I know that. I also know that the Americans and the Japanese have new electronic miracles ready every day, and they implement them sometimes faster than we can appropriate the technology. If I had only been able to persuade the Chairman to turn the schools over to me—but never mind that. Explain."

Bulanin lit a cigarette, then put it out. Borzov would not be able to see what he was doing, and any pause would be interpreted as weakness or guilt. "Very well, Comrade. I diverted them, yes, but only in accordance with orders."

"I don't remember giving orders of that kind."

Bulanin referred him to a document number, that of the order to kill Leo Calvin because of his failure during the Cronus operation in America.

"Since that order carried a higher priority, and I had reason to believe that the subject could be found in a certain location, I sent the men to locate him."

"And you are telling me, then, that they did locate him, but failed to secure his cooperation?"

Bulanin grinned. "Secure his cooperation," he echoed. Borzov kept coming up with these charming euphemisms—he wondered if the man in the basement did it to keep himself from getting bored after forty years of ordering men killed. Or perhaps what passed for Borzov's conscience had come to *believe* that what he was doing was "correcting the man's ideological misconceptions" or "notifying him that his promotion had been denied."

"No," Bulanin said, suddenly stern, in case the grin had been audible in his voice. "We could not—the operatives were not able to secure his cooperation. He proved to be more adamant and more immune to argument than I anticipated."

"More than I would have thought too, Comrade," Borzov said. Bulanin had a sudden spasm of panic. He had never heard Borzov admit error before. Not even the suggestion of it. What did this mean? Was he forgiven? Or was Borzov trying to lure him into a false sense of security before the ax fell?

"Still, we knew he was resourceful," Borzov said

"Yes, Comrade." It was all Bulanin trusted himself to say.

"Still, Comrade Bulanin, you sit in our Embassy. You are a diplomat. You must use your skills to the utmost. You must find resources in yourself greater than those of the man whose cooperation we wish to secure."

"I'll do my best, Comrade Borzov."

"I know you will. You always do. And your other projects have brought us great pleasure here. That is why I know you won't fail to make this man see reason."

"No, Comrade," Bulanin said with the greatest sincerity. "I won't fail."

"Good. If, for some unforeseen reason, the task remains unaccomplished, say, one month from today, perhaps I will have you fly back to Moscow to discuss the matter. We are not so old here that we have run out of ideas."

Bulanin rang off with the sound of Borzov's famous laugh echoing in his ears.

A servant of the Soviet State had to know how to read between the lines. How the positions of the members of the Politburo in the annual photograph reflected their relative power, and their chances at the top spot when the incumbent passed on. Exactly what a euphemistically worded order wanted you to do—a feat of interpretation much easier outside the Soviet Union itself than in it, a fact for which Bulanin was continually grateful. You had to know when to back a superior officer and when to undercut him.

And you had to know where you stood.

Bulanin had a clear idea of that last. *Your other projects have brought us great pleasure.* That, of course, referred to the current coal strike in Britain, now waning perhaps, but not before having wounded the British economy, damaged the rule of law, divided the people, and torn, as the newspapers liked to put it, the Fabric of Society. Bulanin had encouraged the strike; quietly, unobtrusively, but effectively. The men who had called the strike were not paid, conscious agents of the government Bulanin served, but they couldn't have done more damage if they had been. Indeed, they would not have *dared* been so blatantly illegal and so openly dictatorial; they could never have been so bold about working contrary to the interests of the men they were supposed to represent. No, they were sincere, convinced Marxists, Lenin's "useful idiots," and they'd turned on their country on their own initiative, and of their own free will.

All Bulanin had had to do was to nudge them toward the dream of being a hero of some kind of "British Revolution." It was easy enough to infiltrate the picket lines, since miners were being sent all over Britain to intimidate those who refused to join a strike they'd never had a chance to vote for. And, if the confrontation happened to be on the edge of violence, it was a simple matter for one of Bulanin's men to say the right words to get the first policeman to reach for his truncheon, and excuse any violence that might follow.

And all the while, of course, the intelligence must be maintained; the dossiers must be kept. Some of the Britons behind the coal strike might be influential in the government someday. A man already convinced could very easily be converted to a man owned body and soul, if any.

Bulanin could see why Borzov would be pleased with that project. And he could see, too, that Borzov had brought it up solely to let him know that his reward for it was not being required to report to Moscow immediately over the Leo Calvin fiasco. Bulanin knew that a man called home for consultation in circumstances like these somehow never returns to finish the work.

It had been a pat on the back, but a pat on the back with a warning—the *next* hand that touches your back could have a knife in it.

Bulanin put the ashtray and the crushed, unsmoked cigarette out of his sight. He sat back in his chair and closed his eyes. It was all so ironic. He did what he did—exacerbated the coal strike, conspired with the wretched Calvin for the capture of Lewis Alfot—all to serve Borzov, and the Politburo, and of course, the Chairman, in their move to weaken the West. To destroy it, if possible.

To achieve his ambition, he had to do the best job possible. But Bulanin's greatest fear was that he might succeed.

Because, if the words said to him years ago by Borzov had given his ambition substance, his years in Washington and London had given it form. *He would be Chairman of the Communist Party of the Soviet Union. And when he was, he would make peace with the West.*

It was, he saw, the only way the Motherland, and the world, could survive. The United States had a tiny percentage of its people working to grow food, and mountains of surplus moldered in storage. Thirty-five percent of the Soviet people worked in agriculture (he might have quotation marks around his title, but functioning as "Agricultural Attaché" had taught him *something*), and still they depended on food from other nations to survive.

Technological innovation was practically nil; as Borzov had come within a hair of conceding in so many words, the Soviet Union was dependent to a dangerous extent on industrial espionage to keep their industry anywhere near up-to-date. And the industry itself was all heavy machinery and military goods—the old men of the military had too much influence for things to be otherwise. The people of the Soviet Union had a lively black market in what little consumer goods were obtainable. American blue jeans. American phonograph records. American cigarettes.

The army was too big, and kept getting bigger. Morale was bad. Alcoholism was endemic. They had been parked in East Germany for forty years, guns pointing to the West, and they were bored.

There were things to be gained from the Americans, the British, the West Germans, the Japanese. Things to ease the lives of the people of the Motherland. Techniques to make work easier and more productive. Bulanin had seen them. He wanted them for his people. If he became Chairman (*when*, he told himself), he would see that his people got them. He would obtain for them the advantages of the West without the drawbacks—a pesty, obstructionist press, or confusing, energy-wasting multiple political parties.

He did not try to tell himself it would be easy. He would have to "secure the cooperation" of many old men before he was through; he would have to change the habits of a whole generation.

But it would be done. Leo Calvin had had his chance to live by helping put Bulanin in a position where it would be done sooner. He had failed; the chance was now gone. The plan was too important to let someone like Leo Calvin pose a danger to it.

Bulanin buzzed for his secretary. In his mind, he started drafting instructions to his people to rid him of this untrustworthy American.

3

Leo Calvin was puzzled.

He read his newspaper as he sat in the coffee shop and waited for his lamb chop and chips and wondered where all the news was. The news that concerned him, that is.

The waitress brought him the glass of water he'd asked for. She gave him a big smile and an exaggerated swing of the hip as she left him. She reminded him of Margaret, except, of course, for the sexy walk and the makeup. He could use a woman about now—not all of the tension he felt had to do with being in disguise and on the run.

There was a huge hunk of lemon in the water, which would bump into his false moustache if he left it in there. He fished it out with his fingers, squeezed it thoroughly into the water, and placed it in the ashtray for want of a better place to put it. He took a careful sip, making sure the water stayed clear of his upper lip.

Everybody in Oxford drank water with lemon in it, in an effort to disguise the rusty, stale taste. Or they steered clear of water altogether, a luxury that Leo at the moment couldn't afford.

Leo had come to Oxford for a number of reasons. The main reason was, no one expected him to be here. He was a fugitive from British justice. They would be expecting him to try to flee the country. The more Driscoll/Bellman had passed on to them about Leo's past, the surer they would be that he'd try to leave Britain for someplace his face wasn't so well known.

And no matter what Bellman had told the British, Leo *knew* Bulanin would be thinking that way. So Leo knew that every airport would be watched, every dock. If no KGB agent happened to be there waiting for him (and Bulanin knew his disguise—Leo would have to come up with something else), the staff and security officers at each facility would have been made aware of his natural appearance—and you could never tell when someone might see through a disguise.

In Oxford, no one would be looking for him. Oxford was near the headwaters of the Thames, which here was a stream you could almost wade across, right in the middle of Great Britain. You could go nowhere from Oxford except Wales, and that was no help for a fugitive from British justice.

Furthermore, Oxford was a college town. The fact that parts of the University were something like nine centuries old had nothing to do with it. College campuses and college towns were all alike. Leo could function in a college town; in some ways, they were his natural habitat. He had learned to maneuver people and events on the American campuses of the sixties.

So he wandered around. He spent a lot of time in Blackwell's, an enormous bookstore, halls and stadia of books, adjacent to the University. It was warm there. People took him for a graduate student if they paid him any notice at all. He kept his mouth shut, so no one would know he was an American. He sat in the Bodleian sometimes, too, squeezed through the tiny wooden door carved into the enormous wooden door to the library, and sat down. That, though, he did sparingly—he didn't want to get to be known to the point where someone would ask him what he was working on.

In the evenings he went to pubs, a different one every night, again, to avoid regulars. He would sit in a corner and nurse a pint of lager until closing time. He did that because it was cheaper to buy the beer and enjoy the landlord's heat than it was to shove fifty-pence pieces into an ugly gray box on the wall of his room anachronistically called a "shilling meter" to get a few minutes of gas heat.

Leo had unavoidable expenses. He had to pay Benton, who served as his legs and muscle back in London. And he had to pay the other one, the secret one, who served as his eyes and ears in the enemy camp, and gave him the one edge he had.

He spent the rest of his money, what little there was of it, on newspapers and one hot meal a day. And it was beginning to look as if he might as well save the newspaper money.

The only news that related to him was the fact that Sir Lewis, in the guise of the Sussex Cyclops, was losing his touch—he tried some woman in a Brighton hotel, and had gotten her eye instead of her life. No information on the woman, which was surprising. The British press, Leo was learning, had no shame, and could not be muzzled. He was surprised they hadn't offered the woman thirty thousand pounds and a glass eye to have a story called "MY ORDEAL SHOCK HORROR NIGHTMARE WITH THE CYCLOPS," or something equally subtle.

It was all very puzzling. Disturbing. Irritating.

For instance, just how good *was* Bellman? He'd thwarted Leo's Cronus operation; he'd twice escaped Leo-instigated, Bulanin-ordered death. When Leo had learned about that yesterday, he couldn't believe it. He'd known he was in trouble with Bulanin, and nothing short of Sir Lewis could get him out of it, but he thought he'd at least be able to get the satisfaction of knowing Bellman was dead. But no, his eyes and ears assured him, Bellman was very much alive. And Leo was hanging out in pubs.

Another big question was why the hell hadn't the old maniac turned himself in? Leo was the only one who knew Alfot's secret, and he was in no position to say anything about it. Sir Lewis could return home to a hero's welcome. He could tell any story he wanted about his disappearance. He could do his side a world of good by saying he'd been kidnapped by the Russians, which was practically true. He could return to his cozy little cottage and be the people's pride again. He could take that offer to head the commission looking into the Sussex Cyclops case, and spend six months to a year laughing his elderly balls off at the world in general, holding meetings, offering rewards, maybe committing another murder or two when things got dull.

The puzzle—why the hell didn't he?

The waitress came with his meal. "Enjoy your dinner, love," she told him.

Leo smiled and nodded and said, "Cheers." "Cheers" in this context meant "thank you." It also could mean hello, goodbye, I understand, and here's to you. Very useful when you were disguising an American accent.

Leo reached for the square HP Sauce bottle and doused the chop and the chips. It made his moustache smell of tamarind for the rest of the day, but he didn't care, he was hungry.

Leo paused with the second bite to his lips, and put his fork back down on the plate. Maybe the old man *couldn't* go home again. Maybe his former employees at the Section *knew* what he'd been up to.

If that was the case, Leo wasn't dead yet. There had to be an angle for him. Had to be. He picked up his fork again, took the lamb in his mouth, and chewed thoughtfully.

4

Sir Lewis Alfot was sad.

He leaned back against the pillows and watched the afternoon showing of *Falcon Crest* on ITV. Looked at it, rather. He'd given up on the plot. As far as he'd been able to make out, there was enough treachery, violence, and effing in the American wine industry to keep the KGB, CIA, and his own people busy for months. No wonder he couldn't stand their bloody wine.

Even with the door closed and locked, he kept his wig on, and kept the bloody lumps in his cheeks. The door had no deadbolt, so the fellow who ran the place would be able to open the door with his passkey, if he had a reason to do.

The lack of bolts on the doors had almost caused Sir Lewis, in his guise as a businessman from out of town, to reject staying here, but another feature of this place caused him to change his mind. Cloth. Everything bar the telly and WC was covered with some sort of thin cotton material, blue with a flower pattern—furniture, walls, even the windowsill. Probably made the place a damned deathtrap in case of fire, but he wasn't concerned about fire.

He was concerned about fingerprints. Fingerprints, for God's sake.

He was miserable with himself over it. All his experience, all his training of the best bloody British agents since the War, and when he launches a field operation of his own, he *forgets about fingerprints*. Never gave the matter a single thought.

I must be going senile, he thought. I'll be a drooling idiot before long. Whatever I'm going to do about this intolerable situation I've made for myself, I'd better get on with it, hadn't I?

The bit that really hurt was that it was his own people who caught him out, though there was a bit of pride mixed with the pain. But when they tried to ease him out without telling him why, they only made matters worse.

Sir Lewis had known Robert would have a difficult time understanding the importance of this mission and Sir Lewis might not have been able to explain it to him properly in any event. It was extraordinary, that part of it. When Sir Lewis thought about it, it was clear; it was the mandate of the British character; it simply *had* to be done. But when he tried to show his reasoning to someone else, he got maddeningly tongue-tied and angry.

The way he'd been angry at Felicity. It was a shame, what he'd had to do to that girl. No helping it, of course, but it still rankled. And that bloody fool of an American, blundering in before he had a chance to make sure of finishing the job, condemning poor Felicity to spend the rest of her life in actual possession of the blind eye the rest of the country suffered only figuratively. Lord knew she didn't deserve it. Duty could be a rotten thing sometimes.

Still, Lewis Alfot had never shirked his duty. His duty remained clear. The only things left unclear were just what he should do now, and how much time he would have in which to do it. He was a hunted man. It was only a matter of time before Robert would share his knowledge with the police. At least, that was what Sir Lewis would do in his place. The act on Felicity made it mandatory—*you must protect your people*. That was the essence of leadership in this business, and he had trained

Robert personally. He had confidence that Tipton wouldn't let his standards down.

Sir Lewis missed the Section, missed the activity. And until today, he hadn't realized how much he missed London. Right now, the sound of the air hammer down below in the street was more welcome to him than any music might be. And earlier that afternoon, when the lunchtime crowds were thickest, and anonymity therefore greatest, he walked through Harrods; the Food Halls, the book department, furniture, clothing, everything. The clearing house of the world, it was, full of riches and unashamed of it. The symbol of the Britain that was, and had to be again. Owned now, in large part, by a bunch of bloody Arabs.

Sir Lewis sighed. Well, at least the store was still there.

What really galled him was the fact that he could take the lift to the lobby, go downstairs, walk half a block, turn a corner, pay 50p, and ride the Piccadilly Line nine stops to the Tournament Press. That was home as far as he was concerned, and come as close to it as he might, he could do nothing to change the fact that he was now a permanent exile from it.

Because he killed a few people.

No. It wasn't that. He'd killed people in the wrong circumstances. People he had no—how did the Bond books put it—no *license* to kill. Random people off the street. A cross-section of Britain.

Well, he had to be honest with himself. Not exactly a cross-section. The only respectable one he'd done was the postman, and the man wasn't wearing his uniform when Sir Lewis caught up with him—he was beastly drunk, and he'd been trying to pick a fight with a couple of decent Pakistanis as soon as he left the pub. The nation could do quite well without that sort.

For the rest—a whore; a dole-collecting, violent young yob; and a kidnapping terrorist. If it was the cross-section he'd had in mind when he wanted to dramatize the blind-eye problem, he had definitely begun cutting from the bottom.

Except for Felicity, he told himself. But Felicity couldn't be helped.

Sir Lewis was who he was, had been able to help his country (and dammit, he *had* helped his country) as much as he had done, because he *knew*, because he had been forced to learn, that sometimes you had to be ready to kill *without* a license.

For example, in the War. He killed a damned lot of Germans in the War, and a few French collaborators as well, but the most important man he'd killed was an Englishman. The bloody captain in 1940 France. The one who'd lost his nerve, and wanted the men to surrender to the next group of Germans they came across.

He'd actually proposed that to Lieutenant Lewis Alfot. "We have to face the fact, Alfot," the captain had said, "the war's over in France, and the Jerries have won."

He gave orders for Lieutenant Alfot to pass along to the men. Orders Lewis Alfot would never let pass his lips. A captured Luger found its way into the lieutenant's hand, a shot, and it was over. He told the men the captain had committed suicide, but for the sake of his family they would put it about that he'd been killed by the enemy. The men, happy enough to be rid of a coward as commander, had gone along willingly.

And he'd led them to safety. And they *loved* him for it. He led the men through hell to make it to the beach, and they loved him for it. By God, if he could have one thing from his old life with him this second, it would be the loving cup the men had given him.

Lewis Alfot had vowed he would never let the possible results stand in the way of what he felt was his duty.

So. What, then, was his duty now?

It was obvious that Project Blind Eye was over. In his current status as a hunted man, there was no way he could accumulate enough bodies for the British people to see the message and wake up. Furthermore, considering his stupidity over the matter of fingerprints, and his failure to dispatch Felicity Grace effectively, Sir Lewis was no longer fully confident of his ability to do it.

It was manifest, then, that his duty was simply this: To salvage *something* of the mess his current plans were in.

He closed his eyes. He tuned out the air hammer, and the street noise, and the drivel of American voices from the telly. He thought hard about the problem, thought until his head grew so hot that bolt or no, he removed his wig.

132

An hour's hard concentration gave him the answer; he knew what he had to do. It would not be pleasant, but that was not a consideration.

The first step was to get himself captured again.

5

The Sister always smiled at him. He'd come here twice a day for the last few days, and every time, the head nurse on the head-and-eye-injury ward of the hospital smiled and nodded at him.

It had taken Bellman a little while to figure out what was going on. She couldn't have been flirting with him. Sister Pauling (as her nametag had it—it was hard for Bellman to avoid thinking of her as a nun, but here a head nurse was a Sister, and that was that) was built like a brick shithouse—literally. Six feet tall, four feet across, rectangular.

Then it occurred to him that she might just be smiling at anyone who was coming to visit a woman who could afford to eschew socialized medicine and pay for one of the hospital's almost vestigial private rooms. He rejected that explanation because it surely had to be down on some form somewhere that Miss Grace's bills were being paid by her employer, Tournament Press, and Sister Pauling didn't strike him as the type who wouldn't know everything on every form.

On his first visit today, he'd figured it out. The formidable head nurse was a romantic, and she was approving of the way Bellman remained devoted to the victim of a cruel mutilation. Okay by him. It was as good a cover as any. This time he was playing along by bringing a huge bunch of roses with him. Sister Pauling practically beamed at him. He wondered how she'd act, if she knew the truth. That he and Miss Grace both came from a world where devotion was a liability. That the time might come when he might have to use Felicity as cruelly, if not as brutally, as the Sussex Cyclops had.

For the first time, the nurse spoke to him. "There's another young man in there with her," she said. She had a surprisingly gentle voice and manner. "A boy, really. Said he was a fellow employee. He was polite, quite polite."

Bellman noted the surprise in her voice. Sister Pauling was determinedly Not Judging By Appearances.

Bellman smiled. "About so tall? Two-tone hair, brown and yellow? Bovver boots? Ears like a package of M&Ms?"

Sister Pauling tucked a wisp of iron-gray hair under a construction in starched white linen that resembled the Sydney Opera House. "M&Ms?"

"Oops. American candy. Like a bag of Smarties."

She nodded, and the hair came loose again. "That sounds like the boy. I can tell him to leave. That is"—to Bellman's delight, she blushed—"that is, if you want to be alone with Miss Grace."

"No thanks. I know him. I'd like to say hello to him myself."

"That'll be fine, then. I'll send someone around with a vase for the flowers."

Bellman thanked her and walked to the room. He knocked softly and went in. Dave Hamilton shot to his feet.

"At ease, Dave," Bellman told him. "How's the patient?"

"Why don't you ask the patient?" Felicity asked. "Bloody awful. This damned bandage . . . it itches like hell. I must look like the bloody Bride of Frankenstein."

"The Bride of Frankenstein had black hair, actually," Dave Hamilton offered. "With like a gray streak, you know, from the temple."

Felicity managed a smile. It was only half a smile, because the left side of her face was encumbered with a bandage. It was braced by being wrapped completely around her neck and forehead, and her bright red hair shot out from the top of it like flames from a volcano. It was half of a weary smile, at that, but it was the best he'd seen her do since she'd been in here.

"I was telling Dave how sweet he was to have come," Felicity said. "It was such a nice surprise."

"I was glad to do it, and all," Dave said. "You seem miles better."

134

Felicity grunted.

"Well," Dave said. "I guess I'll be running along home. Everton and Spurs on the telly today."

"Can you wait a few minutes for me, Dave?" Bellman said. "I'd like to talk to you."

Dave pursed his lips. "Something to do with work?"

"Something to do with work."

"All right, then. Plenty of football left this season. Take your time. Ta, Miss Grace."

"Goodbye, Dave. Thank you again."

The door closed behind him, then opened again almost immediately as a nurse came in with a vase for the roses. She smiled on them, and left without a word.

"What in hell was she smiling about?" Felicity demanded.

"She caught it from the Sister."

"What are you talking about?"

"It's not important."

"Oh," Felicity said.

"Yes?"

"It just sank in. The roses are for me. You have brought me flowers. Fancy that."

"It's the traditional thing to do," Bellman said. "I hope you like roses."

Love them," she said. "It's been a long time since anyone gave me roses."

"You deserve them," Bellman said.

"I deserve them for decoration on my grave. That's what I deserve."

"That's enough of that," Bellman told her. "I've just come from Tipton. He's got orders for you—stop blaming yourself."

"Easy to say."

"Just follow orders."

Felicity's voice was bitter. She was tracing little impatient, meaningless hieroglyphics on the sheet with one finger. "Yes, sir. No more blaming myself, sir."

"I'll tell Tipton."

"Do that."

"I've got an order for you, myself."

Her eye widened. "Oh? What's that, Mr. Bellman?"

"Stop being so fucking tough."

"I'm sure I don't know what you're talking about."

"I mean let it *out*, Felicity. You're going to kill yourself like this."

"What if I do?"

"No 'what if' about it. You are not going to. This job isn't over yet, lady."

"It is for me."

"The hell it is. When are they letting you out of here?"

"End of the week. They want to do some plastic surgery first. You see, I tried to close my eye when the biro started coming, and my eyelid got torn. Then, too, the plastic pen barrel wasn't as sharp or as sturdy as the other implements the Cyclops had used, and it broke off splinters, so they want to sew me up so that I can cover my false eye prettily. When I get it. Revolting, isn't it?"

"I can take more before I retch," Bellman said. "I'm tough, too."

"Until then, they have cotton in there, soaked with antibiotics and God knows what all, to ward off infection while it heals."

"Okay. When they let you out of here, I want you to move in with me. Or I'll come out to Putney and stay with you."

"Why?" Felicity demanded. "Have you developed a kink for women in eyepatches? Or does sympathy turn you on?"

"I'm thinking about the job," Bellman told her. "Things are going to start happening—I've spent too much time jerking off around here. I'm going to be running around like a man who's mistaken the Ben-Gay for the hemorrhoid cream, and people are likely to be ringing at odd hours to tell me things. I need a trained professional to answer phones—"

"A secretary."

"A professional. To discuss strategy with. To keep an eye on things when I'm not—" Bellman stopped, and listened to himself. "Oh, Jesus," he breathed.

Felicity started to laugh. Harsh, loud, unbridled laughter that had her bouncing off the bed. "To keep an eye on things!" she said, then laughed some more. Then she said, "Oh, God," and started to sob. A tear rolled from her good eye.

"Oh, Jeffrey," she said.

136

"I'm sorry . . ."

"Jeffrey, hold me. Hold me tight."

6

By the time Bellman walked past Sister Pauling's farewell smile, he had everything he'd wanted to get from Felicity. He had the whole story of the night in Brighton. Not much use, perhaps, but at least it showed that the old man was still resourceful, and that he could put across an act. The way he'd lulled her into sympathy with his madman-falling-apart routine before he struck had been masterful. Felicity still had trouble believing how well he'd suckered her.

Bellman also had Felicity's promise that she'd work with him when she got out of the hospital. It had been decided that he'd come and stay with her on Putney Hill. She'd be a semi-invalid, after all, and in her place she knew where everything was, and knew what was there in the first place. That suited Bellman. He didn't know exactly what he'd be doing, but he suspected it would be things he'd be just as glad not to have Tipton know about. The Bloomsbury apartment was altogether too easy to bug; he didn't want Tipton to be tempted.

Felicity's emotional binge had helped her. She was calmer when he left her, and now that some of the tension of shock and horror had been burned off, she'd been ready to go to sleep. Bellman was glad of the slip of the tongue that had brought it about.

He wished, though, that he could decide if it had really been a slip of the tongue. On the one hand, he was not aware of any intention to say anything so tasteless just to provoke a reaction. On the other hand, it had worked, and if he *had* thought of it before, he would have *known* it would work. Manipulation had been drilled into him all his life; he'd done it so continuously for so long, maybe the process had been taken over by his midbrain—a conditioned set of reflexes, like whistling, or riding a bicycle. He couldn't stop if he wanted to. Someone should warn Felicity about him. He should do it himself. He knew, though, that he wouldn't.

Dave Hamilton was waiting for him just outside the hospital doors.

"There you are," Bellman said. "I thought you'd be in the lobby."

"Oh. Sorry. I wanted to keep an eye on my bike." He pointed across the road to a small red Honda. "It's not much, but it's all I've got, know what I mean? I mean, Tournament Press are a fine lot, but I'm not making enough that I can afford to have my bike nicked."

"Nobody pays that much money," Bellman told him. "Look, I've got a car here, the company has fixed me up with a Mini wagon. It'll be a tight fit, but I think we can fit your bike in the back; I'll take you wherever it is you want to go, you save gas, and I get to talk to you."

Hamilton agreed; Bellman went around the corner for the car. In addition to the Mini, Tipton had fixed him up with a special driving license. That, Bellman thought, was an act that might cost more British lives than the Sussex Cyclops.

He drove carefully, looking both ways before he did anything, and made it safely to where Dave Hamilton waited. They got the bike stowed away, and Bellman said, "Where to?"

"Doesn't matter," Hamilton said. "Ever been to Camden Town?"

"That's up around the zoo, isn't it?"

"Not far. Lots of markets and things. I need some stuff. If you don't mind."

"Not a bit. You'll have to give me directions." Bellman looked both ways, and pulled out into the lefthanded traffic.

In between directions, Hamilton talked. At first, he was nervous. "I'm not in trouble or anything, am I? I mean, I know the boss sends geezers around checking up and all, but I haven't been talking to anybody. I barely talk to my own family, anymore."

"No trouble, Dave, relax. I've read your file. I know you haven't talked about your job to anybody, except to tell them you run a computer for a publishing company."

"Played hell with my life, too, if you want to know. I've drifted away from all my mates. Of course, they don't have jobs. Now they can hardly think of anything to say to me bar, 'Oy, Dave, lend us a fiver.' "

"This whole business can be a drag."

"Well, I'm not complaining, mind."

Bellman smiled. "Nobody said you were. And who cares, anyway? Go ahead and complain if you want."

"No, sir, Mr. Bellman—"

"Jeff," Bellman said.

"All right. Jeff. I'm not complaining. If you've read my file, you know how much I need this job. I'd give up five hundred layabouts for the look on my mum's face when I told her I got a job. And good pay, too. I never did anything but take the course at the college because the geezer from DHSS suggested it."

"Miss Grace says you're a natural at computers."

"I've always liked fooling around with gadgets. I don't know if this was in my file, but I used to make spending money fixing tellys and radios and the like for people. Then after my brother got hurt, and my dad run off, I expanded it. Part of the—what d'ya call it—the Underground Economy."

It amused Bellman to notice that as Dave relaxed, his Cockney got thicker. G's were dropped constantly now, and H's were disappearing as well. TH's, F's, and V's started blending together, so that "my brother" became "me bruvver."

Bellman's original accent was American South-coastal, as spoken by his father, the Congressman. He never reverted to it, except on purpose. He supposed he just never relaxed enough.

"It's in your file," Bellman told the boy. There was more there than that. Hamilton's father had run off (he was in Australia, but Dave and his mother didn't know that) because he had brought Dave and his younger brother, Mike, to a football match (Chelsea vs. Liverpool) three years ago, and Chelsea had lost. In the ensuing violence, which probably would have ensued even if Chelsea had won, Mike Hamilton had been hit in the back with a piece of paving rock, which broke his spine and paralyzed him from the shoulders down.

The family undoubtedly would have taken out their anger and grief on the hoodlum who'd thrown the rock, but he was never found, so they took it out on Dad. They were led in this, so the file said, by Dad himself, who began to live down to his own self-image. He drank. He got tough with Dave and Dave's mother. Finally, he disappeared. Dave had taken over. He'd decided the dole payments weren't enough, and he'd gone to the Department of Health and Social Services to demand to know what an eighteen-year-old school-leaver could do to make money that wouldn't put him in jail.

The answer had been computers. Chance had put him in Felicity Grace's class. And here he was.

"I thought it might be in the file," Dave said. "I fixed Miss Grace's telly for her once—she lives right near the college, you know. She just needed a resistor changed. Shop would have charged her a bomb."

Bellman smiled again. "Bad boys rape other young girls . . ."

Dave said, "Uh-oh, I think I'm going to be out of a job. You fix gadgets, too?"

"I don't fix them, I just like to know how they go wrong. Sometimes, you have to break them."

"I read a book about computers that said, 'The first step of fixing something is getting it to break.' " Dave laughed. "I don't know anything else like a machine. If you do it right, you get the right answer. You can put any kind of information into a simple code, and *deal* with it." His voice held regret that life wasn't like that.

Bellman parked outside a big warehouselike building about a block from the Camden Town tube stop. Crowds of punks and tourists and every flavor in between oozed in and out of it like water from a pump. Dave covered his bike with a blanket and headed for the building.

Bellman was just as glad to go inside. It was standard January London weather. The sky looked like the inside of a pewter bowl someone had upended over the city. It would probably start raining in the next half hour or so.

There was nothing Bellman wanted to buy inside, but it was

interesting to look at. There were clothes and ornaments and lots of bootleg tapes. A bobby stood around conspicuously, but it was obvious he was there more to stop pickpockets and purse snatchers than to check into the authenticity of any merchandise for sale.

Bellman spent some time watching a fellow with a hairdo like a Day-glo stegasaurus who stood behind a folding card table in the middle of traffic selling stuff that would turn your hair orange or lime green or electric blue. For a few quid, he would punk you up for the day, guaranteed washable. Bellman skipped it.

Across from the hairdresser was a place that sold earrings. "That's where I get mine," Dave Hamilton told him. He ran a finger down the colored array in his right ear. "Got plenty now, though."

After a stop at a food stand (Bellman got a pork pie—he'd once tasted what the British thought of as a hot dog, and once was enough), Dave announced there was nothing he wanted there today, and that they should walk down the road to the open-air market.

They stepped back outside to find the sky darkened from pewter to cast iron. "Won't be a minute," Dave promised. "Just some gear I want to check at the other place. We can leave if it rains."

The other market had had a previous life as a parking lot—now, with tiny stalls cobbled together from planks, plywood, and corrugated metal, it reminded Bellman of a Brazilian *favela*, pre paint job. Not that bright scenes of city life would especially match the gray street or the gray sky.

The merchandise was much the same as at the indoor market, but even more eclectic. A lot of used things—books, clothes, records. Bellman was tempted by a copy of The Turtles' Greatest Hits, in really great condition, but he didn't want to have to lug it back to the States when this business was (finally) over. There was food in greater variety, and a decent-looking Middle Eastern restaurant across the street. Bellman started to regret the pork pie.

Dave was apparently absorbed in looking through a stall

smaller than the shower in the company flat. They sold military uniforms, all kinds, all countries.

It started to rain. Bellman pulled his collar up, but cold rain made it onto his neck and formed a channel for itself down his spine. Dave was out of the rain, under a corrugated roof that made a noise like a snare drum solo. Bellman decided to give the kid a few more minutes, then suggest they get the hell out of there. In the meantime, he looked around.

After a while, he said, "Who the hell would want to buy a brown balloon?"

Dave jumped as if Bellman had dropped an ice cube in his pants. "What? Oh. Sorry, Mr. Bellman. Jeff. I was looking at this jacket. This is U.S. Marines, innit?"

"Right."

"Too dear for me at present, though." He put it back on the rack. "What were you saying?"

Bellman pointed toward the entrance to the lot on the far side of the one they'd come in to a miserable-looking black man selling balloons. He had a long folding table set up, with his helium tank beside it. Tied in bunches along the table were balloons, trying to float up into the rain.

"Look," Bellman said. "People come here with their kids, so he can sell balloons. But look at the colors he's got. Red, green, blue, sure. The purple is unusual. Nice too. But what kid is going to want a white balloon? Or a black one, or a brown one?"

"He's even got gray ones, see?" Dave said. He seemed as puzzled as Bellman was. Then he shrugged. "We could ask him."

Bellman shook his head and grinned. "I've got enough to worry about without making suggestions to a balloon man."

"Takes all sorts," Dave replied. "Anyway, he won't be selling many in the rain."

"That sounds like a hint," Bellman said. "Sold. Let's get back to the car."

Bellman finally got around to what he had in mind on the drive home. It was simply that he wanted Dave to stand ready to do any processing he might need done in the days ahead.

Dave looked surprised.

"Check it out with Tipton if you want," Bellman said.

"It's not that," Dave protested. "I'll be glad to help you. If that's what you want."

"It might not come up," Bellman said. "I'll let you know."

"Fine with me," Dave said. He still looked surprised.

FIFTH

Each thought he was thinking of nothing but
    "Snark"
  And the glorious work of the day;
And each tried to pretend that he did not remark
  That the other was going that way.

But the valley grew narrow and narrower still,
  And the evening got darker and colder,
Till (merely from nervousness, not from goodwill)
  They marched along shoulder to shoulder.

—*The Hunting of the Snark*
Fit the Fifth

1

The Congressman was just as glad to get out of Brussels. NATO fact-finding mission, so-called. He and his fellows from Capitol Hill were supposed to find out facts, which they did. Every time they went, they found out the *same* damn facts. They found out what our NATO allies wanted: Complete protection from the Russians; no nuclear missiles on European soil for their left-wing political parties to get upset over; big buildup of conventional forces without having to pay any money for it; and more say in the distribution of the forces America was paying for. Also, they wanted Cabbage Patch dolls for their kids.

So he was glad to be taking a break from all of it. He wasn't so sure if he was too happy over what he was doing instead. When he met his agents, he liked to meet them in his office in Washington, the secret one in the basement of a predominantly black apartment building in a part of town where monuments are scarce. He didn't mind entertaining them at his regular place in the New Congressional Office Building. He frequently went for walks with them along the river—in conference with a constituent, or a volunteer worker, or a graduate student or something. In Washington, almost any excuse would be easy to put across.

It was different in the field. You just didn't want to be seen with the boys (or girls) in the field. It was dangerous to the operation; it was dangerous to the agent; and worst of all, it might blow the Congressman's cover, and the effectiveness of the Agency, forever. So he and his son had arranged all this folderol over a scrambled London-to-Belgium phone (still being circumspect—the phones in Europe had a tendency to connect a caller with a favorite number of theirs, no matter what you dialed) just to have a chance to talk face-to-face.

147

Of course, the Congressman had agreed. If Jeffrey was willing to talk to his old man face-to-face, or if there was a course of action he felt he needed to run by him, he damned well *better* talk to him. Once his son was committed to an operation, he wasn't the sort to come back for consultations. He demanded carte blanche and got it, and answered only for results.

Which was the way the Congressman wanted it. The way he had planned it since he'd conceived his son on the not unwilling (at first) body of a captured Russian spy going by the name of Rebecca Underwood. The boy (or girl) was to have the best genes available, the best training, and then would be sent into the world to do a job for his country no one else could.

The only thing the Congressman hadn't foreseen was that his son wouldn't like the work. Or rather, that he would convince himself that he *shouldn't* like the work, and try to stay away from it. That he'd hate the part of himself that kept dragging him back to it. To the Agency. To the Congressman.

The boy blamed it all on his father, of course. The Congressman had learned to live without his son's love. He had his respect, and he had his fear. The Congressman suspected that he was the only thing his son *did* fear, aside from his own nature, his own destiny.

So they'd meet, and the Congressman would find out what was going on. The Congressman had promoted a Belgian-built Chevy from the NATO motor pool, and, disdaining a chauffeur (raising eyebrows on a few of his more perquisite-mad colleagues) had driven himself up to Dunquerque, where he boarded the ferry for Dover.

The ferry was a confection of airplane-style windows, swept-back smokestacks, and white paint that gleamed in the lights of the harbor. It looked like something that had been sculpted out of a bar of Ivory soap, and it bobbed on the waves like one. A Frenchman on the dock assured him it rode flatter when it was under way.

The Congressman drove the car into the garage section of the ferry, directed by a disheveled docker with the shape of a bowling ball and the imperiousness of Charles de Gaulle. He parked, took the keys, and went looking for his son.

The Congressman had to admit that for a boat designed for

nothing but endless two-hour trips, they had done it up. The seats (all facing forward, again like an airplane) were covered in some kind of imitation leather. There was a duty-free shop, a restaurant, a snack bar, and God help us, a disco. There was also, he saw in scoping out the bathroom, a convenient cubicle containing a low porcelain receptacle, something between a sink and toilet, in case the Channel trip cost you your lunch. The Congressman noted it for future reference, and hoped that the ship would get under way soon. He took a seat close to the bathroom, and decided that son or no son, if Jeffrey stood him up, he was a dead man.

A few moments later the throb of the engines turned into a low-frequency hum, and the boat began to slosh its way across the Channel. As the docker had promised, it was better. Slightly. The Congressman resolved that the next time he crossed the Channel he would go by helicopter.

Bellman joined him just after the Congressman decided it was wiser not to look out the windows. "Where the hell have you been?" he demanded.

His son smiled at his discomfort. He held up a canvas shopping bag from Harrods. "I've been doing some marketing for an invalid. Lots of English people do it. Prices are a lot cheaper in France, especially for cheese and poultry and things like that. French butter."

The Congressman knew what the little bastard was doing, but he wouldn't give his son the satisfaction of letting him know how the thought of food was affecting him. "What did you want to talk about?"

Bellman sat down next to him. "The first thing I want to do is bring you up to date." The Congressman listened as his son recited the whole dismal story. If the Congressman didn't feel so sick, he would be shouting, swearing mad. He could get away with it, too—there was no one else in the compartment with them. Probably, he thought with an inward groan, they were all at the disco.

The Congressman knew that the state-of-British-Intelligence report by Sir Lewis had two remaining chances of doing anybody any good—slim and none. And slim was looking mighty poorly. There was just too much going on. With the Congressman's old friend gone crazy, there were too many things that could go wrong, publicity bombs that could go off with a loud noise when touched by the wrong fingers.

No, they were going to have to solve that particular little problem some other way. Or leave the British to clean their own house, and face up to what might happen if they didn't. Which, he knew, he couldn't afford to do either. America had few enough friends. Sir Lewis had been one of the ones the Congressman had the most confidence in.

The Congressman shook his head. He didn't like to make mistakes. He didn't like to feel fallible.

"Are you listening to me?" Bellman demanded.

"I'm listening," his father said. "The girl was sent home from the hospital yesterday, and you're movin' in with her. Gettin' domestic."

"It's the best way to work toward the objective," his son told him coldly. He always reacted coldly when the Congressman accused him of ulterior motives.

"I'd like to know what the hell the objective is just now, son."

Bellman opened his mouth to tell him, but the old man said, "Wait a minute. Can we get up on a deck somewhere? I never was much of a sailor; I need some air."

"It'll be cold as hell," his son warned. "Also wet, with the spray and the drizzle."

"I don't care. Let's go. Leave your bag. Ain't nobody going to steal it. Anybody who can think about eatin' on a trip like this deserves it."

Bellman took him up two flights of sandy-surfaced metal steps to the top deck of the ship, a crowded place of tubes and fittings, life boats and air intakes. The air was cold, and seemed to reach places in his lungs the queasiness had sealed off. The spray in his face was refreshing.

"The objective now," Bellman told his father, "is to get Sir Lewis out of circulation without this whole mess blowing up all over the front page."

The Congressman looked at the wake alongside the ship, then up into the distance. There was nothing to see but blackness. He looked back at the wake. "That strikes me as an excellent assessment of the situation, boy. Any amount of publicity that

150

gets out over this is going to be a mess. That Sir Lewis is the killer is bad enough. Once that bunch starts sniffin' around, who *knows* what they'll turn up? If they get hold of the espionage connection around that old man, it will take years to fix up the damage. If it can *ever* be done. Is that England already?"

His son's eyes followed his father's pointing finger to a hazy group of lights off in the distance. "No," he said. "That's another ferry heading to France."

"Wishful thinking," the old man murmured. He spit over the rail. "Anyway, son, what are you going to do about it? As far as I can tell, this sack of shit can break open any day now."

"Any minute."

"What's that supposed to mean?"

"I heard from Leo Calvin."

The old man looked at his son. Jeffrey had never been one to go in for leg pulls, and there was no indication in his face that he'd changed his mind. Besides, the boy wouldn't joke about Leo Calvin. The only thing that had gotten him back on the job was the chance to neutralize Calvin before Calvin could get around to neutralizing him.

"What do you mean you *heard* from him?" the old man demanded.

"He left me a tape, care of the American Embassy."

"Just like last time."

"Just like last time," Bellman agreed. "Only this time it's in his own cultured voice."

"How do you know? You never spoke to him."

"You're right. Put it this way: if it's not Calvin, it's somebody he coached. He mentioned things about the Cronus business— for instance, the wording of the note he left me on Miles's body—that no one in the world but the two of us would know."

"All right, let's say it's him. What did he want?"

"His life."

The Congressman snorted. "Is that all?"

"No. He wanted money and a new identity."

"And he asked *you* for it? He must be cracking up. He must know you wouldn't give him the time of day if you ran the Naval Observatory. What did he offer you in exchange?"

"A threat. He's put it together about our friend the Cyclops. He'll go to the papers with it if we don't play along with him."

"Sweet Christ," the Congressman said reverently. "What do you intend to do about it?"

"I don't know yet. He offered a promise, too—he'd tell us everything he knew about Russian and Cuban operations. Which must be quite a bit. He wants to meet. He left me a code to use—I'm supposed to place a personal in *The Times* two days from now to tell him where and when. If I don't show up, or if anything happens to him, the information goes to the tabloids."

The Congressman looked off into the blackness again and rubbed his chin. "Goddam," he said, "this is what comes from meddlin' in someone else's business. It's bad enough to step in your own messes—listen, son, do you think Calvin has any proof?"

"Who needs proof? You know the English papers. Sir Lewis is missing, the murders are happening, they'll love it. And they'll dig. And they won't stop."

The Congressman just grunted. He spat again into the Channel. He turned to his son and asked him again what he intended to do about it.

"I think I'm going to arrange the meet."

The Congressman looked grim. "I suppose there's no help for it. It could be a trap. Calvin doesn't care for you any better than you do for him."

"It could be a trap," Bellman conceded. "But we do know the Russians have been after him."

"They've been after you, too,"

"But I'm only supposed to be their enemy, right? Calvin in their eyes is a *traitor*—he messed up the Cronus project. He's got no choice—he has to go *somewhere*. And who else has the muscle to save him from the Russians?"

"I taught you from the beginning never to let the other side call the shots, son."

Bellman smiled. "They won't, Congressman. At least not all of them."

The old man listened while his son told him what he had in mind. After a while, despite wind, cold, and the relentless motion of the waves, the Congressman was smiling, too.

152

2

Sir Lewis stood quietly under the bus shelter across Putney Hill from the big old house and watched the lights in Felicity Grace's windows. The drizzle had stopped, but a cold, wet wind was blowing off the Thames, and it was nice to have the protection of the glass panels and metal roof. Every few seconds he glanced farther up the hill to see if a bus was coming. He had no intention of taking it, and would move to another vantage point as soon as he saw one. The last thing he needed was for some nosy Parker of a driver to remember the strange old man who scorned the bus on a cold night.

Cold and uncomfortable as it was, Sir Lewis's vigil had already paid off. An hour or so ago, the American, Bellman, had turned up carrying a bag of food. He hadn't emerged, and Sir Lewis was sure he was in for the night. Sir Lewis would have given a lot to know where the young man had been all day, but he was happy enough to know where he'd be when Celeber's men turned up tomorrow morning.

Sir Lewis was amazed at how long it had taken him to think of going to Celeber. Not the man himself, of course—Sir Lewis had had no idea of his existence before he'd found the name in the classified directory earlier today—but some other private detective. Once he'd decided that the American was the best possibility to lead him back to this Leo, to this other American who'd made such a mess of things, the idea of a private detective fairly shrieked out.

But Sir Lewis hadn't heard. He'd let the events of the past year alienate him, turn him into a rogue animal, unused to the idea of friends or helpers. He'd been lying on his bed in the cloth room late this morning when it occurred to him that friends and helpers *needn't be the same people.* He had plenty of money; he could *hire* help.

It had to be done carefully, of course. Carefully at every step. For instance, it made him decide, once and for all, what the plan was to be. He had to take his chances with the American. He could hardly walk into the office of a private detective and offer to pay him to shadow the Agricultural Attaché to the Embassy of the Soviet Union every time he stepped out of Number 18 Kensington Palace Gardens. At least he couldn't do it without causing ripples that would bring attention to him. Sir Lewis wanted attention, and fully intended to get it. But not quite yet.

It was important, too, for Sir Lewis to pick the right detective. Securicor, or one of the other big agencies, would be out of the question. They'd request too much information, and they might be tempted to check it. And they had too many official friends with whom they would want to maintain the proper relationship. Not that they would ever violate the legitimate interests of a client—it was a matter of what one meant by "legitimate." No, the big security companies would be too damned ethical to suit Sir Lewis's present requirements.

On the other hand, he needed an outfit large enough to maintain a twenty-four-hour daily surveillance until further notice, and competent enough to keep their operations secret, even from a fellow professional.

Celeber Security was the fifth place Sir Lewis had tried, and he had known as soon as he'd walked in the door of Hugh Celeber's office that it was the right place.

It was Celeber's eyes that had told him. Sir Lewis had prepared for his little shopping expedition (in another piece of careful planning) by adopting a new disguise. He walked in wearing a beard, spectacles, wig, homburg, gloves, overcoat, and scarf. He also carried a stick. He looked like a rich London Jew circa 1915; he looked like a man wearing the most blatant disguise imaginable. It was bait.

And what it was designed to catch was the look in the detective's eyes. He saw through the disguise immediately—no one was trying to fool anyone on that issue—but he said nothing except "Good afternoon," and "How may I help you, sir."

Sir Lewis begun to tell Celeber the story he'd prepared. Sir

Lewis gave him the name "George Smith," the verbal equivalent of his disguise. He said that wasn't his real name.

Celeber was a deceptively young-looking man, tall and lanky, with an innocent face, guileless brown eyes, and a suit and a head of hair in matching shades of beige. "Your real name will be on your check, Mr. Smith," he said. His voice was respectful, and boasted a studied lack of regional or class accent.

"There will be no check," Mr. Smith had said. "Cash. In advance. I shall phone you daily for reports—you will tell me when you require more money, and a messenger will bring it. Here is two thousand pounds for a retainer."

There was a flash of something in the guileless eyes. "What do you want me to do?"

"There is a young woman," Sir Lewis began.

Celeber nodded. It gladdened Sir Lewis's heart. He knew his lie would go over—it was common enough, and unsavory enough that anyone with a normally soiled mind would believe it.

"There is a young woman," Sir Lewis said again. "My interest in her is known to no one, but it is considerable. *And* it is backed by a serious financial commitment."

Celeber nodded again. His face was impassive, but the phrase "dirty old man" was so strong in his thoughts Sir Lewis could almost hear it.

"This young woman was recently injured in an accident. Nasty business. Lost an eye."

"That is nasty," Celeber conceded.

"That bit's even nastier. She was with a man at the time. A young man. An American named Bellman. She *says* it's innocent. Someone she knows from work. Maybe so. I want to be sure."

"A perfectly reasonable attitude," the detective assured him. "What is it exactly you'd like me to do?"

"She's home from hospital now. Watch her flat. I'll give you her address—place in Putney. I'll get you a description of this Bellman character as well. Watch her place. If Bellman shows up, follow him when he leaves. I don't care where he goes. If he wants the woman, fine, but I suspect he's playing up to her to get at my interests, and I won't have it. I want to know where he goes, whom he sees, whom he talks to. I'll pay what it costs, but I'll want my money's worth."

"I think we can make each other happy, Mr. Smith," Celeber said.

And so it was arranged. Celeber would call in operatives and brief them and have them on the job by 0700 this morning. Mr. Smith would ring every evening at half past seven for his report. And, though no specific words were spoken, Mr. Smith was given to understand that it was the policy of Celeber Security that the client be exclusively the *beneficiary* of their investigations, never the subject.

That suited Sir Lewis Alfot fine.

Sir Lewis looked to his left up the hill. High headlights and the double row of wide, lighted windows told him a bus was coming. He left the shelter of the bus stop, pulled his head down into his scarf, and headed up the hill to the corner, where he could watch Felicity's window (the lights were still on, though it was well past midnight) from the cover of a privet hedge. He was grateful for the protection from the cold offered by Mr. Smith's beard.

Sir Lewis reflected, not without pride, that he was getting a feel for functioning under the new rules he faced. In the old days, he could have ordered wiretaps and surveillance on Felicity, the Russians, *and* the American, with resources limited only by his own discretion.

Still, he'd had done all right. One night of discomfort, then he could retire to his hotel room once more while Celeber and his men kept track of Bellman for him. With luck, it could lead him back to Leo, which was where, in all the world, he most wanted to be. They could do the work—he would be working on backup plans. A good agent always had backup plans.

The bus was gone, but Sir Lewis decided to wait awhile before returning to the shelter. He looked up again at Felicity's windows. He wondered how she thought of him now.

He wished he knew what was going on up there.

3

What was going on up there was an argument.

No, Felicity thought, *not* an argument. It takes two to argue. What we have here is me making a fool of myself in the presence of a man. Something, she reminded herself, she had made a solemn vow never to do.

Something she couldn't stop doing, either.

"Can't you see how dangerous this is?" she demanded.

"It's dangerous," Jeffrey conceded.

"You can't take all this on yourself," she insisted. "You need support. You need backup. *Tell* Mr. Tipton."

"I intend to. As soon as everything is set."

"But you've already told Bulanin!"

"Not me personally. I sent him the message through a double agent he trusts. He'll check it out—and he'll learn the time and place of the meet, of course, if he isn't in on it in the first place—and he'll find out the information is accurate."

He came over and sat next to her on the sofa. "Look, Felicity, I'll go through it all again. Either Bulanin is in on this little ploy of Calvin's or he isn't. If he is, we let him think none of us suspects him. If he isn't, we get him involved, get him thinking what we might do, what Calvin might do. What kind of publicity might come out of this."

Felicity put her hand to the side of her head. Under the bandage, the empty eye socket itched as though it would drive her mad. "Do you understand all this yourself?" she asked wearily.

"I'd better. I'm not having much luck making you understand it." He smiled briefly. "I'll quote the Congressman. 'Best thing to do with a potential arsonist is set fire to him.' "

"Fight fire with fire," Felicity said. "I've heard it."

"That's it. From Bulanin's point of view the worst thing that could happen would be for Leo Calvin to start telling us everything he knows. It could destroy him, and all his work. Bulanin is the type to care a lot about his work. He'll take steps to protect it. We watch what he does, and we learn something. The worst that could happen is that our double agent gets his reputation enhanced. When are you going to be able to make love again?"

Felicity closed her eye and shook her head. It had been a wretched day, big things and little things. Jeffrey had been gone, of course, off to France to do the marketing and whatever other mission he'd set for himself. He had moved in with her, but that didn't mean he would tell her any more than he wanted to.

Despite that, it had been unsettling not to have him around. He was very solicitous, and he had a way of talking that kept her mind off the obscene hole that had once provided her with half her information about the world. She shuddered and felt ill every time she thought of it, every time she pictured herself with the biro sticking out of her eye.

But it was fitting, in a way, too. Since Derek had died, Felicity had *felt* diminished, incomplete. She felt about two ounces less than a whole woman. The lost eyeball was a perfect physical representation of that fact.

And leaving everything emotional aside, it was just a bloody nuisance. She had no depth perception—the world was as flat as a cinema screen. The doctors had warned her to expect it, told her that in time her brain would adjust and she'd hardly remember the difference, but that was no help when she'd pour tea all over the table. It was heaven to be allowed (with proper precautions) to wash her hair at last but she seemed to knock over the shampoo in the bath every time she reached for it.

And of course, the world of objects had chosen this time to revolt. The drain in the tub had backed up. She hadn't trusted herself to use lye to fix it—probably would have spilled it all over her wet skin and burned herself horribly. Jeffrey had taken care of it when he returned. He cleaned the whole place while he was at it, scrubbing, mopping, using traditional British thick bleach to clean the WC. He laughed at Felicity's injunction to him not to mix them. He told her he'd studied basic chemistry a long time ago.

One thing he couldn't fix was the telly, which had also decided to go haywire. The picture was washed out in a blaze of brightness. That, Jeffrey couldn't fix, though he did diagnose the problem as a burnt-out resistor. To her surprise, he suggested she forgot having the regular man round, and rang Dave Hamilton instead.

Ordinarily, Felicity would have let it go for days or even weeks—she didn't share the national preoccupation with the box (only the Americans watched more), but since the incident in Brighton she had been obsessed with *seeing* things. Motion. Color. Form.

Then the special light had flashed on the telephone. Jeffrey had installed it to signal when one of his informant's calls was being forwarded from the number he had given them to ring to this one. Jeffrey had picked up the phone, listened for a few seconds, said good, and then rung off.

Felicity, without really thinking, had asked him what it was all about.

And he told her. He was making sure the Russians knew exactly what he was planning. That news had outraged all her professional instincts, and had started the nonargument, during which Jeffrey agreed with all her objections, but changed his mind not a bit.

And finally, this. He wanted, he said, to make love to her. Was it pity? Or was he one of those sick bastards who enjoyed doing it with mutilated women? No, she told herself, he was a good commander, concerned about her morale. The way, for example, Sir Lewis Alfot had always been.

"It will be some time," she said, "before I'm ready even to *think* about sex again."

"Anytime you're ready," Bellman said. "I'll be available." He spoke softly, but Felicity heard him. She went off to the bedroom while Jeffrey took a shakedown on the couch.

She thought about him for a long time before she went to sleep.

4

Leo Calvin was beginning to believe in the brain drain.

In America he had worked with British men and women, and had been impressed with their quality. English, Scottish, Welsh, and especially Northern Irish, they tended to be intelligent, cool in a crisis, ruthless enough for any purpose, and (rare, for Leo's usual line of work) they even seemed to have a sense of humor.

That was in America. Now that he was here, all his effort and most of the money he had left had gone to secure the services of Stan Hope and a man who admitted to no other name that Grunter Martin.

They were not, in Leo's expert opinion, terrorists. They had no political leanings, not even an understanding of the causes they had ostensibly enlisted in. They were in it for the money, but they weren't mercenaries, at least not in the professional fighting man, dogs-of-war sense.

What they were was hoodlums. If it weren't for the coal strike, Leo would never have heard of them, and that would have suited him fine. Beggars, however, could not be choosers, and Leo needed help.

Specifically, he needed Stan Hope. Hope had been out of place along the violent fringes of the coal strike. Not because of the violence. There were numerous tarts, gambling debtors, and people late with interest payments who could testify that Stan could be, when the spirit was on him, an artist of violence, a sculptor who carried a slim, sharp engraving tool in the same pocket as he kept his gold cigarette case and lighter. It wasn't the violence; it was the fact that if there was one thing not at issue in the recent dispute, it was that digging coal was hard work. Stan

Hope would always look out of place around anything that even hinted at hard work.

Stan was willing to listen to Leo's offer because Leo was the one who'd thought of the best way to make use of him during the strike. That was to send him around to wives of working miners. Let him talk to them. Let him make the veiled (or unveiled) threats about violence to their husbands, violence or worse to themselves or their children. There was a greasy elegance about the man, with his slick black hair, wavy red lips, and wide white smile, that made a threat from him terrifyingly credible.

Leo was sure it was a class thing. He had no idea what Stan Hope's antecedents might be, but he looked and acted like an aristocrat gone horribly wrong. Unlike the miners, or the hoodlums who *might* be miners (Grunter Martin, for example), the recipient of a threat from Hope could make no cultural connection, appeal to no kind of shared interest. Stan Hope would smile, and threaten anything. And he would do anything, and still smile.

Leo's idea had made a useful man of Stan Hope, and that had earned him a lot of money. He was ready for some more. Leo knew the signs. The expensive scent masked the smell of a body that hadn't been bathed in quite a few days. Stan Hope was living in a place with a shilling meter, too. The shirt was custom-made, but it was soiled and beginning to fray. Twice he had seen Stan go for the gold cigarette case, something the chain-smoking Mr. Hope normally did every five to seven minutes. Each time, Stan had caught himself, and had instead drawn a crumpled pack of Benson & Hedges from the side pocket of his leather-patched tweed jacket.

Leo was glad to see it. That had to mean the gold case was in a pawn shop. He mentally reduced the offer he was about to make. He would give Stan Hope no more than necessary. Leo loathed Stan Hope. But Stan was the only man he knew smart enough to keep quiet, and (if he were well paid) dependable enough to do what was required of him.

Not so dependable, however, as to let Leo take him for granted. That was the reason Grunter Martin had been asked along.

"You give Stan more money than you give me," Grunter said. There was no anger in his voice, or hurt or surprise, just the statement of fact. Grunter Martin was broad and brawny. His name came from the noise he made when he hit people, which he did with a detached professionalism whenever the money was right. He never showed, or, as far as Leo could tell, had any emotion whatever.

"Yours is just a retainer," Leo told him. "I'm going to give Stan a particular job to do. For that he gets paid once. I want you to work for me on a regular basis; you'll get this much every week."

"Until when?" Grunter asked. He had tiny bright blue eyes that could gleam with shrewdness just when you were about to dismiss him as an idiot. Grunter dressed like an American truck driver, a look he'd picked up from the cinema. Right now he wore blue jeans, a gray sweatshirt, and a black zip-up cloth jacket. His brown hair was crew-cut length all over his head, except for his forelock, which he combed down over his brow. Combined with the eyes, it gave him the look of some malevolent Kewpie doll.

"Two weeks at least," Leo told him, hoping he'd be out of the country by then. Turning himself in to Bellman would be unpleasant, to say nothing of dangerous, but it would at least protect him from the consequences of having told a lie to Grunter Martin.

"All right, then," Grunter said.

"What's the job?" Stan Hope asked. He did the cigarette routine again. Leo noticed that he lit the new cigarette with the butt of the old one, which meant the gold lighter was probably in hock as well.

Leo took a manila envelope from under his coat and handed it to Stan. "The job is simple. Take this. Keep it for me. I will ring you every day. I—"

"Sorry," Stan said. "Phone's out. You could ring me here at the Duke's Head."

"All right. What's the number?"

Stan offered to write it out for him, but Leo said he would remember it.

"All right," Leo said again. "Eleven-thirty A.M. every day. Be there. Wait until afternoon closing if for some reason I don't call. If you still haven't heard from me by the time they chuck you out, bring that envelope to *The Sun*."

Stan raised his eyebrows and opened his mouth to speak, but Leo cut him off.

"Don't wonder what's inside it. Don't look."

"No fear," Stan assured him. "I only get curious when I'm poor. You'll make your first call tomorrow?"

"That's right."

"Not to look a gift horse in the mouth, but this seems quite a bit a money for a job a trained dog could do."

"A trained dog could forget. Or see a bigger bone. You're too smart for that, Stan. Aren't you?"

"Oh. Of course."

"Good. I may have another job for you, but we can talk about that later. I'd want you, too, Grunter."

"This fall under the money you give me every week?" Grunter asked.

"No, there'll be a separate payment for it if the job comes up."

Leo might have told him the time. Grunter nodded once, raised his pint, drained it, put the mug down with a clatter on the scarred wooden table, and licked ale foam from his lips. "Good," he said. "The only thing you haven't told me is what I do for my weekly paycheck."

"Ah," Leo said. "I was coming to that. The first thing you do is to stay available in case I need some extra muscular backup. I don't expect that to happen."

"Easy money so far."

"For the rest, all I want is for you to stay with Stan. Keep people from bothering him. Don't let him lose the envelope. Listen in on my daily phone calls to him."

"Yeah?"

"And if he opens the envelope, or I don't call one day, and he fails to bring the envelope to the newspaper—"

Stan held up a hand. "This is quite unnecessary, you know. Leo, you know—"

"If he doesn't do it," Leo said.

"Yeah?" Grunter asked.

163

"Kill him."

Grunter shrugged. "I thought that might be it. Got time for another pint, Stan?"

5

I don't like this, Dave Hamilton thought. I shouldn't be here like this. Couple years ago I was just a kid in her class, now here I am in the lady's apartment. Posh place, but not flashy. Class.

Not the sort of place I belong.

It was also embarrassing to have Mr. Bellman there. Dave knew by now that the American was living here with Miss Grace, and he was more embarrassed by it than either of them seemed to be.

Not that Dave was wet enough to think a woman like Miss Grace wouldn't have a geezer or two around. He wasn't a virgin himself, if the truth be known, though since he'd stopped running with the old crowd he'd been relegated to the amateur ranks as far as that went.

And if there was going to be a face around, there was no reason it shouldn't be this American. He was a nice enough sort but he just didn't understand. He kept trying to treat Dave like some kind of pal, and couldn't seem to see that it wasn't on.

They weren't lovey-dovey or anything, at least not in front of Dave. It was plain, though, that they were comfortable with each other. It was the way they looked at each other that told the tale, the way the American took care of her. Dave's knowledge of the real business of the Tournament Press was strictly limited (and Dave got happier about that every day), but he'd seen enough of what the real professionals went through to know that people in that line of work seemed to go through life with their briefs too tight. They *never* got as comfortable with each other as these two seemed to be.

Dave was there to fix the telly. When they'd rung the flat and told him what they wanted, he felt queer, like he knew the way he'd feel when he got here. Too wide a gap between him and a posh bird from Gloucestershire or whatever. The American might as well come from Mars. He couldn't know about them, they couldn't know about him. He'd been about to say he couldn't make it.

But then he thought it over. Mike was having his pains again, and trying not to cry about it. It didn't seem fair—if he couldn't move his legs, couldn't feel anything else about them, why should he feel pain? It made Dave want to cry himself, something Mum had given up trying not to do.

Dave did all he could for his brother, but he couldn't do a thing about this. Medicine didn't help. The doctor said it was all in Mike's mind, but he was a bloody Paki from the National Health; what did he care? He got his packet whether he made anybody well or not. Someday, Dave would put enough money by to have Mike looked after by a real doctor.

Not that Dave wanted money from Miss Grace. He definitely did not want money from her, not now. Wouldn't be right somehow. But he did want to get out of the flat. And while he couldn't do anything for Mike or for Mum, he could help Miss Grace. He'd swallowed a couple of times to force the queer feeling back down to his belly where it could be contained. Then he told his mum he'd be back soon, put on his jacket, and rode his bike to Putney.

It had taken him more time to get upstairs to the flat and get the back off the box than it had to fix what was wrong. Dave gave the solder a few seconds to cool, then wiggled the cylinder (about as big around as a cigarette and half as long) to make sure it was secure. He placed the solder and flux back in his toolbox, and leaned the iron against it, point up.

"I'll let that cool for a moment, then I'll be off."

"Done already?" Miss Grace asked.

Dave shrugged. "It wasn't much. Mr. Bellman—Jeff had already put his finger on the problem by the time he rang me. It was a resistor, same as I fixed for you last time. I think there's something in the circuit that's burning them out, but it's more trouble than it's worth to pull the set apart to find it. Resistors are cheap enough." He handed her the old one. She held it up to her unbandaged eye (Dave had an uncomfortable flash of what must be behind the bandage) and looked at the colored circles painted against the overall beige of the cylinder.

"It's a color code," Bellman said. "Resistors are all pretty much alike, but they can't print numbers on them to tell them apart, because you might have to put it into a circuit numbers down."

Miss Grace nodded. "And you'd have to take the whole thing apart to read it."

The soldering iron was cool now. Dave packed it neatly in his toolbox and closed the lid. "I'll be off, now," he said.

Bellman was reaching for his pocket, and there was a question on his face, but Dave cut him off. "No charge," he said.

"Dave," Miss Grace said, "you must."

"I won't hear of it," Dave insisted. "It's a get-well present. I couldn't get you flowers. . . ."

He stopped because Miss Grace had come up to him and kissed him on the cheek and told him he was sweet, and Dave couldn't think of an appropriate response other than flight.

"Well," he said at last, sure he was blushing and angry at himself for it, "I've really got to go now. Me mum will have her hands full with Mike."

"Thanks, Dave," Bellman said. "I owe you one."

"It's nothing." Dave could feel himself bouncing on his knees in his anxiety to be out of there, like a kid waiting for permission to use the WC. "Enjoy the telly. Ta ra."

And mercifully, he was out the door. He stood there a moment, knowing he'd made a proper charlie of himself, but unable to feel anything but relief.

He heard voices from inside. Bellman's asking if she really wanted to know about this stuff; Miss Grace assuring him she did.

"All right," the American said. "All you have to do is remember this: 'Bad boys rape other young girls, but Violet gives willingly.'"

"Charming," Miss Grace said.

166

"Mnemonic device. To remember the color code. Black, brown, red, orange, yellow, green, blue, violet, gray, white. Black is zero, brown is one, red is two . . ."

Dave left. He already knew about this stuff, maybe even better than he wanted to.

6

Bulanin was pleased. Perhaps his luck was changing. He certainly deserved a change in his luck. Had been deserving one for a long time now.

But at least his informant's tips had been correct. *Both* the tips had been correct—the one that said that Leo Calvin had contacted the American, and the one this morning, telling him where and when they were to meet. Two in a row. A winning streak, as the Americans said.

And, as the Americans would also say, Bulanin was crowding his luck. He was handling this himself instead of trusting it to subordinates. It was a risk, but Bulanin, as always, had reasons.

One was that his subordinates, or those hired by his subordinates, had been failing rather miserably against this Bellman and his lady friend. The other was a matter of pride. Bulanin had somehow allowed Leo Calvin to lead him around by the nose, to use him to an extent it caused him shame just to think of—as though the KGB were a murder-for-hire organization, like some bunch of American gangsters, to be used to settle private disputes. The fact that the murders had failed didn't serve to change the basic fact—Leo Calvin had played on Bulanin's ambition and led him to pervert the mission of the organization he served. And the nation the organization served, if it came to that.

This, strictly interpreted, was a Crime Against the State, and no one but Bulanin had committed it. Therefore, no one but Bulanin should provide restitution, and that he planned to do.

Bulanin was not a fanatic, and he was not insane. He had no intention of turning himself over to Borzov for punishment—that would serve no one, the Motherland least of all.

But Leo Calvin had seduced Bulanin with promises of the head of Sir Lewis Alfot, alive and crammed with priceless secrets. He had made Bulanin perform like a trained bear, but he had not delivered the reward. Instead, he was treating with the Americans. With Bellman, the mad American, who had broken all the rules of recognized behavior, and who might, for all Bulanin knew, spray the Embassy with nerve gas the next time he took it into his head to visit.

So be it. Calvin had made his choice. Let him live with it. Or die with it. If Bulanin couldn't deliver Sir Lewis Alfot, he would deliver Leo Calvin. Not alive. Not alive. Bulanin knew how persuasive Calvin could be; he would not have him carrying tales to Borzov about how Bulanin had made a mess of his opportunity to capture alive the Motherland's greatest British enemy.

Calvin would die tonight. If possible, he would die slowly in the basement of the Embassy, but he would die.

Bulanin still wasn't sure what to do with Bellman. How big an incident would the death of this man cause, if any? Whom would the Americans kill in retaliation? Bulanin sighed. If he could answer those questions, he would already know what to do.

Bulanin hunched himself farther into his coat, cursing the January cold. Moscow was far colder than this, but there was something in the London damp that lingered uncomfortably in his bones long after he had gone inside again and locked it out behind him.

Tonight, the chill would have a chance to sink deep. Bulanin had placed himself on this bench, near the winter-deadened garden of the flower walk in Kensington Gardens, some ninety minutes ago. His blood felt like treacle someone had left too long in the refrigerator. He couldn't have moved fast if his life depended on it. At least he wouldn't be able to get off to a fast start.

This is how you show your age, he thought. Not in your face, in your legs. Bulanin hoped there would be no running tonight.

He was seated so that by looking around the twigs of a leafless bush he had a view of the Albert Memorial, where, in—Bulanin consulted his watch—five minutes Bellman would meet with Leo Calvin. It was not possible to appreciate the Albert Memorial in the dark, but Bulanin had come to look at it many times in daylight, and it never failed to fascinate him. It looked like the skeleton of a church spire, a Gothic one, lacking only the flying buttresses. Otherwise, every inch was carved or ornamented. Inside, was a seated statue of Prince Albert of Saxe-Coburg and Gotha, Prince Consort to Queen Victoria. It amused Bulanin to think that Karl Marx might have watched the workers ("The Grateful People," who erected the statue, according to the legend in gold that adorned it) erecting the structure, and felt all the surer of the eventual collapse of capitalism.

The Memorial was, to be sure, a memorial to bad taste. But it was also a memorial to obsolescence. Albert himself had been defunct before they started. But neither did Saxe-Coburg nor Gotha exist anymore. Not as separate principalities. And the Empire, the one the sun never set on, commemorated in four elaborate groups of statuary at the corners of the monument, was a memory, too. Europe, Africa, America, Oceania, each represented by a woman riding a wild beast, surrounded by worshipful aborigines, had forgotten Albert. Had probably forgotten the Empire.

They had been so *strong*. No power could have brought them to their current state except themselves. It was a mistake Bulanin would not let his own nation repeat.

It was quiet in the park, but not deserted. It was still early enough—not quite half past seven. The sun set early in the winter. People were still making their way home from work, and many walked across the park. Some, coming apparently for the quiet, and willing to pay the price of the cold to get it, sat quietly on their benches as Bulanin sat on his. A young black man on roller skates cut intricate capers around the statuary, fence, stairs, and benches that surrounded the Memorial. When he came close, Bulanin could hear him making rhythmic, breathy explosions with his lips, the rhythm of the music being pumped into his head by the small black box clipped to his belt.

Suddenly, the young man stopped and spoke to a newcomer, a tall man with the hood of his anorak covering his head.

"Pardon me, mon?" he said. Jamaican, Bulanin thought. Somewhere in the Caribbean, anyway. Far from home and making the best of it. Like I am, Bulanin thought.

"Yes?" the stranger said.

"Is your name Bellman?" It came out Bell-Mon.

"That's me."

Bulanin knew the voice. It was Bellman, all right.

"Fellow give me a fiver to give you a message," the Jamaican said. "He told me you'd give me another to hear it."

Bellman skinned his hood back, and Bulanin could see his grin. Bellman hiked up his coat and reached into his wallet. "Sorry," he said, "no fiver. Here's five ones." The black man took them; Bellman made a joke about spending them while they were still good.

"Who's the message from?" Bellman asked.

"All he told me was Leo. You know him?"

"Not as well as I'm going to. What's the message?"

"He told me to say he'd meet you down dere." The Jamaican pointed to the Alexandra Gate, his finger indicating a short diagonal to the southeast corner of the Gardens.

"Anything else?" Bellman asked.

The young man gave an eloquent shrug. "That's all, mon."

Bellman shrugged back and took off at a brisk pace. Bulanin didn't wait long before starting after him. By the time Bulanin's legs got limber, Bellman's head start would be big enough.

7

Chalk one up for Leo, Bellman thought. He'd arranged things so that their first face-to-face meeting would come with bars of good vintage British Iron between them. Leo had stationed himself outside Kensington Gardens completely, out on the pavement on the corner of Kensington Road and Exhibition Road. Serves me right, Bellman thought. Two feet away, but with the locked and chained Alexandra Gate between them, he might as well be in Canarsie.

Leo looked different from the way he had when Bellman had gotten his only previous glimpse of the man, across a burning warehouse in a town called Draper, Pennsylvania. Leo had a moustache now, and his hair was darker, but Bellman knew the grin. He'd know the grin anywhere.

Bellman walked close to the bars and said hello.

The grin widened. "And which one is the monkey?" Leo asked. "I've looked forward to this. Should I call you Driscoll or Bellman?"

"Call me whatever you like. Just tell me what you want."

"What I *want*?" Leo shook his head and sighed. "My friend, the gap between what I want and what I can have is enough to make me cry. For instance, I *want* to kill you."

"You've tried. Or had it tried."

"You're very lucky. Or very good."

"A combination."

"Of course, I don't dare kill you now. You're my only hope. The only consolation I have is that you want me dead as much as I want you dead, and you can't kill me, either."

"Plenty of room between the bars for a bullet to get through," Bellman said. He put his hand into the pocket of his coat. He had nothing in there but a couple of pound coins, but Leo didn't have to know that. Bellman had a perverted urge to push the terrorist, see what he'd do.

The answer was, he behaved like a professional. "You're too smart for that, my friend," he said. "The reason we can see each other so nicely is the lights from all these cars. The reason we're talking so quietly is that we don't want to disturb all these passersby. Do we?"

Bellman made a face.

"I didn't choose this place by accident, my friend. There's a busy Underground stop nearby; three bus lines run through here—no, four. I know you're not alone, but if you or any of your helpers do anything to me, it will draw a crowd. And even if it doesn't, the secret of the Sussex Cyclops will be all over London—all over the *world*—by tomorrow."

So much for pushing. Bellman couldn't shoot, or give the signal for the men he'd requisitioned from Tipton to shoot, either. The sidewalk was crowded—something doing at the Royal Albert Hall just down the block, no doubt. Calvin could take one step backward, and have a shield, a veritable fortress, of innocent human flesh around him.

Bellman faced a fact he'd been facing at two-hour intervals since he first got the news that Leo wanted to see him: There was nothing he could do but play along.

He faced it, he didn't have to like it. "All right," he said irritably. "Why don't we cut out the macho bullshit spy talk and get down to business?"

Leo grinned again. "I thought you'd never ask. The first thing you should know is that I'm going to want money. Lots of it."

"Define lots," Bellman suggested.

"Seven figures. American dollars. Swiss bank."

"Dreamer."

"A lot of it will go for bribes. I'm too big a patriot to ask Uncle Sam to protect me for the rest of my life. Plastic surgery. Things like that."

Bellman was getting impatient. "Maybe you just better spell it out."

Leo spelled. He was offering Bellman's Agency himself as a hostage for six months. Hostage and information source. The money had to be paid in advance, but they didn't have to let Leo out to collect it.

"I talk. Twelve, fourteen hours a day, if you want. I know a lot, and I can figure more. Russians, Cubans. Terrorists. You check out the information. If I've done enough, you let me go and enjoy my money. You'll always know where I am, and I'll always be available for more questions."

"I can't negotiate something like this."

"No negotiations. This is it. Anything else, I'd just as soon let the Russians catch up with me."

"What if we take you up on it, pump you, then lose your body when we've done?"

"Then the information on Sir Lewis goes in. I have to check in at intervals, but there's no limit on this. There's no time limit on fingerprints."

A lifetime of training kept Bellman from reacting, at least externally. How the hell had Leo found out about fingerprints? It wasn't something he had time to puzzle over now.

"I've got to get back for authorization on this."

"Naturally. I didn't expect you'd have five million bucks and a pardon in your pocket."

"How do I get in touch with you?"

"I'll reach you. There'll be a personal in *The Times* addressed to The Captain and signed Snark. It'll carry a time and a telephone number. Got it?"

Bellman nodded.

"Good. I never dreamed it would be such a pleasure doing business with you. Do I need to point out the consequences if I'm bothered in the meantime?"

"No."

"Then goodbye. I'll be careful crossing streets."

Bellman watched him turn and walk away. He also picked up one of Tipton's men, the one who would follow Leo back to wherever he was staying. Not that it would matter. Leo would expect to be kept under surveillance. Bellman doubted he'd even make an effort to shake the tail. The newspapers were all the insurance Leo needed.

Bellman sighed. His father had warned him about letting the other guy call the shots. He turned and headed down the path toward Queen's Gate, so he could get the hell out of there and get on a Number Fourteen bus back to Putney.

The voice came from behind a tree. "Wait a moment, Mr. Bellman."

Bellman jumped. That was involuntary, even though he'd been expecting something like this. Bulanin had seen him jump, too. That was bad. The idea now was to be supercool and get back even.

"Hello, Bulanin," he said. "Is that a gun in your pocket? Or are you glad to see me?"

Bulanin didn't jump, exactly. He did flinch. The file on the Agricultural Attaché was thick and explicit, and the Congressman's comments in the margins had suggested that Bulanin was not proud of his sexual exploits. Particularly the homosexual ones.

"You will come with me," the Russian said stiffly. "Immediately."

"Grigori Illyich," Bellman said. "You're far too handsome to resort to hard pickups in the woods."

"You are not funny," Bulanin said.

"You are. Agriculture or no agriculture, you are not an outdoor agent. You want me to come along to ask me questions, get me to tell you things. I'll tell you right here. First, that was Leo Calvin I spoke to. Obviously, he tipped you off we were going to meet, or saw you found out. Probably another effort to get you to kill me—he'd be damn near unbeatable if he didn't hold these grudges. Second, I'm not going to tell you what we talked about, because it was a lot of bullshit—you familiar with that term?—a lot of bullshit, and I don't trust him any more than you do."

Bellman took his hand out of his pocket, slowly. Bulanin wasn't flinching now—the handsome face was impassive. But he was thinking. Bellman could almost hear the buzz of neurons firing in the Russian's brain.

"Third," Bellman went on, "you can shoot me, if you like. If that *is* a gun in your pocket. But I'm not alone. Maybe neither one of us has a whole lot of respect for British Intelligence, but as marksmen, they're perfectly adequate. There are a least three of them with a bead on you right now. They don't know who you are, so they'll have no compunction about shooting you down if you do anything to me, even if it *does* start World War III.

"Four. I'm leaving now. It's a cold night, and I'm hungry. I suggest you do the same. Five. If you want to speak to me about Leo Calvin or anybody else, leave a message at the American Embassy. I'll be delighted to talk to you, Grigori Illyich. Any time."

"You are laughing at me," Bulanin said.

"Who?" Bellman demanded. "Me?"

"I have been laughed at before. The laugher has always regretted it."

"Good thing I'm not laughing, then."

"You are laughing. And you will regret it. I, too, hold grudges, Mr. Bellman."

Bulanin melted back into the woods. Bellman asked himself what he'd accomplished so far tonight. He'd been outmaneuvered by Calvin, and he had in turn outmaneuvered Bulanin. It was now confirmed that Bulanin had *some* knowledge of what Leo Calvin had been doing, and it was the next best thing to confirmed that it concerned Sir Lewis Alfot.

Did Bulanin think he was being double-crossed by Calvin, or was the Russian's appearance here tonight a charade for Bellman's benefit? Bellman was inclined to believe the former, if only on the basis of the Russian's facial expressions and body language.

One thing for sure—he'd have to run Leo's demands by the Congressman. Leo knew a lot of secrets, as he'd said, and Bellman suspected his father would forgive a lot to get his hands on them. It was the nature of the business.

It was also depressing as hell. Bellman sighed, then followed his smoky breath out of the park. He sat on a bus and let it take him home to Felicity.

SIXTH

"My poor client's fate now depends on your votes."
  Here the speaker sat down in his place,
And directed the Judge to refer to his notes
  And briefly to sum up the case.

But the Judge said he never had summed up before;
  So the Snark undertook it instead,
And summed it up so well that it came to far more
  Than the Witnesses ever had said!

—*The Hunting of the Snark*
Fit the Sixth

1

No book or film about private investigators ever mentioned the blessed paperwork. Hugh Celeber sometimes thought he would have been better off going in for accountancy. Then, at least, there would be some professional interest to the forms that piled up on his desk. Invoices. Payment records for his operatives. Copies of the payment records to satisfy Inland Revenue.

Reports.

The reports that sat on his desk now were what was keeping him late in the office tonight, as much as he would have preferred it to be the routine paperwork. Specifically, the reports for his client, Mr. Smith, on the activities of a certain Mr. Jeffrey Bellman of the United States, and the people he spoke to in Kensington Gardens last night.

Mr. Smith, when he had made his nightly telephone call this evening (the events in question had occurred too late to make last night's report, more was the pity), had been told that there was something Mr. Celeber wanted to discuss with him. Something personal and urgent. The one bright spot in this whole business was that Mr. Smith had taken it like a lamb, and had promised to be there at nine sharp.

Celeber looked at the grandmother clock near the door. Nine-fifteen. He tightened his lips and forced his attention back to the Inland Revenue forms.

Hugh Celeber was a cautious man. He made a tidy living for himself and his Aunt Dorothy, with whom he had lived since age ten, but he did it cautiously. He followed husbands for wives and wives for husbands. He followed American boyfriends for Dirty Old Men, which was how Smith had presented his case. He found witnesses for solicitors, and arranged to keep an eye on witnesses solicitors had already found. He did it all cautiously. He kept his nose clean. He stayed in business. Aunt Dorothy could have unlimited scones and lemon curd with her tea.

Celeber made a noise that might have been a growl, then shook his head as if to chase the noise away. Cautiously (the thing was sharp, and he had once hurt his hand), he reached to the bodkin and removed the next paper his secretary had spindled for his attention.

Three papers later, the bell rang. "Finally," Celeber said, and he rose to admit Mr. Smith.

"I had trouble finding a taxi," Smith said by way of greeting. Celeber decided it was probably a lie. A man who would wear that cartoon-anarchist disguise more than once would lie about the day of the week.

There was one change in his appearance tonight, though a minor one. He wore new spectacles. These were even heavier, with massive, thick frames. The left temple had been mended with bandage tape just where the tortoiseshell disappeared into the false hair around his ears.

Celeber showed his client into his office. "You're here," he said, pointing to a chair. "That's the important thing."

"The important thing," his client corrected him, "is whatever it is you have to tell me. Urgent and personal, I believe you said."

"As personal as it is possible to be, I'm afraid, Mr. Smith."

"I don't follow you."

"I'm afraid I'll have to insist on knowing your real name."

Did the eyes widen behind the flat glass of the spectacles? It was hard to tell.

"Out of the question," Smith said.

"I am forced to insist," Celeber said. "You told me you wanted this man followed because you believed he was getting too close to your lady friend—"

"And that he had designs on my money, don't forget that."

"I never forget anything said to me by a client, Mr. Smith. Or whatever your name is. The point is, what you said to me was, to put it kindly, not the complete truth."

"I'm paying you enough to take my word for it."

"Ordinarily, yes." Celeber gave him what he hoped was an

amiable nod. "A private investigator's life consists largely of listening to people tell him lies. Most of them are inconsequential, designed to protect the ego or to salve the conscience."

"Let's just say that's what I'm doing and leave it at that, Celeber. Is this all you had to tell me?"

"No, Mr. Smith, I'm afraid it is *not* all I had to tell you. And I am not prepared to let it go at that, as you put it."

Now the eyes *did* narrow. "Why not?" Smith asked. His tone was calm, even amiable, but Celeber didn't like it at all.

He didn't like *any* of this at all. He reached for the reports, held them up, and shook them. "*This* is why we can't let it go, Mr. Smith. You say this Bellman is trying to move in on your business?"

"I am," Smith said, "getting weary of saying it."

"Then what the devil *is* your business?" The exasperation in the detective's voice was sincere. It was a business where surprises were endemic, but not this kind. Not the kind that had you out of your depth the instant you found them out.

He shook the reports again. "Your Mr. Bellman has indeed been spending time with your Miss Grace. He has, as we've told you in our nightly reports, been living with her. You seemed to take that news with equanimity, Mr. Smith."

He was still taking it with equanimity. "Go on," he said.

"Last night, Bellman went to Kensington Gardens. He was followed."

"That's what I'm paying you for, blast it."

"He was followed," Celeber repeated, "by men other than mine. At least four of them, possibly more. Do you have another detective agency on this case, Mr. Smith?"

Smith said, "No."

Celeber blinked. The last thing he'd expected had been a straight answer. "Well, *someone* was following him. My men followed instructions in spite of this. Bellman spoke to two people, one through the Alexandra Gate. Fortunately, they spoke long enough for one of my men to get in position to follow the man he spoke to when the conversation finished. He tailed him to an address in Fulham. He gives the name Frank Smith— a relative of yours, perhaps—and he seems to be another American."

"I want that address! Tell me immediately!"

"It's in the report. I'm afraid you must hear me out, and satisfy me, before I let you see it."

The eyes glared. Celeber was glad the glass was there to filter some of it before it reached him.

Celeber swallowed. The man was disconcerting, comedy get-up and all.

"The other man Bellman spoke to," Celeber went on, "was followed by another of my operatives."

"I want that address," Smith said ominously.

"The address the second man went to—"

"Bugger the second man, damn you! I want the Fulham address!"

"—was number Eighteen Kensington Palace Gardens. This is the Soviet Embassy, Mr. Smith! The man your instructions had us tailing was Grigori Bulanin!"

"I am not interested in Grigori Bulanin. I want—"

"*I* want," Celeber said, "to know why you have given me instructions that have led to my putting a tail on the man who is reputed to be the top KGB operative in Britain. I demand to know who you are and what you're up to. I—"

Smith rose, and with one quick motion snatched the reports from Celeber's hand. He was saying something about the last payment being delivered tomorrow, but Celeber wasn't listening. In reflex, he grabbed his client's wrist. Smith, in turn, clawed at the hand that held him.

The two men struggled across the desk. Even as he realized the absurdity of the situation—real-life private investigators did not scuffle with clients!—he was planning ways to win the fight. He decided to see if the man in the comical disguise would guard his identity as fiercely as he guarded the papers he held.

Celeber grabbed the false beard and pulled. He blinked at what it revealed. "Sir Lewis!" he gasped. Celeber, for the first time since he'd entered the business, felt himself completely at a loss. There was no conceivable explanation for Sir Lewis Alfot, of all people, involving him in these melodramatics.

"Sir Lewis," he said again. "I'm afraid I don't—"

He didn't get to finish. Sir Lewis had let go one hand, and with dexterity better than a pickpocket's, had reached into his greatcoat, pulled out a sand-filled sock, and used it against the side of the detective's head.

Celeber went down, dazed. His chair skittered away as he hit it on the way down. Celeber blinked a few times, and was just about to gather his legs under him in an attempt to rise when Sir Lewis struck again.

This time, the man Celeber had known as a newspaper celebrity–philanthropist gave a yell like a savage and overturned Celeber's desk on top of him.

The edge bit into the detective's thighs. The pain dazed him as effectively as the cosh had. Celeber was sure that one of his legs was broken. Perhaps both.

Celeber tried to move, to wriggle out so he could crawl away from this madman, but the desk was too heavy. It was a paperweight, and he was tissue. If he struggled too hard, he'd tear himself in half.

Sir Lewis looked at him, blinking behind those absurd spectacles. The beard dangled from the left side of his face.

"Can you move?" he asked solicitously.

That was the limit. That was the last straw. *"No, I can't move! Get me out of this, you bloody madman!"*

"I didn't think so," Sir Lewis said calmly. He began patting his beard back in place.

It occurred to Celeber how often, in normal conversation, he used the phrase, *I'm afraid*. He didn't say it now. He merely felt it.

Celeber noted that Sir Lewis still had the reports in his hand. Good. Let him take them and leave. Then—the phone should be on the floor here somewhere, Celeber could hear the dial tone. He'd squirm around and get it and ring 999. . . .

Then Sir Lewis did something odd. He removed the spectacles and started taking off the tape. Then he saw something that made him stop. He replaced the spectacles. He said, "Ah," and walked around the desk. He stooped to pick something up. It made a fluttering sound as it moved through the air.

When the old man walked back around the desk, Celeber could see what it was. The spindle. The bodkin from his desk. The fluttering was the sound of the still unprocessed Inland Revenue forms held in place by that nice sharp point.

2

Bellman stood to the side of the door with a gun in his hand and demanded to know who it was. It shouldn't have been anybody—all Felicity's visitors had to be announced.

"Mr. Bellman?" a puzzled voice said from the other side of the door. "Is that you?"

"Who are *you*?" Bellman demanded.

"Maurice Stingley," the voice said. "DI Stingley. From Sussex."

Bellman closed his eyes. He recognized the voice now. He had three choices—he could fire through the door, which was tempting but probably counterproductive; he could tell Stingley to bugger off, which would only irritate him and make him more persistent; or he could let him in.

Bellman took off the lock and the chain bolt and opened up.

Stingley walked in wearing an expression he'd swiped from the foreclosure officer at the bank. He took off his hat (a homburg—Bellman would have thought a bowler would suit him better) and put his gloves and scarf in it. Bellman took them, and the policeman's coat, and draped them over a chair. Stingley's face showed disapproval, but Bellman didn't care.

"To what do we owe the honor?" Bellman asked.

"May I sit down?" Stingley asked.

Bellman reflected that this guy's mother must have been strict when it came to manners.

What the hell. "Of course. Pardon me. Please do. Would you like some tea?"

Stingley gave him a that's-better-no-reason-we-can't-be-civil-about-this smile. "Thank you, no. I—um—was expecting to find Miss Grace here."

"She's still asleep. Medication. I'm looking after her during her convalescence."

"Kind of you," Stingley observed. "Any chance of my talking to her?"

Bellman shrugged. "If she wakes up."

"I consider a talk with Miss Grace as unfinished business. Shortly before she left my patch—before *both* of you left my patch, in fact—she told me about three unidentified bodies in a sand pile, and promised me an explanation the next day. Now, our caseload in Sussex in such that three bodies more or less isn't *such* a great number, but I'd still like that explanation."

"That was also the night," Bellman reminded him, "that Miss Grace ran into the Sussex Cyclops."

As soon as he closed his lips behind the final *s*, Bellman knew he'd made a tactical error. No reference to the Cyclops was going to make Stingley any easier to deal with.

"I know," the DI said. His tone was still amiable, but he was now talking without moving his lower jaw. "I mean to have a chat with her about that, as well."

Bellman said, "I don't know if that's going to be possible."

Stingley caught hold of his temper by the tip of the tail. "Now, see here," he began heatedly, then took a breath and relaxed. "Look, Bellman. I know you're America's answer to James bloody Bond, and Miss Grace is Modesty Blaise or whatever the hell. I'm just a simple copper, trying to catch a maniac before he does a better job on the South East of England than William the bloody Conqueror. Doesn't that strike you as a noble enough end? Shouldn't I get a little cooperation? Or failing that, the reason no one higher up seems to want him caught?"

He leaned forward and looked Bellman square in the eye. "I'm not a fool, you know. I know what National Security is all about, but no one has mentioned that to me yet. You've come the closest, with your bloody international terrorist. Of whom, I might add, neither hide nor hair has yet been seen. I have been on this case for over a year, and I have boiled it down to one question: *What the bloody hell is going on here?*"

Trusting Stingley wasn't the problem. They'd trusted him before, and Tipton's men had been running constant checks on

Stingley since. He'd passed no word along, not even to his superiors. He was a clean, honest cop. A true-blue Briton. The reports told him that, and Bellman's instincts backed it up. The trouble was, he was too clean, too honest, to be told a nasty little secret like this one.

"I'm a visitor here," Bellman said. "It's not my story to tell."

Stingley made a face and gave a tight nod in the direction of a copy of that morning's *Times* that lay in a heap on the floor where Bellman had dropped it when the doorbell rang.

"He struck again last night," the policeman said. "Here in London. Skewered a private dick with the bodkin off his own desk. Can't get fingerprints off a bodkin, but the stroke is right. Our boy's expanding his field."

"That's why they called you to London?"

"Nobody called me to London," Stingley said bitterly. "I bloody well came. Was about as welcome as a hedgehog in a pair of tights, but they didn't actually try to chuck me out. What do you know about it?"

"Just what was in *The Times*," Bellman said.

Bellman had been reading *The Times* assiduously the last two mornings. Particularly the personals column. He was looking for an ad addressed to The Captain signed Snark. The Congressman wouldn't decide whether to meet Leo's demands until the second meeting had to be arranged.

The ad hadn't appeared yet, just the story of Sir Lewis Alfot's latest peccadillo. It was more of the same—all it did was refresh the story in the minds of the press and public, and add weight to Leo's threat to blow the lid off.

"There was nothing new," Stingley said. "Well, one thing. This Celeber, the victim, had a wisp of false hair caught under his ring. So perhaps the Cyclops wears a disguise. The *Yard*"— Stingley said it like the name of a disease—"the *Yard* are finding out if Celeber used it in his detective business."

Stingley slapped his knees with both hands and stood up suddenly. "So. There you have it. I came to get information, and I find I've been giving it out. Perhaps there's more to you spy chaps than I thought."

Bellman handed him his things. As he put them on, Stingley said, "So long as I'm giving out the information, let me tell you this. I'm a patient man, Mr. Bellman, but everything has a limit. I don't *like* these killings. They are sick; they are nasty; they turn my stomach. I think they could be stopped, but something the government or whoever have in mind is letting them continue. I don't pretend to know more than the people in power, but my conscience is itching, Mr. Bellman, and the itch gets stronger all the time. Eventually, I will be forced to scratch it."

Stingley put his hat on. "Kindly pass that along, will you? And give my regards to Miss Grace. I still hope to have that explanation someday."

Bellman let him out, locked up behind him. He stood looking at the door, reflecting on Leo Calvin's sense of humor.

Snark, he thought. Lewis Carroll's mystical, unseeable, unknowable menace, hunted across an enchanted island by a collection of madmen led by their Captain, the Bellman.

But the reality was madder than Carroll's nightmare. *This* hunt had no readily defined quarry. This one was each against all. Bellman hunting Calvin; Calvin hunting Bellman. The Russians after Calvin and Sir Lewis. Leo after Sir Lewis. The Americans after the British and the Russians, and the British and the Russians each after the other two. And God alone knew who Sir Lewis was hunting. Besides more victims.

Who *was* the Snark? In the poem, to look on him (it?) was to "softly and suddenly vanish away," provided the Snark was a Boojum.

Maybe that was the answer. In *this* nightmare, the Snark was the last one unvanished.

3

By the time Grigori Illyich Bulanin had stopped being a Raven, he thought he had had his fill of sex for a lifetime. He was wrong. Borzov had been right when he'd told him that sex is the most powerful of desires—neither indulgence, nor overindulgence, nor forced overindulgence to the point of disgust had been able to destroy Bulanin's sexual needs.

But his previous life had had its effect. Bulanin was all too aware that a man's sexual or emotional attachments might be used against him. He was positive that given enough time, they would be.

So Bulanin would form no attachments. He had nothing to do with American women when he had been stationed in Washington. He had nothing to do with English women while he was here. It would be all too easy for the CIA or British Intelligence to slip a Swallow in on him. As demeaning as he had found it to be the one to play that sort of trick, Bulanin was sure it would be even worse to be the victim of one, and he wouldn't take the risk.

For the same reason, he would have nothing to do with the women who worked at the Embassy, though some were attractive, and more seemed to be interested. Bulanin knew that anyone could be turned, given the right pressures. He had no intention of becoming intimate with a woman who had been seduced by the other side, and would defect as soon as she had accumulated all the knowledge from him she could. You might as well, he thought, hand a woman a gun and let her point it at you while you are naked.

He also refused to go to prostitutes. That could be a trap as well, the one-way mirror, and the camera whirring behind it. Or a newspaper photographer might see him emerging from the home of a known prostitute and snap a picture then. The photographs were certain to make their way back to Moscow and offend old men Bulanin simply could not afford to offend. All the powerful old men would hold it against him—some because they were strait-laced old fools whose sexual urges were sublimated into power games. Imprisonments. Liquidations. Others would be against him, and justifiably so, Bulanin thought, for being foolish enough to allow himself to be embarrassed in such a way.

Bulanin knew that the closer he came to realizing his dream, the more men would be against him. That was the nature of power, and the nature of the struggle to obtain it. Bulanin wasn't the only young man with this dream; he had to have power within reach before he made too many enemies. In the minds of many who could help lift him to the height he intended to reach, his past, especially the sexual element of it, was something he *might* be forgiven. If he proved valuable enough otherwise.

So Bulanin turned to the one source he knew would not recoil on him. Every three months or so, he had Borzov send him a woman. She would be assigned to the Embassy in some menial capacity—typist, telephone operator, even maid. That was for the British, who had approval over diplomatic personnel.

For Bulanin she was therapy. In three weeks or a month his sexual tensions would be released, and she would be sent back to Moscow, with the thanks of a grateful KGB.

The new one had arrived yesterday. Her name was Magda. They were all named Magda or Olga or Natasha, and they lived up to their names. Common. Forgettable. Details changed, the overall impression remained the same.

Magda dyed her hair blond. Her face was quite pretty, and her breasts were large. Her waist and legs were thick, but Bulanin had stopped expecting anything else—Borzov seemed to think that after you made love to a woman you were supposed to harness her to a plow and take to the fields.

Bulanin didn't mind. Ordinarily, he wouldn't even have noticed. Now, however, he was noticing everything. Did Magda seem a little smarter than her predecessors? Was it possible that she would report to Borzov about him? The thought had occurred to Bulanin before, but before he never worried about what Borzov would think of his actions. That was no longer true. Bulanin scowled.

"I don't please you," Magda said.

"You please me to death," Bulanin told her. "Keep doing what you have been doing."

Magda smiled and bent her head. Bulanin gave her a pat to encourage her. He didn't want her running to Borzov with the news that Bulanin had lost interest in sex.

He looked around at the walls of the hotel room. The hotel was a modern one in North London. American-style. Air-conditioning in the summer. Coin-operated machines in the hallways for soft drinks and wine and crisps. Free ice, there for the taking. Color television.

Bulanin always stayed in this sort of hotel when he had a woman on his hands. Somehow, it felt more prudent not to do it within the confines of the Embassy. It was also, Bulanin thought, more exciting. Bulanin had frequently heard Americans decry this sort of place, but he'd never been able to understand why. What was the excitement of staying in a building with no pillows on the beds, or antique plumbing? To Bulanin, this style of place offered comfort and convenience, and more, *predictability*. When he came to this place he knew what to expect, just as he knew what to expect when Borzov sent him a woman.

Which was more than he could say about the rest of his life, lately.

There had been too many surprises, nearly all of them unpleasant.

"Don't bite, damn you," he said. Magda murmured an apology.

The latest and perhaps most unpleasant surprise had been his reaction to what had happened with the American the other night. It was not at all the correct response. The correct response would have been fury, either cold or hot. Plans for revenge, not necessarily violence, mind you, but determination to find a way to make the American feel as foolish as he'd made Bulanin feel.

Instead, he felt fear. It was an empty sort of fear, a melancholy. A mourning perhaps for the death of his dream.

"No!" he said aloud.

Magda looked up quizzically at him. Bulanin said nothing.

Magda emptied her mouth and sighed. "Comrade," she said. "This is not going well."

"Never mind how it's going," Bulanin told her.

"Comrade, I would not tell you how to be a diplomat. This is not going well. You are too *tense*. You must *relax*."

"I have too much responsibility to relax," he told her. And, he thought, I am in too much trouble. Potentially. If my bungling of the past few weeks gets whispered in the proper ears.

"If you don't relax, you won't be able to carry out your responsibilities."

Bulanin looked at her. She *was* smarter than the others.

Braver, at least. None of the others would dare to talk to him that way. "Why do you dye your hair?" he asked her.

"Sometimes I like it this way, sometimes I like it the natural brown. Here, Comrade Grigori, let me rub your neck. It will relax you." She scuttled around behind him and began to squeeze the muscles at the base of his neck.

"You *are* tense," she said. "We'll soon have these lumps softened up. You'll feel better."

Soften them by all means, Bulanin thought. They'll be easier for Borzov to cut through when I am recalled to Moscow for failing to deal with Leo Calvin.

Magda continued her work. She was good at it. As Bulanin relaxed he solved his problems by deciding to quit worrying about them. He would deal with the American as best he could; he would have his agents on the alert for Leo Calvin, who surely had to die, and he would trust his Destiny to see him safely through.

He felt much better. He told Magda to lie down.

A few minutes later she said, "You see? This is much better."

"You were right. I needed to relax." He resolved to stay that way.

The resolve lasted until his return to the Embassy, where he found the message from Leo Calvin waiting for him.

4

There had been two tails on Leo Calvin when he'd left the meeting with Bellman. Now there were none. The first dropped off the second day after the meeting; the second one was taken off the job this afternoon, when Leo had pulled him up an alley, ducked into a doorway, jumped out, chopped the guy in the

Adam's apple, pulled him into a hallway, chopped him twice more, and finished him.

He almost hated to do it—it had been such a nice, friendly setup. They had been keeping tabs on Leo to see if he intended to keep up his part of the proposed bargain with Bellman's people. And, since Leo, for once in his life, had had every intention of doing so, it made no difference to him. It was an unusual, low-pressure situation. Leo had begun to enjoy it.

It made a difference now. Leo was on his way to make a phone call to Bulanin's special number at the Russian Embassy, and no flunky of Bellman's was going to have any chance of knowing about that. Furthermore, Leo could no longer afford to be followed. By anybody.

This guy was apparently British. He had no credentials on him, but then, a spy wouldn't have. His driving license was made out to Anthony Edge, which to Leo sounded like something from the cover of a spy novel. He was unarmed. He had sixty-two pounds thirty on him, which Leo pocketed. That was primarily to keep the bobbies happy, but it was nice to have the money, too. Benton and the other still had to be paid.

The right people would know this was no robbery. Bellman and his British friends would find out soon enough. Let the body serve notice that all bets are off. Leo Calvin was going back to Bulanin.

Back to Bulanin. Leo laughed out loud at the thought—a couple of old people turned to look at him. To hell with them. Laughed again. A day ago—two *hours* ago—the very thought would have seemed like suicide.

It was still dangerous. Leo wasn't kidding himself. But he could work it. If he did it right, he could have everything he'd set out to get at the start of all this—Bellman/Driscoll dead, the Russians off his back, money, security. Plastic surgery. A new identity. Back to America. Back in business. Those bastards hadn't seen anything yet.

All right, he told himself. Relax. First things first. You were busted, but now you're back in the game. You got hold of another ace. The *same* ace.

You've got Sir Lewis Alfot again.

The old man had been waiting for him when he'd come back from making his daily phone call to Stan Hope. Leo hadn't recognized him at first. He'd been wearing tape-repaired spectacles, and hair on his face and head. And he was holding a Colt .38-caliber police special when Leo walked through the door.

"Mr. Calvin," the old man said, and Leo knew who he was. The thought that ran through Leo's head was "time to say your prayers," which was ridiculous. Leo had said no prayers since before the last time he'd washed dishes.

But Alfot didn't pull the trigger. Yet. He waved Leo away from the door with the gun, then got up off the thin bed and circled around the room toward the door as Leo went in the other direction. Still covering Leo, Sir Lewis closed and locked the door.

"That's better," he said.

Leo kept trying to figure the odds, but the machine always registered "no sale."

There were too many factors, relative values unknown. This man was a brilliant agent; he was also a homicidal maniac. When Leo remembered Sir Lewis was sixty-nine years old, he wanted the old man to come for his eye, just get close enough for Leo to be able to do something. He wouldn't be caught by surprise the way Margaret had been.

When he thought of poor, stupid Margaret tied in that chair with the hypodermic sticking out of her eye, Leo almost wished the old man would shoot.

"Sit down, Mr. Calvin," the old man said. Leo followed the gun's commands and perched in the dent on the blanket where Sir Lewis had been.

"I see you've changed your appearance," the old man said.

"So have you," Leo told him.

"Circumstances," the old man said. "I want to kill you, Mr. Calvin. It has been forty-four years since I have wanted to kill a man so much." The gun rose.

Here it comes, Leo thought. He was amazed to learn how afraid he was of dying. He'd always thought that killing and dying were much the same thing if you had a certain kind of mind—*his* kind, needless to say—and once that mind became inured to the one, it had no trouble dealing with the other.

Not true. Not true. Not yet. Don't kill me, for God's sake. They were in his brain, but they never made it to his mouth.

It wasn't the blast of a revolver that cut him off—just the old man's voice. "But I don't dare. Kill you I mean."

Leo worked hard at making his voice sound calm, and succeeded. "Why not?" he said.

"Because I need you."

"Need me," Leo said.

"Of course I need you, you fool. I've come to give myself up to you."

He *was* insane. "You *are* insane," Leo heard himself say.

The old man might not have heard him.

"I need you," he said, "to turn me over to the Russians."

It even made sense. In a way.

"They're on to me," the old man said. "That's why they put me out to pasture in the first place." He sounded hurt.

"And you doubt they'll do that again."

"I know fucking well they won't do that again!" The anger on Alfot's face could be read through any disguise. "I wouldn't let them if they would." The scowl smoothed. "There's no fear of that, in any case. It would be an institution for me, after this. They wouldn't even need to mention my project to put me away."

"You mean the killings," Leo said.

"You will not speak of them," Sir Lewis said sternly. "You are a mercenary and a terrorist and God knows what else. You have no conception of duty or honor or the good of the Nation. You are not equipped to understand. You will be quiet."

The old man still had the gun. Leo shut up.

"They would simply say," Sir Lewis went on, "that I had turned senile and wandered off, and had to be under strict medical supervision, and could talk to no one." He scratched under his beard. "Damned uncomfortable thing. I'll be glad when I can get it off."

He adjusted his spectacles, taking care to be sure the tape held the temple together. "They might," he said, "even kill me. I wish they would, but I doubt it. Lord knows I'd rather be dead than in a straitjacket." He gazed steadily at Leo. "*You* convinced

194

me of that. You may be glad I can't afford to repay you for those weeks of bondage."

Leo asked him just what he wanted. Somewhat to Leo's surprise, the old man had it all worked out.

"You will turn me over to the Russians as originally planned. I come to you instead of going to them on my own because I don't know whom you've been dealing with, and I don't want to go through a rigamarole about my bona fides."

He went on to say that he was sure Leo was getting in hot water by now for not having made delivery, and that this was his chance to straighten matters out. Leo thought, old man, where were you a week ago?

Sir Lewis was willing to make concessions. "You undoubtedly think I'm mad," he said, "but I am not unreasonable." Leo would be permitted to tie the old man up when he left the flat, and when he slept. ("Satisfy yourself of your personal safety, by all means.") Sir Lewis had funds, in case any were needed while Leo made the final arrangements with the Russians. ("Within reason, mind you. I want to be in Moscow as soon as possible. I can be of use to them, and the sooner I get cracking, the better I'll like it. Philby is a KGB general, with a lovely flat and a big pension. . . .") Sir Lewis also offered his word of honor not to try to escape, but he didn't think that would mean much to a man like Leo.

But there were conditions.

"No drugs," Sir Lewis said. "That is a damnable thing to do to a man, and I won't have it again. No physical abuse. No outsiders until you actually turn me over to the Russians."

Leo fought a smile as he let the old man rave. If he were going to allow Leo to tie him up, how was he going to enforce his conditions? Leo's word of honor? Leo was planning ways to use the old man's money to get a new supply of tranquilizer for his captive when the old man showed he might not be so crazy after all.

"—A hollow tooth, you see. Filled with cyanide. Been there for years," the old man said. "One could almost forget it's there. But not quite. Something we learned from the Russians in the old days. I volunteered to have it done to me first—can't ask your people to do things you aren't willing to do yourself, can you? It's perfectly safe unless you bite down on it in a special way. Or try to remove it. You can also crush it against a gag designed to keep your mouth open. It's my insurance, you might say." The false beard parted in a smile. Leo looked at the teeth with new respect.

He didn't doubt the old man for a second. As far as Leo could tell, he was insane enough to have *all* his teeth filled with cyanide.

"If I see a hypodermic," the old man elaborated, "I will kill myself. If you manage to drug me anyway, I will kill myself at the earliest opportunity. If you try to remove the tooth, you will have done the job for me. Any questions?"

Leo had two. The first—how long does cyanide keep its effectiveness?—he thought it wiser to keep to himself. He asked the second, more because he thought Sir Lewis was expecting him to than for any rational reason.

"Why didn't you use it before? When I had you down in Brighton."

"Don't be dimmer than you can help," the old man said with contempt. "And don't act as if you think *I'm* dim. I told you before—I *may* be mad. I am not stupid."

Leo apologized. Sir Lewis sniffed. He seemed to have decided, on mature reflection, that Leo *was* dim. He answered the question.

"The reason I didn't use it when I was your captive was that I was *planning to escape*. You couldn't hold me indefinitely without my cooperation, and I knew it. I found my opportunity, and I took it.

"But it's different now," the old man said. "*This* is my escape. If I fail now, there is no other choice. This is my one and only opportunity, and I have reduced it to it's simplest terms— succeed or die."

With that, he'd handed the gun over to a still incredulous Leo, had Leo search him for other weapons or poison, and made himself at home. Leo had taken about twenty minutes to think things over while Sir Lewis made himself a pot of tea.

This, Leo realized, was his opportunity, too. Succeed or die, indeed. He'd tied an unprotesting Sir Lewis to a radiator, slipped outside, attended to the surveillance problem, and made his phone call. That done, he came back to the flat, released Sir Lewis, took custody of the money, and removed them from the premises before the dead agent's colleagues could turn up.

He'd spent the hours in between looking at the old man sleeping peacefully on the hotel bed and counting the minutes until he could no longer resist calling Bulanin again to see if his message had been received.

SEVENTH

Down he sank in his chair—ran his hands through
    his hair—
  And chanted in mimsiest tones
Words whose utter inanity proved his insanity,
    While he rattled a couple of bones.

"Leave him here to his fate—it is getting so late!"
    The Bellman exclaimed in a fright.
"We have lost half the day. Any further delay,
    And we shan't catch a Snark before night!"

                —The Hunting of the Snark
                Fit the Seventh

1

Leo Calvin had, over the years, abducted or kidnapped upwards of twenty people, but he'd never had a "victim" like Sir Lewis Alfot before. Either time. For you or against you, mad or sane, drugged or otherwise, this was one resourceful old man, and you could forget that only at your peril.

It was, Leo had to admit, much nicer once he was on your side, or at least working toward the same end—in this case, a smooth exchange with Bulanin and the Russians.

A few days ago, Leo had been low on money, ideas, and hope. The best he could think of to do was turn himself in to the U.S. Government—the government he'd been trying to destroy since back in the days he was a terrorist because he had *ideals*—and try to convince himself he was happy about it. Now, thanks to the old man, he had money, clothes, a warm place to sleep (as warm as anyplace in Britain was to sleep in, at least), weapons, devices, and a new deal with Bulanin. When Alfot promised to cooperate, he really delivered. He must have been squirreling stuff away for years, in anticipation of just such a situation. It was a pleasure to deal with a true professional. Before the old man had lost it, he must have been awesome.

It had not been easy, of course, to come to an accommodation with the Russian. Bulanin had been burned too many times since this business started to be ready to jump back in. He was good and mad, so much so that he forgot to hide it.

Leo was ready for him. "Yes," he told Bulanin over the phone. "I met with the American. Whom were you tailing, him or me?"

"That is not relevant. What were you doing meeting him?"

"Buying time, my friend. He had a lead; he was getting close,

I offered to turn myself in, tell them all the secrets about you I had."

"Why did he not shoot you? Arrest you?"

"I know some secrets about their side, too, my friend. Secrets they couldn't stand to have revealed. As they would be if anything happened that I didn't like."

"I have lost good men in an effort to kill this man at your instigation. . . ."

"And you want to know why I didn't shoot him? He *wasn't alone*—he had British agents all over him like stink on shit. Secrets or no secrets, I would have been dead in five seconds, and that wouldn't do anybody any good."

"That is a disgusting expression," Bulanin said. His voice sounded as if it were coming through a wrinkled nose.

"I apologize," Leo said. Bulanin grunted. Leo went on. "I made him an offer—it bought me a few days, but my time is running out. I have the goods and I'm ready to deliver. The rest is up to you."

"And after all that has happened, I am to trust you." The idea disgusted him more than the simile had.

"No," Leo conceded sadly. "You are not expected to trust me. And, at the risk of offending you, I don't trust you, my friend. I think there is an excellent possibility that when the time comes, you will relieve me of my prisoner and kill me."

"Then we are at an impasse," Bulanin said. His voice betrayed no eagerness to end it.

"We will think of a way to accomplish our business in mutual safety," Leo said. Bulanin grunted again. Leo heard a match being struck, and the hiss of a flame.

"Very well," the Russian said at last. "We will discuss it."

Leo kept the smile out of his voice, and said he'd call back.

It took a little over ten hours; seventeen telephone calls, each from a phone box distant from the previous one. Between times he returned to the hotel, dreading each time that Sir Lewis had been left alone too long, and had bitten the poison out of spite, or boredom. Then Leo would listen to the old man complain about the amount of time it was taking to get this done, and almost wished he *would* bite the poison.

During the negotiations, Leo ate twice—some McDonald's

hamburgers with Sir Lewis in the hotel room, and a Cornish pasty from a fish and chips place near Piccadilly Circus. The pasty gave him heartburn, but the heartburn helped keep him awake.

It started to snow about the same time the Underground closed down for the night. He walked through the weather from booth to booth. He was cold, and his feet were wet, but he couldn't afford to use the same phone twice (Bulanin might be able to trace it) and he didn't want to be a memory in some cabbie's head. So he walked.

By six A.M., it was finished, a complicated system of live and dead drops, observation opportunities, private and public transport, checks and double checks, all designed to get all concerned feeling safe enough to agree to a rendezvous to be announced by Leo at the last minute.

And it was all, of course, a farce. A necessary farce, though, because each had to make the other believe he could now justify this meeting. And if there were no meeting, Bulanin would not be able to double-cross Leo, as he undoubtedly intended to do. And Leo would have no opportunity to double-cross Bulanin, which he would do if it seemed desirable or feasible.

It was all supposed to happen tonight. Leo had some time to weigh the possibilities. He was exhausted, but he wouldn't sleep. *He'd* use a drug, even if the old man wouldn't. Sir Lewis, Leo had discovered, slept soundly *without* drugs.

Besides, Leo had to be awake to make his call to Stan and Grunter. He had another job for them.

2

The stuff Leo had got for them was a bloody miracle. A bit of gray paste smeared in the keyhole, stick in the fuse, stand back.

The lock melted out with no more noise than a hiss like bacon in a pan.

But Leo forget to tell them about the glare, a white streak of eye pain like a carbon arc. Stan and Grunter managed to look away in time, but a few seconds went by before Grunter's vision cleared enough to enable him to find the door again. It made a difference. Two thumps of his shoulder did for the chain bolt, but through the field of dazzle, all he could see was the redhead with the bandage over her eye scrabbling under the sofa cushions. Leo had warned them she might have a gun.

Grunter didn't wait. He dove across the room, grabbed her by the waist, and threw her across the room into a bunch of expensive electronic equipment. The telly, a big one, was knocked off its stand onto the floor with a crash like a brick through a jeweler's window.

That was bad. The idea was for no one to know they were there. Fortunately, most of the people in the building were at work, this being a weekday. Stan had pushed the door to by now (it would no longer latch, of course), and Grunter could see the smile on his face as he walked over to where the woman lay sprawled on the floor.

"Stand up," he said. He gestured with the gun Leo had given him.

She obliged him. She got unsteadily to her feet and walked carefully away from the broken glass, lest she cut herself. Her face was grim, what Grunter could see of it. She had her head down, her face tilted like a chicken looking for corn, so that her good eye had a better view of the floor.

She bunched the floor-length blue velvet house robe in her hands, too, to get that out of the way. She was a tall bird, taller than either Grunter or Stan, and she showed a lot of leg, all of it quite admirable. Grunter was beginning to be glad the American wasn't here yet. If he had been, the orders were to kill him and the woman and bugger off. As it was, they had a little leeway. Some discretion.

"Come out of it, then, love," Stan said.

She looked hatred at him, but said nothing. She tilted her head at the floor again and walked carefully away from the shards of glass.

Then she took a sharp breath, and with no more warning than that launched a wide, swift, sweeping kick at Stan's head. The bare foot caught Stan across the chin and sent him sprawling. Stan's gun went off (more bloody noise) and the bullet knocked plaster loose from the ceiling.

The woman turned on Grunter. "Now, you bastard," she said.

Grunter wished Leo had had a gun for him as well.

Mrs. Pettison heard the noise from the flat upstairs, the thump of something heavy hitting the floor, the crash of broken glass, and wondered if she should go see if everything was all right.

Mrs. Pettison hadn't much *experience* of being a neighbor. For thirty-two years, since the first days of her widowhood, Frances Pettison had been the clerk for Selwick Brothers—*Fine Boots for Gentlemen*. She had made appointments for measurements and fittings. Kept the payment records and sent the bills. Ordered fine leather and silk for uppers and soles and linings. Maintained the file of plaster casts of customers' feet, so that they might order a new pair of custom boots sent wherever in the world they happened to be. She reminded old Mr. Selwick of birthdays and bank holidays and the like. She had been too busy and too important to the business to know much about her neighbors, or how to behave toward them in unusual situations.

Now, though, with Mr. Selwick nearing seventy and ready to retire, and no one interested in taking over the business (because no one cared about *quality* anymore, as Mr. Selwick frequently lamented), Frances Pettison had been made redundant. Terrible word. Made you sound like an extraneous clone of someone who was actually useful.

Terrible fate, too, for a woman who was used to being busy. Not that she'd have to eke out an existence on the old age pension. Mr. Selwick had been *quite* generous, and she had some money put by. But she was stuck in the *flat* all day. She liked to travel, but there was only so much traveling you could do. . . .

More noises from upstairs. Good heavens, a firework or something, and two months and more past Guy Fawkes Day. She really should go see if Miss Grace was all right.

She hated the idea of becoming an old busybody. That young American, Mr. Bellman, seemed to take excellent care of her,

205

and Mrs. Pettison didn't *care* that they had begun to live together. Of course, it would *look* as if she did, if she kept going up there.

But didn't she see Mr. Bellman leaving an hour or two ago? Yes, she did, or at least heard his step on the stair, recognized his whistle—it was amazing what you became familiar with, home all day.

Miss Grace was probably alone up there. How could she be making all that noise? Mrs. Pettison listened. No more glass or fireworks, but plenty of thumping. After her terrible accident, she shouldn't be exercising. She herself had told Mrs. Pettison that what she needed was rest.

Perhaps it was drugs. None she shouldn't be taking—Miss Grace wasn't at all the sort for that—but something the doctor had prescribed. Something she'd had a bad reaction to. The poor thing could be rolling around in a convulsion or something up there.

It was the sort of thing a neighbor should look into. Mrs. Pettison resolutely climbed the stairs and knocked on Miss Grace's door.

It hadn't been latched. It *couldn't* be. Mrs. Pettison saw the scorch marks around the lock. The door swung open. The noise was louder, now.

Mrs. Pettison poked her head around the door. "Miss Grace . . ."

Felicity was angry. She was breathless and in pain, too, but mostly she was angry. These two villains were nothing, or should have been, no matter how they'd got into her flat. Gun or no gun, she should have been able to handle them in no time at all. And she would have.

But she had no depth perception. She wasn't used to living with the one eye. The same flat field of vision that caused her to knock over the pepper grinder at dinner caused her to kick the man with the gun in the chin and stun him, instead of in the throat, to kill him, the way she planned.

Now she had to deal with this pig, the stocky one. And it wasn't working. Her blows would land, but not in the right spots.

She'd claw at him and hurt him, but never enought to put him out of action.

And he was no fool. When he hit her he went for the left side of her head. Several of the blows had landed—her vision was no help to her there, either—and now there was a dull ache in the depths of her head. Visions of hemorrhages or of God knew what else came to her mind, and she fought the fear and the cold tightness in her stomach.

And the man went for her good eye. Again and again.

The fear of blindness, of being violated in that way *again*, was too big to fight. Instead, she channeled the impulse to panic into fury, and increased the pace of the fight. As they grappled and spun, Felicity saw the room as a collection of blind eyes. The curtained windows. The bullet hole in the ceiling. The jagged, gaping hole in the television screen.

The man grunted, and clawed for her eye again. Felicity, this time, was ready for him. As he reached high, she pulled back and reached for him low. Again her aim was off, but she kept her hand on his body until she found the right spot. She squeezed. Hard.

The man stopped grunting and squealed. He doubled over and clutched at himself. Felicity knew she had him now, and she could feel a grin of animal malice on her face as she moved in for the kill.

A voice said, "Miss Grace . . ." There was a small scream, a crunch, and a thump. Felicity looked up to see the smaller man holding a gun over the head of a dazed Mrs. Pettison.

"Come out of it," he said. "Come out of it right now, you bitch, or I'll crush her skull like a box of raspberries." He raised the gun higher. A trickle of blood ran down Mrs. Pettison's face.

Felicity came out of it.

"Over there," the man with the gun said. "No, not the couch. The chair. I know you've got a bloody gun hidden in the couch. You all right, Grunter?"

The stocky man wiped tear-streaming eyes. "Shoot her, Stan," he said. "The bitch."

The one called Stan wiggled his jaw. "Not yet," he said. "Not for a while."

Stan held the gun aimed straight at Felicity's eye. "What the bloody hell do you want?" she asked.

Stan smiled. It made him wince. "I want," he said, "a lot more from you than I did when I came through that door. And I intend to get it. But first things first. Where's Bellman?"

3

Bellman was on the carpet in the office of Robert Tipton.

Tipton was standing. He was leaning over the desk on his knuckles. He was not yelling. Tipton knew that if he began yelling, he would follow with screams and violence.

The American sat in his chair in an attitude of respectful attention—feet together, back straight, eyes on Tipton's lips. He's probably bloody *studied* it, Tipton thought. The bloody Congressman probably stuffed it in the heads of all his men— Appropriate Body Language to Adopt When Receiving a Deserved Dressing-Down. The whole attitude seemed to be I-listen-to-your-opinions-with-respect-sir. It made Tipton want to puke.

Bellman had listened with respect while Tipton told him that the body of the man they'd had tailing this Leo Calvin character had been found in an alley earlier that afternoon. He listened with respect when Tipton told him that he had been a good man, one of the best.

When Tipton had announced that as far as he was concerned, it was all Bellman's fault, the American had disagreed. Respectfully.

"I don't think so," he'd said. "Calvin is a dangerous man. I told your man that."

"Oh," Tipton said. His voice was getting hoarse from

repressed rage. "*Did* you, now? How *kind* of you. It's the only bloody thing you *did* tell us, though, isn't it?"

Tipton slammed a fist into the desk, knuckles down. He ignored the pain.

"You come in here, and you take over the whole bloody section. Co-opt my people, cost my best agent an eye—"

"Oh," Bellman said, "come *on*, now." The respect was getting thin. Childishly, Tipton was glad. He didn't want this arrogant bastard's false respect. He wanted a no-holds-barred *fight*, to use up some of his anger and frustration.

"You come in with your American money and power and arrogance and lord it over us without even the simple courtesy of telling us what you were doing."

Bellman leaned farther forward, and his eyebrows went up. A total movement of perhaps three inches, maybe half an inch for the facial muscles. It changed the body language completely. Tipton got the message—hostilities begin shortly. He welcomed it.

"I tried telling you what I was doing," Bellman said. "And your best agent lost an eye."

"What are you—"

"I asked you for a surveillance team, told you the subject and where to find him, and your man was killed. And the subject, who kidnapped Sir Lewis and started this whole mess in the first place, got away."

"What are you saying, Bellman?" Tipton could feel the muscles in his arms shake. His voice was cold.

Bellman's was bland. "I'm telling you what happened when I had the simple courtesy to tell you what was going on."

"You are accusing me of treason."

"I am telling you there is a leak in your organization."

Tipton took his fists off the desk. He sat down, massaging his knuckles. He looked at the American. The one secret Tipton had kept from Bellman (after he'd learned the reason for the old man's retirement, that is) was something Sir Lewis said about their being "something wrong in the Section." Tipton had chalked it up to the vaporings of a madman, but mad or not, Sir Lewis was an expert at this sort of business. His intuitions weren't something you could laugh off.

Apparently Bellman had intuitions, too.

"Nonsense!" Tipton said. He was rather more vehement than he'd intended; he wasn't entirely sure whom he was arguing with.

"Don't tell me nonsense," Bellman said. "There's a leak. There's no other way around it. Wherever I go, Calvin or the Russians turn up. Too goddam many coincidences."

"Then you must think I'm the traitor."

Bellman smiled. "You and Hollis, right? Not necessarily."

"But you've seen the reports! Everyone's been checked, double checked. Followed. Interviewed. Family and associates vetted. It can't be. This is a small Section. I know, within reason, every contact every one of my people has made."

"Within reason," Bellman echoed. "You know as well as I do, you can only reason with the facts you start with."

"And what does that mean?"

"It means someone is doing something you *haven't* thought of."

"They don't speak to anyone. They don't correspond or talk on the telephone. Not to anyone we can't vouch for. What do you suggest, telepathy?"

"I suggest you get off my back. It's not really my problem. I was just explaining why I'm reluctant to share my plans with this Section."

"I suppose you expect me to feel honored you came in when I summoned you this afternoon."

"No," Bellman said. "Not honored. Look, Tipton. You know what kills you in this business. It's the dead dreams, that lack of illusions. Trust is tempered and temporary. You can never be a hundred percent sure of anything."

"I know my people," Tipton said. He sounded like a fool to himself as he said it. The history of espionage, especially the recent history of British espionage, made that statement a bad joke.

Tipton admitted as much to the American. "But," he said, "I have been doing this sort of work since before you were born, and I couldn't go on if I didn't *resist* what you were saying. I have to resist it with all my might, or I will be lost. Perhaps we all will. I . . . ."

He stopped because Bellman wasn't listening to him. He was leaning back with his eyes closed; his face was clenched in pain.

"Jesus Christ," he said.

"What is it?" Tipton demanded.

"Resist," Bellman said.

"What?"

"Mr. Tipton, I need young Hamilton."

"You do?"

"Now. I'll tell you why in one hour. Maybe less. All right?"

Tipton didn't notice that he'd said anything, but Bellman was thanking him and bolting from the office before the Action Section Chief could say a word.

4

What with the snow and the wind, Sir Lewis was even more grateful for the false beard. It kept his face warm (perhaps a trifle too warm), and it kept the snow from getting down the front of his topcoat.

It had been snowing ever since Leo Calvin had hauled him out of the hotel (the last cloth-walled hotel room, Sir Lewis reflected, that he would ever stay in), and began this bloody Eskimo trek of tourist's London. The Tower had been cold, but at least he could get out of the elements. The Abbey had been fine, of course. But now, here at the zoo, Sir Lewis was beginning to wonder if he was going to make it through the day to the completion of his plan.

He knew why they were doing it, of course. It was a flirtation between the American and the Russian, a peeping at each other from behind fans. Leo would see Bulanin (it *was* Bulanin, much to Sir Lewis's delight); Bulanin would see Leo. Bulanin would be able to tell if Leo had other people with him, people who might spring a trap. Leo was supposed to be able to tell the same thing, but with the communications capabilities a fully funded organization could command, Bulanin could have hidden away a Red Army division in another part of Regent's Park, and arranged to call them in with one word into a microphone hidden under a flower in his lapel.

Lord, it was cold. It never seemed to get this cold before.

The animals didn't seem to mind. Some of them seemed to be reveling in it. The polar bears, of course, but the rest of the bears, too. Tigers. A cute little creature called a red panda, much more attractive than the great lumbering black-and-white kind. Sir Lewis hadn't even known it existed. About the size of a raccoon, fur about the color of Felicity Grace's hair (and how *was* she doing, the old man wondered) with a white face, feet, and bands on the tail. It would come out of its little house on the tree, walk around the stone circle that penned it in a couple of times, grin at Sir Lewis, then climb back up into the treehouse. Soft life, Sir Lewis thought.

A particularly nasty gust of wind chilled the back of Sir Lewis's neck, where the beard didn't cover. He pulled his head down deeper into his collar and thrust his hands down into his pockets.

As long as he was feeling around down there, he decided to feel through the coat lining for the Device. For a few seconds it eluded his fingers, and Sir Lewis felt a flash of panic until he caught hold of it in the corner of his front pocket. Sir Lewis chided himself for a fool. He had deliberately worn loose pants, huge and baggy with pleats, of some hideous purplish-gray material. He had practiced, both before he rejoined Leo and after, twisting them around on his body, pulling them up or down or whatever, to make it possible for him to get into the pockets no matter what. Sir Lewis was now certain he could get hold of the Device, when necessary, no matter how he was bound. Unless they tied his hands to the top of his head, or something equally bizarre. He doubted they would.

The Device itself was quite simple. It was about the size of a golf ball, and resembled a blob of gray plasticine. It was similar to the substance Sir Lewis had given to Leo, except that this particular material was designed to explode rather than to generate any great heat.

Sir Lewis's greatest risk had been keeping it concealed. He couldn't go without sleep, after all, and he knew that Calvin was going to take the earliest opportunity to search him, his case, his clothes. Sir Lewis had bet that Leo would not think to search his *disguise*. The explosive had been concealed under the adhesive-coated burlap that attached the beard to his face. Sir Lewis made a great show of removing the beard whenever he was ready to go to sleep, and putting it on again, after shaving, next morning in the loo. This morning, he had peeled off the burlap, removed the layer of explosive, formed it into a ball, placed the detonator in it, and tucked the Device neatly away in these ridiculous trousers.

The detonator, simply a small device capable of making a spark, had been concealed in Sir Lewis's mouth, tucked away between his cheek and gum like some of that vile American sucking snuff. The story of the cyanide tooth had effectively forestalled any search there. There had been one anxious moment when it had come free in the night, and Sir Lewis woke up choking on the bloody thing, but he had coughed it up and managed to keep Leo from seeing it. The coughing fit itself had aroused no suspicion—he was an old man, wasn't he?

Yes. He was old. He was cold. He was tired. And he was, in large measure, a failure. His campaign to awaken the Kingdom to the dangers of turning a blind eye on the things that were wrecking society had not worked in the slightest. And it rankled.

But this, Sir Lewis reminded himself, was no time to brood. He had one last task left. He had the Device. He had Leo Calvin. He had the determination, but then he had always had that.

All he asked was that he be brought into the company of the Russian, Bulanin. He'd show them yet. He'd take a couple of deadly bastards with him.

Lewis Alfot would go out, by God—literally—in a blaze of glory.

5

Felicity sat on the chair, forcing herself not to look toward the door of the loo.

She looked at other things—she took a tour of the blind eyes she had noticed during her scuffle with the stocky one. Grunter, his friend called him. The friend's name was Stan.

She looked at the two of them, as well. Studied them. Memorized their faces, not that she expected it would do any good. These bastards had no intention of leaving Felicity or Mrs. Pettison alive to remember anything. They were talking too freely.

Felicity looked at them anyway. It was good for her resolve to see them punctuating every sentence with a waving gun, see Grunter's face attacking a sandwich cobbled together from the contents of her refrigerator, watch his jaws work with a rotary bovine grinding that alone would have been enough to make her want to kill him. She wanted to watch Stan's face go through its repertoire of smug, nasty smiles behind the constant curtain of cigarette smoke.

And she watched them guzzle beer. Grunter drank more, but Stan drank his share, putting the can down from time to time to light a new cigarette with a fancy gold lighter (the other hand never let go of the gun), but he always picked it up again. That was good. It was important than Stan drink enough beer.

Grunter drained a can and clinked his gun against the empty. It was Bellman's gun, or one of them. The one he slept with. He'd been sleeping on the sofa. He'd been perfectly welcome to sleep in the bed with Felicity if he wanted, but he hadn't wanted. Bellman slept on the sofa, with a gun tucked down in the cushions near his head. If Felicity had been able to reach the gun in time, the situation would be considerably different.

But she hadn't, and Grunter had the gun, and he tapped it against an empty beer can.

"What is this piss?" he demanded.

Felicity said nothing.

"Come on, darling," Stan said. "Answer the man."

"It's all written on the can," Felicity said. "Can't he read?"

"Of course I can read," Grunter said. " 'Schlitz,' " he read, " 'Lager beer. The beer that made Milwaukee famous.' What the bloody hell is Milwaukee?"

"It's a city, Grunter. In America. She got it for the Bellman character, doubtless. He'd probably sit in front of the telly on a Sunday evening, watch American Football on Channel Four, drink American beer, and pretend he was back home."

"It tastes like piss," Grunter said.

"Where is Bellman, miss?" Stan said.

"I don't know," Felicity said.

"I'm tired of this bitch," Grunter said conversationally. "When can we ring Leo? I want to finish here and get going."

"Seven o'clock," Stan said. "What's your hurry? I'm sure our charming hostess will be much more talkative when her neighbor wakes up."

Mrs. Pettison lay at his feet like a trophy rug. There was a slow trickle of blood from her scalp. Stan prodded her with a toe. She groaned.

"Must have hit her harder than I thought," he said. "I was upset. Still, she'll come round. I want her awake. It's important for her to be awake when I ask you questions. Grunter, any more of the American piss left?"

"Bloody gallons."

"Give us another, then."

Good, Felicity thought, drink up. She looked toward the hallway, to the end of it, where the door to the loo was. It was innocent and white, and looked as if nothing at all was going on behind it.

Damn. All right. The thing to do now was not to jerk her head away, but to turn away smoothly. Her head hurt where Grunter had hit her; it hurt worse from all this thinking.

Leo. They were going to ring Leo at seven o'clock. When they'd been talking about it, she'd seen Grunter pat the side pocket of his jacket. Undoubtedly the telephone number. If she could get hold of it, she could find out where Jeffrey's friend Leo would be at seven o'clock. He *might* have a lead to Sir Lewis, which would make the Section happy.

All she had to do was get it. All she needed to do that was a little luck.

Grunter had his face pressed to the metal circle at the top of another beer can. "I'm leaving off this garbage," he said, throwing the can to the floor. "It smells of bloody bleach."

"You're just put out because it's American beer." Stan smiled at his friend through a haze of smoke, the smoke, Felicity realized, that was keeping him from picking up the faint, but detectable odor of chlorine. Dammit, how much beer could these bastards drink before one of them had to go to the loo?

They'd let her go, earlier. Just after the fight. Stan had been a proper gentleman about it. He had Grunter cover her while he went inside and checked for concealed weapons and made sure the window was too small to get out of. Then he'd held the door for her like a Harrods Green Man and told her that if she came out any way but sweet she was dead.

"I'll be standing far enough away from the door so that you won't be able to reach me with soap or bleach or whatever, throw it in my face. But a bullet will reach you, so be careful."

Felicity had been careful. She'd had no intention of coming *out* of the loo with anything. As soon as she closed the door behind her, she'd got the can of drain opener Bellman had left inside, broken three nails getting it open. She used the facilities (she knew she wouldn't get another chance), flushed, and used the noise of the tank refilling to cover her next actions. She poured the rest of the drain opener into the bowl, about two cups. Then she got the plastic bottle of thick bleach she used for cleaning the bowl, and poured that in.

Bellman had laughed at her when she'd warned him not to mix them. The drain opener was sodium hydroxide. The thick bleach was basically chlorine dissolved in water. Bellman had called it basic chemistry. Dissolved in water, the drain opener would free sodium ions. These in turn would work on the water itself, both in the bowl *and* in the bleach. This would serve to liberate chlorine gas.

Felicity heard the hiss of the reaction, and saw the first faint greenish-yellow wisps of chlorine before she hurriedly left the loo and shut the door behind her. Stan ushered her back to the parlor, where he and Grunter drank beer.

And Felicity waited for the gas to build up in the little room.

Chlorine gas. Poisonous. Caustic. Extremely flammable.

It had to be thick in there by now. Felicity's nose fairly itched with it. It was hard to believe even the cigarette smoke could keep Stan from smelling it.

Maybe he *should* smell it. Maybe he'll go to investigate. It would be best if it were Stan, but she could deal with things if it was Grunter who went. One eye, sore head, broken, bleeding nails and all—she could deal with it. She was a trained professional, after all, and these two were just thugs.

But one way or another, for one reason or another, if *one* of them didn't open the door to the loo, and damned bloody soon, Felicity was going to go mad.

6

Dave Hamilton didn't know how to take it when the American asked him to come next door to the flat. Dave hadn't even known there *was* a flat, and he wasn't sure that Mr. Bellman had the authority to take him off the job in the middle of the day. In as polite a way as he could manage, Dave told him as much.

Bellman smiled at him. "It's all right, Dave. Pick up the phone and clear it with Mr. Tipton. Tell him I want to take you to the company flat. He'll understand."

"If you're sure it's all right . . ."

"Of course it's all right. What's the matter?" Bellman assumed the air of someone extremely narked. "Think I'm a faggot or something, after your body?"

It had never crossed Dave's mind until this instant.

"Relax," the American told him. "It's the *British* spies who are poofs. Americans sell their country out for money. At least," he said, "that's the way it usually happens."

"Er . . . do you mind waiting a little while? I've . . . er . . . just got some of these accommodation lists to finish up—"

"Nope. Can't wait. You ring Mr. Tipton's office and tell him. Come on. Time's wasting. For Queen and Country, and all that."

Dave rang up, and to his surprise, was connected with Mr. Tipton in person. The Acting Section Chief seemed dubious, especially when Dave told him it was Mr. Bellman's idea to clear it with him, but he said Dave should go ahead, by all means.

Dave spent the first few moments in the flat just looking at it. He thought you had to be a character on the telly to live in a place like this. When he thought of his mum and Mike and him living in a cramped, cold Council flat, he envied the person who lived here. Then he remembered it was a company flat, and *no one* lived here, and he didn't know whether to laugh or bust up the place.

To hell with it, he thought. I don't like this. I don't like being around this man, for some reason never have. Let me just see what he wants and get back to my keyboard.

"There's an awful lot of work waiting for me, Mr. Bellman," Dave said. "So if you'll just tell me what you want of me . . ."

Bellman's fist hit him in the jaw and cracked his head back like a boxer's bag. The salty taste of blood filled his mouth as his teeth sliced into the soft flesh of his inner cheek.

The actual *pain* of the blow hadn't had a chance to register yet when Bellman hit him again, in the belly this time. The air whooshed from him, bringing with it a fine spray of blood. Dave thought he was going to be sick. He clutched at his stomach and sank to his knees on the thick white rug.

He tried to speak. "The matter with you? Bloody crazy?"

Bellman bent over, jammed his thumb into the flesh below Dave's ear, just behind the jawbone.

The pain was like nothing Dave had ever imagined in his life. Globes of colored light danced on a field of red. He could hear inarticulate moans —"ahh—ahh"—like a dumb animal whimpering. Was that him? Dave couldn't tell. There was the pain, and nothing past that could make an impression.

The pressure against his jaw stopped, and the red drained from in front of his eyes. With it went the strength that had been keeping him up. He flopped over sideways and whimpered. It made him ashamed, but there was no fighting it.

"What do you want?" he demanded. "Why are you fucking *doing* this?"

"We're going to talk, Dave," Bellman said. His voice was calm, matter-of-fact, as if he did this sort of thing every day. In a way, it was worse than the pain. The pain was now—this voice promised trouble for the future. For *all* of the future.

"I'm going to get information from you, and this is how I'm going to do it. I could trick it out of you. I could drug it out of you. You're an amateur, I'm a professional, there are a dozen ways I could do this. They'd all work. But they all take time. I haven't got time. I'm going to get it out of you by beating it out of you. How much of it you stand depends on you."

"That's . . . that's bloody *torture.*"

"How about that?" Bellman asked. He cracked his knuckles. Dave heard himself whimper again, cursed himself for a coward.

"What do you want to know?"

"For openers, how much have you been getting to sell out the Agency? And was it worth Felicity Grace's eye, or the other man's life?" He reached down and slapped Dave across the face. "Was it?"

7

It was insidious, this spy business. It was like a drug that your body could manufacture for itself. All you had to do was let it. And then ride the high. Watch yourself figure out how knowledge of your whereabouts had been reaching Leo Calvin, and through him (when he wanted it to) the Russians. Feel the pieces fit together in your mind.

Hear the poor stupid kid yell as you beat on him.

Bellman hated himself at this moment. It never should have come to this. He should have known. He shouldn't have let himself be dragged back into the game, Leo Calvin or no Leo Calvin. It was worse than that—he had volunteered. Maybe his father was right; maybe it was in his genes too deep for him ever to be free of it. "You tryin' to stay out of the game, son, is like a duck tryin' to fly *north* for the winter. Just can't be done."

It was beginning to look that way.

And, if he *had* to come back, he should have come back all the way. Suspicious of *everyone*. Thinking the worst, imagining worse that that, about anyone he happened to meet.

Bellman had made an unforgivable mistake. He *liked* Dave Hamilton. He liked this kid because he seemed to have faced some tough breaks with courage, and had taken steps toward taking his future in his own hands. Britain, he had thought in his smugness, needed more people like young Dave Hamilton.

So Bellman had sat there and let the kid sell him out. And Sir Lewis remained at large. And Felicity was blind in one eye. One of Tipton's men was dead. The Section Sir Lewis and Tipton had built was in big trouble. And what was going to happen to Dave Hamilton didn't bear thinking about.

It didn't take much more to get him talking. Bellman hadn't

expected it to. When Dave took hold of the future, he grabbed more than he could hang on to.

"I did it for me brother," Dave said. "He needs better doctors. Smarter. Who care more. Than the bloody National Health. The job was good, but it's not enough. I didn't expect Mike to walk again or nothing, it's just the pain—"

"I don't care why you did it," Bellman said.

"I thought he was a *journalist*. He said he was a bloody *journalist*. He told me I wouldn't be doing no harm. And he paid me. A lot. Told me it was leads, you know, so that he might find stories, and all. I saved up a lot of money from what he paid me."

Dave was sitting on the floor. His back was against the front of an overstuffed armchair, his head thrown back on the seat. It was if he were talking to the ceiling, or to God. Now his head snapped forward, and anger flashed in his eyes.

"I never *told* him anything! Nothing. I just told him the bloody hotel rooms I booked. How can all this be my fault?"

Bellman shook his head. He could almost believe the boy had been that naive. Almost.

"Don't try that on, Dave," he said. "You knew it was your fault when you visited Miss Grace in the hospital. When you came to fix the resistor on the TV set. If I had any brains, all I had to do was look at you to know."

Bellman looked at him now. "Was it an American?"

"Who?"

"The person you told. The one who recruited you for this business. Or was it the balloon man?"

"No. It was an American. The . . . the first time. I don't know about the balloon man. Whether he was an American. Once the system was set up, I never had to speak to anybody. I just went to the market on Sunday."

Bellman nodded. He could see the way Leo had set it up; or at least he could see the way he himself would have set it up. You hang around, you listen. You talk to people. You hear who's getting the Civil Service jobs, or who's already got one. You come on as a journalist—an American journalist, no less. You offer money for information.

It doesn't have to be earth-shaking information. You can get useful intelligence just by looking at a list of who's studying what in technical schools—that kind of thing can show you what fields of research are hot in the target country at the moment. Bulanin's job as Agricultural Attaché was a cover, yes, but that didn't mean he didn't want to find out how much food Britain would grow in a given year and how much it would have to import. That situation would affect the pound, which would affect politics, which would affect everything.

You could build yourself a nice little network of low-level informants, each passing you secrets worth far more than the people providing them suspected. If you're Leo Calvin, you're looking for something, anything, that will please the Russians enough to get them off your back.

The one day you hit pay dirt. You find a kid who is in charge of booking rooms, flats, houses, and hotels for the agents of a spy organization. Of course, he doesn't tell you it's a spy organization. Maybe he doesn't even know when you sign him up. But *you* know, thanks to your Russian friends, that anything Sir Lewis Alfot is connected with, or had been connected with, is hot. Anyhow you can trace any of the people who work there.

And you get even luckier. The kid needs money. It never occurs to the kid (it wouldn't, Bellman thought) to go to his boss and explain his concern over his brother, and try to get help that way.

Besides, it's *exciting* to be a mole for a journalist. Real cloak-and-dagger stuff. If you get found out, you do a short stretch in jail, and the newspapers call you a hero. And when you *start* doing it, you think you're only working for a publishing company. By the time you find out otherwise, it's too late. The system has been set up, and the kid is caught in it.

And the *system*, Bellman thought. The system was beautiful. The kid works with computers. As Dave himself said, the fascination of computers is that *anything*, any kind of information, can be reduced to a string of numbers. And numbers, in turn, could be represented by anything. Letters, as in a department store code. Sounds, as in a touch-tone phone.

Colors. As in the resistor code.

Bad boys rape other young girls, but Violet gives willingly. Black, brown, red, orange, yellow, green, blue, violet, gray, white. Zero, one, two, three, four, five, six, seven, eight, nine. That's all you needed. He should have known as soon as he saw the brown balloons. *Nobody* wanted a brown balloon for a decoration, but you needed the digit for the code.

Bellman wanted to know just how the code worked. Dave explained that the system worked various ways. The balloons would code out a question like "Anybody working in Brighton" . . .

"Brighton," Bellman said.

Dave swallowed hard, and continued. Or lately, they'd want to know where Bellman was. "Mostly, he'd give me a phone number and a time to call it," he concluded.

"Sometimes you'd pass a coded message back by way of your earrings, though, wouldn't you?"

"Sometimes. Not much." Dave swallowed again. He'd managed to pull himself together a little during the questioning, but he hadn't forgotten the pain. Or that it could start again at any second.

"Could . . . could I ask *you* a question?"

"Ask," Bellman said. "No promises that I'll answer."

"What's going to happen to me?"

"What do you think?"

Dave bit his lower lip. "Oh, Christ," he said. "Oh, Christ."

"No, I'm not going to kill you," Bellman said.

Dave looked at him. "You're not?" Then the face fell. "Oh, right. That's Mr. Tipton's department, and all."

"Tipton's not going to kill you, either."

"He will when he finds out. Unless . . ." Dave was fighting a hope he didn't dare let himself feel. "Unless you're not going to tell him."

"I don't have to tell him. He already knows. This place is bugged."

"That's why you told me—"

"That's why I told you to let him know I was taking you here. He's heard it all. Probably seen it, too."

"Then . . ." Dave licked his lips. "Then what *is* going to happen to me?"

"Something that will make death look good by comparison," Bellman told him. "You're in it, now. Leo Calvin has probably told the Russians about you, or he's told them enough to make them believe you when you go to them."

"*I'm* not going to go to—"

"You have no choice!" Bellman was surprised at the anger in his own voice. "You can stay alive, because you can be of use. You can sell false information to the Russians for Tipton. You'll have no friends. You'll be able to trust no one. You'll get no promotions, because you've shown nobody will be able to trust you. If you try to get out, you're a dead man. If you get caught by the Russians, you're a dead man. And you'll be thrown to the wolves the minute someone decides you'll be of more use that way."

Bellman shook his head. "Welcome to the world of espionage. You stupid, stupid fool. You had a chance—the hell with it. You're stuck now. Life in the shadows, no parole."

The doorbell rang.

"I didn't know," Dave said. "I didn't know . . ."

"Now you know," Bellman said. Dave kept murmuring.

"Shut the fuck up before I hit you again. When's the next time you're supposed to get in touch with these people?"

Dave looked surprised. "Why, tonight. They gave me a special phone number. A new one—not one of the usual phone boxes."

He told Bellman what it was. The doorbell rang again.

"You are about to receive your first assignment. You are going to refrain from making that phone call tonight. Come on, let's go." Bellman pulled the dazed boy to his feet.

He pulled the door open as the bell rang for the third time. Tipton was there. In person. There was an angry look on his face, and his skin was as gray as his hair.

Dave looked at him and worked his mouth. "Mr. Tipton . . ." he said at last, but he couldn't manage anything more.

"I want to talk with you for a second, Tipton," Bellman said.

Tipton spoke to the agents with him. "Take him to my office. Wait with him until I get there."

They took Dave away. Tipton looked at Bellman and said, "What a bloody mess."

"I don't make them," Bellman said. "I just smell them out."

"Don't expect me to love you for it."

224

"You may go directly to hell, Mr. Tipton. I've heard a lot of stuff about British pride out of you. I think you ought to save it until you've got something to be proud of. You are amazing. You give the kid a sensitive job, and you think because *he* doesn't know what he's doing, he's not a security risk. By the time he knows, he's in too deep, and *everybody* is in a bloody mess."

"See here, Bellman," Tipton began.

"*You* see here. I want three things from you. I want a phone number traced."

"All right." Tipton was still seething. "What else?"

"I know you have to use the kid."

"You outlined the situation very nicely."

"Go easy on him."

"Are you mad?"

"Go easy on him, I said. He never had a chance. You set him up and sent him out there naked. Go easy on him. I mean it. The poor bastard never had a chance."

"Good Lord, man, are you *crying?*"

"No," Bellman lied, "I am not crying. The third thing I want is top-flight medical care for Hamilton's brother."

"Oh?"

"Don't give me 'oh.' Just see that he gets it. Send the bill to the Congressman if you want, but see that Hamilton's brother gets taken care of."

"The Congressman," Tipton promised, "will hear about *all* of this."

"You got *that* right. You'll tell him about it. And so will I." Bellman nodded, like a notary stamping a document.

"Come on," he said. "Let's find out who that phone belongs to."

8

Bulanin looked at his watch. Almost time. This absurd charade would soon be over.

Bulanin was in Paddington Station, leaning against a glass case holding an enormous effigy of a bear. It looked altogether too friendly to represent the Russian Bear, but he approved of the symbolism, just the same.

Aside from minor differences (like the bear), all of the railway stations in London were the same—huge, high-ceilinged, barnlike structures, with red-signed shops crouching against the walls like derelicts, or standing forlornly in the middle of the cement floors like bewildered travelers.

All of Bulanin's chosen observation points had been British Rail stations. They fit all of Leo Calvin's criteria—they were large, so that the parties could see that the other was alone without having to come into premature contact; they were public, to make an ambush less feasible; and they were easily accessible.

Also, they sheltered him from the snow. If Bulanin had wanted to run around in the snow, he could have asked to be assigned to Moscow.

It seemed to Bulanin that he was choosing better places for Calvin's purposes than Calvin himself was. The zoo had been deserted—if Bulanin intended to betray Calvin at one of the sightings, he could have done it there. The same with the Tower. It made no sense.

Still, Bulanin faithfully executed his assigned steps in this little dance. Calmly, he watched the American and the ridiculously bearded Sir Lewis. (And it had better *be* Sir Lewis, Bulanin thought grimly. Not, he admitted, that it would make a difference to the fate in store for Calvin.) They walked calmly across the station, like a man showing his peasant grandfather the wonders of the metropolis. Calvin paused at a sweets machine about fifty yards away from where Bulanin stood, worked the machine, and peeled and ate a piece of chewing gum. He offered one to the bearded man with him, who declined. Then he looked directly at Bulanin, caught his eye, and nodded soberly, once. Bulanin returned the gesture.

When the two men had walked far enough away from the machine, Bulanin walked quickly over to it. He found the note in the coin return slot. It read "LAST STOP—THE TOMBS. BRING THE MONEY."

Bulanin smiled. He'd been led on a day-long paper chase through the snow in order to be assigned a rendezvous at the usual meeting place. Leo Calvin had a sense of humor, it seemed.

Bulanin rubbed his nose. As he did so, he spoke into a small FM transmitter concealed in one hand. "The Tombs," he said. He would dispose of the transmitter before he arrived at the rendezvous. Calvin might insist on searching him before going through with the transaction, and the sight of the device might cause a problem.

But by then, Bulanin wouldn't need it anymore. His men would be in place. Sir Lewis and the money would be exchanged. Then the men would strike. The money would be retrieved. Bulanin would deliver to Borzov both the old man *and* the American. Leo Calvin would have tried to be clever once too often.

Bulanin had a sense of humor, too.

9

Mrs. Pettison groaned and stirred. Felicity could see her eyes move under her eyelids. She'd come round soon.

Stan grinned and nudged Mrs. Pettison again with his toe. "Come on, darling, wake up. I want you to be a good neighbor and help me convince the young lady to tell me where her boyfriend is."

Stan was no fool. He knew (or had been told) that Felicity was a professional. Physical duress wouldn't make her talk; it was a waste of time even to try it. But the torture of an innocent bystander might just work. Even if it didn't, the smile on Stan's face said he'd enjoy it all the same.

In a few minutes, Mrs. Pettison would wake up, and Stan would go to work. And Felicity would watch. And say nothing. She *had* to wait them out, had to let her trap work, if it was ever going to. It was the only way to get out of here alive, if not necessarily in one piece.

Stan drank the rest of his umpteenth can of beer—bladder like a bloody *camel*, Felicity thought—then went through the gold-plated ritual of lighting yet another cigarette.

Mrs. Pettison's eyelids fluttered.

Stan's eyelids widened when he saw it. "That's better," he said. "Grunter?"

Grunter looked up from one of Felicity's BBC Basic computer language manuals, in which he had apparently been absorbed. "What, then, seven already?"

"About twenty till," Stan said. "But the old woman is coming around—we might still have something to tell Leo."

"Great. Let's get started, then."

"In a minute. I'm off to the loo."

Felicity almost cheered. She tensed her muscles for action,

then forced herself to relax. She didn't want to tip anything off before the last second. His hand on the doorknob would be time enough.

"After all," Stan went on, "we don't want any interruptions once we start to work, do we, now?"

Grunter looked at him with disgust. "If you had any taste in lager, it wouldn't be a problem."

Stan smiled. "Won't be a minute. Just come sit here, hold the gun steady, and don't let her try anything funny."

"There's nothing bloody funny about any of it." Grunter settled into the chair and glared at Felicity. He was not happy about the way she'd handled him in their earlier scuffle, and Felicity could see his hands twitch with the desire to even things up.

Felicity watched Stan walk down the hall. When he was about two feet from the door of the loo, Felicity tensed and leaned slightly forward. She licked her lips.

Grunter saw it, didn't like it. Something in his shrewd, deadly brain put the observations together with an intuition and strong sense of suspicion and came out with one word—TRAP.

"Stan!" he called. "Don't go in the loo!"

Mrs. Pettison threw her arm across her face, shielding her eyes from the light. Felicity died inside.

Stan stopped with his hand on the knob. "How's that again?" he asked.

Grunter opened his mouth to repeat himself, but Stan didn't wait for an answer before he opened the door.

Stingley was ready to give up and go home. Actually, he was ready to go back to his brother-in-law's home, just down the road a bit in Richmond, where he'd been staying the past few days.

Two things were keeping him close to London—the Cyclops, and his conscience. He just didn't want to go back down south while the man he'd been hunting had last struck in the capital. He knew it was foolish—what if he struck next in Cardiff, or Glasgow, or the Shetland Islands, or France? Stingley could spend the rest of his life chasing this bloody maniac and never see his wife again. But, Stingley thought, logic be damned—as long as the Cyclops seemed most likely to be holed up in London, Stingley would be, too.

It was his conscience, though, that had him here, in particular, staked out on the block of flats where Jeffrey Bellman had been stopping. What the hell, he thought, there's nothing better to do. It wasn't as if the bloody Yard had any use for him or anything.

And he'd meant what he'd said to the young American the other day, every word of it. Soon, *bloody* soon, he would have to make a fuss about what he knew. Unless, of course, someone showed him a damned good reason not to. So he was standing in the snow, walking around the neighborhood. It was even more ridiculous than staying in London trying to be near his quarry, but he was looking for *something*, just one little tiny something, that would either let him call it off or give him the push to do what he threatened.

What made it worse was that Bellman probably wasn't even there. Surveying the place when he'd first arrived about forty minutes ago (like a good policeman) Stingley had noticed that Miss Grace's car wasn't there. Since it was unlikely that she'd be on the road so soon after losing an eye, and in a blizzard besides, it was probable that Bellman was out, and the lights in the windows indicated that Miss Grace was convalescing quietly at home.

Stingley toyed with the idea of paying her a call, but decided against it. To hell with it. Go back to Fred's and let him brag about how good a cook his wife was. Stingley held his stomach, where the homemade black pudding she'd served him for lunch was resting uneasily, and reflected that Fred must be hopelessly in love.

Stingley walked back to the car, and took one last look at the windows of the Grace woman's flat. By way of a goodbye, he supposed.

That's when he saw the explosion. The noise followed almost immediately.

"Jesus Bloody Christ," Stingley whispered, and he sprinted for the entrance.

Stan hit the floor blazing. He screamed four or five times, then stopped. Mrs. Pettison picked up where he'd left off, the result of going under because of a rap on the head, then waking to find herself in what must have seemed a circle of hell, complete with explosions, and fire, and flaming, tormented souls.

Felicity had no time to worry about her. Two things had happened in the instant the coal of Stan's last cigarette ignited the chlorine gas—Grunter had reflexively turned his head to see what had happened, and Felicity, who'd been watching for just that reflex, took the opportunity to jump him.

And still, Grunter recovered in time to stop Felicity from finishing him off with a smash to the throat, as she'd intended. Instead, he'd ducked forward, and the blow landed on his nose. Felicity could feel the cartilage squash under her hand, but it didn't slow Grunter for a second.

It devolved into round two of their previous fight; the tall woman and the stocky man grappled around the room. Broken glass crunched under their bodies as they struggled. The smell of burning—carpet, paint, flesh—was growing stronger. Mrs. Pettison screamed repeatedly, without variation, like an air-raid siren. Grunter made his animal noises. Felicity was silent.

Externally. Inside, her brain was screaming at her. *Don't let him go for your eye. Don't let him hit you in the head anymore; the next one will knock you out from the pain. End this. Get Mrs. Pettison out of here. End it. Get out before the fire makes this all irrelevant. End it. End it!*

Then, as if in answer to a prayer she wasn't aware of making, she saw a way to do it. They were almost in position; she almost had the leverage. If she could just get out from under and plant her foot . . .

Felicity brought her right leg out to the side of her body. Grunter's weight still pinned her shoulders. He was trying to control her enough to enable him to get a hand free to finish her. Now Felicity wanted him to succeed.

She planted her foot against the carpet, ignoring the slivers of glass that sliced into her skin. That done, she stopped struggling.

Grunter's victory was warm on his face. Felicity could see him smile as he held her throat with his left hand and raised his right to smash her.

Felicity moved. She arched her back, using her shoulders and right foot as supports. It lifted Grunter's bulk only a little, but it was enough. With his hand in the air, he had a far less secure base than he'd had a moment before.

Now, when Felicity lifted her body and turned inward toward Grunter, there was nothing to keep him from going over sideways. He hit the floor, sprawling. A dribble of blood appeared where a piece of glass cut his chin. He cursed under his breath, then aloud, as he started to scramble to his feet.

He never made it. Felicity got up first. As Grunter rose, she grabbed his belt and collar like a chucker-out at a pub. She pulled the belt and pushed the collar to keep him off balance.

Grunter's best move would have been to go back down, but he was too angry to be smart. He tried to fight his way to his feet, which was just what Felicity wanted. He was still fighting when she ran his head through the broken front of the television set. Grunter's scream turned into a gurgle, and a sheet of bright red washed down the front of the box.

A voice said, "*Jesus* Bloody Christ!"

Felicity looked up wearily. "Stingley," she said.

"Come out of it, before the fire cuts you off!"

Felicity paused just long enough to find the gun Grunter had dropped when she'd jumped him and to take a piece of paper from his pocket. She made her way past a wall of flame to where Stingley stood in the doorway.

"What the bloody hell is going on here?" the policeman demanded.

"Mrs. Pettison," Felicity said. "I've got to get Mrs. Pettison out."

"Relax, I've got her out at the head of the stairs. Bloody good job I got here when I did, or she'd have been roasted. She's smoked like a bloody gammon joint as it is."

"Let's get her out of the building."

"You're bloody brilliant, you are," Stingley said. He was already on his way. He slung Mrs. Pettison, who was too bewildered to protest, or even question, over his shoulder and started downstairs. Felicity pounded on doors and shouted fire; one neighbor had already noticed and called the fire brigade.

Felicity acknowledged with a nod, and continued downstairs amid the increasing traffic.

Outside, Stingley got Mrs. Pettison a safe distance away from the building and put her down on the seat of a car belonging to one of the other fugitives from the fire. The neighbor said, "Hit her head, poor thing," and began taking care of her.

"Do you have a car?" Felicity asked.

"Where's a phone box? I have to call the fire brigade."

"That's been seen to. Where's your car? I need you to take me somewhere."

Stingley was disgusted. "Don't be bloody ridiculous. You're bleeding. You're scorched. You're standing barefoot in the middle of a bloody blizzard. If I'm going to take you anywhere, it'll be right back to hospital!"

"You will take me to the Tournament Press in Bloomsbury. This is a vital national matter. I don't have my credentials with me, but you remember them."

"What vital matter?"

Felicity cracked. *"The matter I set the fire and killed those two sods over!"* She had hold of his coat with both hands. There was blood on the hands. "Now get me the hell out of here before company gets here and ruins everything."

Stingley grumbled and swore, but he took her.

EIGHTH

Erect and sublime for one moment of time,
  In the next, that wild figure they saw
(As if stung by a spasm) plunge into a chasm,
  While they waited and listened in awe.

"It's a Snark!" was the sound that first came to
    their ears,
  And seemed almost too good to be true.
Then followed a torrent of laughter and cheers:
  Then the ominous words, "It's a Boo—"

—The Hunting of the Snark
Fit the Eighth

1

The snow scattered Bellman's headlights, and the wind howled so loud he had trouble remembering he was supposed to be driving on the left.

He was heading for the Tombs, a wax museum or something just south of the Thames, somewhat to the east of Putney. That, it seemed, was the phone number Dave Hamilton had been supposed to call. Some efficient fellow at Tournament Press had written out directions for Bellman; he'd find it.

What he was worried about was his inability to stop thinking about Dave Hamilton. Maybe he should have . . . God, he was doing it again. Not only was it stupid, it was a waste of time.

It was guilt that made him do it, the guilt of having jumped all over Tipton for having made the same mistake Bellman himself had made. Tipton had *liked* the Hamilton kid, that's all. And had therefore trusted him, too much or too little, it didn't make much difference. Now everybody paid the price.

It occurred to Bellman that this post mortem was a stupid waste of time, too. He ought to be thinking about what he'd do when he caught up with Leo Calvin. Assuming, of course, that he survived the drive down there. He checked his directions, navigated into a tricky corner (no easy corners in London), fishtailed on the snow, gentled the car into line again, and went on.

What he wanted to do (why did he *ever* waste time thinking about what he wanted?) was to kill the bastard. That was what he'd wanted from the beginning. How could he do it, though, without the tabloids getting hold of the *Sordid Spy Cyclops Shock Horror* story?

The only way to do it, he decided, was to catch hold of Leo,

take him to a soundproof room somewhere, and get him to tell
who had the information, and how to stop that person from
completing delivery.

The question was, could he do it? Leo was no Dave Hamilton.
Leo was a total professional, a dedicated terrorist. He had wrung
more information out of people than even Bellman had. There
would be somewhere between (Bellman estimated) twelve and
twenty hours to make him talk. Did Bellman want to wager,
God help him, the Future of the Alliance on the possibility that
he knew enough drugs, tricks, and ways of causing pain to make
a hardened assassin spill his guts inside twelve hours?

Well, he decided, yes, he wanted to. But did he dare?

He was still working on that one as he drove across the bridge,
then counterclockwise around the the block where the Tombs
was located. He always tried to scout out scenes of possible
trouble. It made him feel better. Sometimes it even paid off.

As it did this time. On the second time around, Bellman saw
two men walking through the snow toward a heavy oaken door
set into the concrete of the bridge. A sign above the door bore a
grinning skull and the words THE TOMBS. The taller of the two
men raised the heavy metal door knocker and let it fall. It was
supposed to be past the museum's closing time, at least if you
believed the sign on the door, but the door opened, and the two
men went inside.

Bellman stopped working on the question of whether he
dared. It was no longer relevant. Bellman had poor eyesight, but
good eyes, with the lenses. There had been some attempt at
disguise, but the Congressman had begun training him to see
through disguises when he was three.

There was no doubt about it. The tall one was Leo Calvin.
And unless all the pictures, films, and verbal descriptions were
wrong, the stocky one with the beard and glasses was Sir Lewis
Alfot.

Bellman drove once more around the base of the bridge. Then
he left the car up against a nascent snowbank, and circled the
building on foot. He was looking for a way in. He'd find one if
he had to claw through the concrete. Calvin and Alfot in one
place was an occasion he refused to miss.

2

His captor tried to pass the time before the Russian arrived by talking, but Sir Lewis wasn't interested.

"You'd better be more talkative in your new home, old man," Calvin said.

Sir Lewis still wasn't interested. What he was interested in was the man who had opened the door, a lithe, muscular black man. Leo Calvin called him Benton. Benton was dressed, Sir Lewis couldn't help noticing, in a striped pull-on shirt and three-quarter-length white pants. His feet were bare, and he had a gold circle in his right earlobe.

"What is he doing here?" Sir Lewis demanded.

"Earnin' money," Benton said with a smile. "Better money than they pay me here to scare the tourists. Today I was a pirate. Sometimes I wear a hood, and I swing an ax, and chop the heads off dummies. I always stay and close the place up. Except when Leo got business."

That settled that. Sir Lewis need have no qualms about the man's presence. The more the merrier. Idly, Sir Lewis reached in his pocket and touched the Device. He touched it lightly, in case it was the tiny detonator that came to his fingers. The Device was not to go off until Bulanin arrived.

Leo kept talking, oblivious that Sir Lewis had lapsed back into silence. He was asking Benton about telephone calls, and looking at his watch. Benton reported that there had been no calls. Leo looked at his watch again and murmured that it was past seven o'clock. He seemed to be worried about two idiots who might have let him down.

Leo had just about decided to make the phone call himself when the door knocker sounded, hard and hollow, like the gavel at the Last Judgment. The knocker fell five times—three then two. Leo waited until the last one, then nodded at Benton, who went to stand by the side of the door.

When the Jamaican was in place, Leo opened the door. Bulanin stepped inside and shook snow from his hat. He didn't offer to shake hands, just made a little bow. There was a large valise handcuffed to his wrist. He looked at Leo, then at Sir Lewis. Alfot could see a gleam of triumph-long-delayed in the Russian's handsome face. Sir Lewis suppressed a smile.

The Russian said, "Good evening. I see that you are ready to conclude the bargain at la—"

The last word was swallowed in a noise like thunder as Benton slammed the door behind Bulanin. There were two more noises, loud clicks, as the black man shot home the metal bolts that would secure it.

Sir Lewis had seen it coming, but he had still jumped when that noise exploded through the dimly lit interior of the Tombs. The Russian, unprepared, had almost buckled at the knees and collapsed. He recovered quickly, Sir Lewis had to give him that. Anger was already replacing fear as Bulanin turned to face the source of the sound. The exchange was completed when he saw Benton's gun, and the grin of triumph that went with it.

Bulanin turned to Calvin. "What is the meaning of this?"

Leo told him to relax. "Just a little insurance, that's all. He works for me, and he works here. Why do you think I always met you here? Benton is all that remains of the trumpery little organization I was able to put together here in England, and how many KGB people can you command? A hundred? Two hundred?"

The last count Sir Lewis had heard had been a hundred sixty-seven, including Bulanin himself. He was tempted to tell the American so. Why not? He had the Device. He could take control at any second. Why not?

No, he thought. Not yet. This was his last triumph, or setting off the Device would be. In one clean, purifying flash, he would destroy the terrorist scum who had kidnapped him and one of his country's deadliest enemies. He would, as well, end his own life on a note that could (God willing) arouse some belief in the British mind that courage and dedication weren't extinct in Britain. They had never understood what the Cyclops mission was trying to tell them; surely, they couldn't fail to see the lesson in the way Sir Lewis Alfot had met his end.

He would be redeemed. He would be a hero again. It felt good, and he wanted to hold the feeling just a little more.

Bulanin was talking. "What has the number of men I can command to do with anything?"

"It never does either of us any good to be coy, Grigori Illyich. I'm sure that a number of your people are nearby, taking up positions around the building and surrounding us. They wouldn't have been there ahead of time, because I might have spotted them." Leo smiled. "I or the legendary bald eagle of British Intelligence might have. He's old, but he's full of tricks.

"But they're there now, Grigori Illyich, I'm sure of that. We don't want them butting in on our last meeting together. They don't understand our agreement; they might try to take Sir Lewis away from me and prevent you from giving me the money. That wouldn't do."

Bulanin's lips were tight. He said nothing.

"But there's no problem, now," Leo went on. "I trust *you*. I won't even search you, provided you show me the money right away. I won't even insist on sanctuary in Moscow, anymore. Somehow, I don't think I'll get as warm a welcome as I'd like."

Bulanin's face said he'd been expecting something like this, and was willing to make the best of it. "That is very perceptive of you," he said. "But what is my insurance you will not take the money and keep custody of our friend?"

"I've got no more use for him," Leo said. "He travels fastest who travels alone."

"Indeed. I cannot answer for Moscow, not anymore. But *I* will not pursue you."

Leo nodded. The amount of belief he put in Bulanin's promise was not determinable.

"I'm going to reach into my pocket now," Bulanin said.

"Slowly," Benton said. Sir Lewis had nearly forgotten he was there.

"Of course," Bulanin replied. "I'm getting the keys to the valise. That is where the money is. Two million American dollars in one-hundred-dollar bills. You may count it if you wish."

"That won't be necessary," Leo said. "I'll just want to see it."

Bulanin opened the valise and spread it open on the floor. Calvin knelt and selected a few bundles of money at random, checking it to see if it was genuine, insuring against consecutive serial numbers.

He seemed to be satisfied. "It's real, Benton," he said. "And because you've done such a good job for me, you get an extra hundred grand. You'll be living like a king for the rest of your life on three hundred grand."

"I won't say no," Benton told him. He took his money and stuffed it into a Sainsbury's bag, which he placed in the control room. He never took his eye or his gun off the Russian.

"You are a generous man," Bulanin said.

"It's so rare that one can afford to be," Leo told him. "With this kind of money, I can spare the hundred G's, and Benton is a good man. I may need help again."

"You are not following Sir Lewis into retirement, then."

"Not me. Not now. I'm going back into business. If I was able to pull this exchange with you, I don't honestly think there's anything that can stop me. This is seed money. In a year, you'll come looking for me to ask me favors, not kill me."

Now.

"I don't think so," Sir Lewis said. He held the Device in his right hand with his hand on the detonator. With his left hand, he skinned off his disguise. The beard, the hat, the wig, got thrown to the floor. Only the mended old-fashioned spectacles stayed on his face. He still wanted to see, for these last few minutes.

"You may shoot," he said to Benton, "but when you do, the plastic explosive goes off. They call it," he added, "a dead-man switch."

He looked from face to face. Leo was feigning calmness, Bulanin looking with impotent fury at the American. Inside, they had to be crawling, cursing themselves. It was a sweet moment, very sweet. Sir Lewis enjoyed it. It was perhaps the best moment of his life. Better than the moment in France, so many years ago, when he'd seen his duty, and taken a life to save the lives of his men. Better than all the triumphs as head of the Agency he'd created. Those triumphs had been secondhand and remote—this was immediate and personal. Better than the

242

Cyclops mission. Much better. Whatever the elation of success-fully providing a demonstration case, and there was much each time, it always was washed away in disappointment when he realized no one understood.

No one had to understand this. The validity was in the act itself. All he had to do was let go the button on the bomb.

And then Leo Calvin did a strange thing. He turned to Bulanin and said, "Did you bring the antidote?"

"Shut up, you fool," Bulanin said.

"Did you bring it?" Leo might have been talking to a child.

"Yes, I did, but what good will it do?"

"There's no antidote for a bomb," Sir Lewis said. His thumb itched to let the switch go.

"Yeah," Leo said. "There's also no bomb." He turned to Bulanin. "You'd better debrief him quickly, he's losing it. He actually thought I wouldn't search his things while he slept. He had plastic explosive concealed in that ridiculous beard. I took it away one night and replaced it with modeling clay. They call it Plasticine here. I mixed some rubbing alcohol in it so it would smell right."

"*Liar!*" Sir Lewis shouted. He was pressing the switch and letting it go over and over. The Device was mashed into mean-ingless shapes from the force of his hands.

He kept pressing the button until they took the Device away from him and handcuffed him behind his back. Bulanin poured some liquid into Sir Lewis's mouth. It had no taste, or Sir Lewis failed to taste it. He stuck a needle in the old man's arm.

"That will take care of any cyanide tooth he might have. It is a good thing you told me about it."

"Sure," Leo said.

Sir Lewis might have heard, but the words would have meant nothing. He would not have thought to use a cyanide tooth even if he had one. Which he had not. That had been a bluff.

Which had failed.

As the Device had failed. As everything had failed.

It was not to be borne. Failure. Failure. Failure.

He had taken it upon himself to make the Nation remember how to be great. Instead, he had just shown them another way to failure.

Sir Lewis heard bitter laughter. He looked at the American, the Russian, the Jamaican and saw it was coming from none of them. Strange. And the laughter didn't stop. It grew louder, and more bitter.

Sir Lewis's thumb kept pressing against the air.

3

Robert Tipton spoke by car radio to a computer operator back at the Tournament Press. Not Dave Hamilton.

Felicity was sick over Dave Hamilton. She'd brought him to Tipton's attention, she'd sponsored him, rooted for him. She knew she'd let someone down—Dave, the Section, maybe both.

Just another, she thought, in a long series of balls-ups on this operation. The last straw. The news about Dave had led her into open rebellion with the Acting Head of the Section.

Felicity had marched in, demanding clothes. Stingley had waited outside, bewildered, but determined not to be shunted away from the action. Tipton had looked at her, heard a brief report of what had happened at her flat, including the likelihood that she now knew the current whereabouts of Sir Lewis, and began to shout orders into phone.

"I want a team assembled immediately, to be ready at a moment's notice. Surveillance. Possibly assault. I'll decide that on the scene. Yes, I'm going. I said on the scene. I want a phone number traced. Felicity, what's that bloody phone number?"

She told him.

Tipton looked at her. "What was that?"

Felicity repeated the number.

Tipton told the phone never mind about the number. "And I

want an ambulance called round—Miss Grace is going back in hospital." He hung up.

"No," Felicity said.

Tipton didn't seem to hear her. "It's the same bloody number. Our American friend beat a phone number out of Dave Hamilton early tonight, and it's the same bloody one."

Felicity's head hurt. "He did *what* to Dave Hamilton?"

"It must be important, with Calvin's risking leaks from *two* sources."

"*What happened to Dave Hamilton?*" Felicity fairly screamed it. She had to get a grip on herself. She had to get some clothes. Her feet were freezing, and the bottom of her robe was soaking from the walk from Stingley's car.

Tipton told her about Dave Hamilton, and that settled it. Her no when the subject of going back to hospital had come up had been reflex—now she was adamant. She was *not* getting in the ambulance; she was coming with him. It was her fault, and she was determined to fix it. She had too much invested in this case, she said. An eye, for instance.

Tipton never actually acquiesced. Felicity simply announced her intentions, ran down to Disguises and Wardrobes, and dressed herself. Thick socks, lace-up boots. A workman's jumpsuit over her nakedness. A scarf, and an anorak like the one Bellman had been wearing. She felt like a bloody paratrooper.

A glance at Natalie's makeup mirror showed her that her bandage had come loose, dangling from a bit of adhesive stuck to her eyebrow. She pulled it the rest of the way off and had a look in the mirror. The socket of her left eye looked like a recent wound, but it wasn't bleeding. Grunter hadn't damaged her as much as she feared.

Felicity couldn't help noticing what it did to her face, that red mess collapsing in on itself in the middle of it. Her other eye burned with held-back tears until Felicity told herself there was work to do and put it from her mind. She found the first aid kit, and taped a gauze pad in place over the hole, doing, she told herself, fully as good a job of it as any doctor could.

She returned to Tipton to find him trying to get into his greatcoat while speaking on the phone. Stingley was in the room now, with the air of a man who has won a point. He gave Felicity a thumbs-up sign as she entered the office.

"*Bugger* the Special Branch," Tipton said. "We are not telling the Special Branch. They have the power to make arrests, fine. We'll call them to make their precious arrests as soon as we get this sorted out. Now, get moving. We'll be in the lobby."

Tipton hung up the phone. "If we *can* get this mess sorted out," he mumbled. He looked up at Stingley and Felicity. "Do either of you know what the hell's become of Bellman?"

Silence.

"I didn't think so. We have him to thank for this. Him and the rest of the bloody Americans."

The bloody Americans had occupied conversation in the command car until they started spotting the Russians. The Section people were in four cars—two people in each, except for the command car, which carried a driver, Tipton, and the two interlopers. Three of the cars reported over the radio that they had seen men in parked cars in the immediate neighborhood of the Tombs, a neighborhood not likely to have much traffic at that time of night. (Stingley had been the one in Tipton's car to spot them, a fact that irritated the Acting Section Chief no end.)

The license numbers of the parked cars had been radioed in to the Tournament Press. Tipton, impatient, had just called back for results.

Which he got. They were the plate numbers of known or suspect KGB vehicles in London. Every one of them.

Tipton switched channels and spoke to his team. "All right. Talk to them. Hard. Approach C. Detain by force if necessary. As soon as you're free, rendezvous with my car at the target. Bring prisoners, or guests, we better call them." He clicked off, and spoke to Felicity in the back seat. "There, something for the Special Branch to do. We'll arrest them on arms charges. They'll all have diplomatic immunity, but it will make a nice splash for the newspapers." To the driver he said, "All right, enough mooching around. Target, now."

It took less than half a minute to get there, even with the snow. As they drove down the block toward the museum they saw a car parked directly in front of it.

"Of all the cheek . . ." Stingley breathed.

The streetlamp reflecting from the snow lit the scene like daylight. As soon as they showed signs of stopping, a figure dashed from the doorway of the Tombs and jumped into the car, which sped off, throwing a rooster tail of snow behind it.

"Follow them," Tipton ordered.

"*No!*" Felicity said. "Stop the car!"

"Are you mad?" Tipton began, but Felicity cut him off.

"It's a *decoy*," she said. "They're still inside."

"Of course they are," Stingley said. "It's an old cracksman's trick. A confederate leads the coppers a merry chase, and you arrest him for reckless driving, or some other heinous crime, while the other waltzes away with the swag."

"All right," Tipton said. "But it may not be." He asked the driver if he could still catch the fleeing car.

"Sure. He'll be a wreck if he keeps to that speed on these roads."

"We'll split up. You chase him, the three of us will go inside."

Tipton had the driver wait only long enough to get something from the boot, then took off in pursuit of the other car.

Stingley grinned when he saw it. "Handy," he said. "Metal jaws, like the fire brigade use. Powerful. I was wondering how we were going to get inside through oak doors, but that thing will have them open like a tin of sardines."

"That was the idea," Tipton told him. He handed the machine to the policeman. "Here, you invited yourself, earn your keep."

Stingley blew on his gloveless hands to warm them, then took the metal jaws. He was about to ask where Miss Grace was, but a quick look around showed that she was already at the door, touching it with flat palms as if she intended to push it in single-handed.

Tipton and Stingley ran to join her.

247

4

When Bellman found the way in, it was so easy it made him suspicious. It was a louvered wall vent, set nearly flush with the slope of the road that ran alongside the building. When he tried the cover experimentally, it came free. The fan blades and the machinery that ran them swung away on a hinge. Silently, as though the hinge had been newly oiled.

The opening was a comfortable fit. There was even a chair placed on the floor below the opening to make it easier to get down.

Bellman took a second to figure out what the hell was going on. If it was a trap, it hadn't been designed especially for him, since no one had known he was going to be there. Not even him. Especially not him.

Then he realized what was going on. All this hadn't been arranged to make it easy for Bellman to get in. It had been designed to aid someone in getting *out*. Someone, for instance, who expected the place to be under surveillance. Someone who was concluding some kind of deal with some kind of foreign power . . .

Bellman coughed, and cursed himself for making the noise. The air was fairly pungent here, even with the vent. He sniffed tentatively, and fought the urge to cough again. It didn't smell like tear gas, or anything he'd smelled before, but then, you only smelled the lethal ones once. Maybe this *was* a trap.

His eyes had adjusted to the darkness by now, and he looked around. What he saw was chemical tanks and air pumping machinery. Taped to one of the control panels was a recipe for "Simulated Smog," which settled that.

Bellman opened a wooden door, and found himself stepping

onto damp cobblestones. A sign over his head read THE BOAR'S HEAD, with a clumsily executed painting to match.

A London bobby stood about three feet away.

Relax, Bellman told himself after the initial shock. This is a *wax museum*, remember? In the dimness of the emergency lights he could see other figures now, including one of a shabbily dressed woman looking backward over her shoulder in fear. A Jack the Ripper tableau, no doubt. Someday they'd do something about the Sussex Cyclops. Bellman smiled. And fought another cough.

Foul-smelling mist swirled around his knees, probably the Simulated Smog settling out of the air now that the machinery was cut off. It was bad enough. It stung his eyes, the inside of his nose. Bellman realized that people used to live with this as a matter of course.

He also realized he couldn't stay in here. It was a shame, because his best move, the high-percentage move, was simply to stay by the window until the one who'd prepared the way out (presumably Leo Calvin) tried to leave. That wouldn't work if Bellman were busy coughing, or wiping teary eyes. He couldn't wait outside, either. If the place was under surveillance, by the Russians say, or even the British, at least some of it would be the moving sort, and the dullest of lookouts could spot a man standing in a snowstorm watching a ventilating duct.

He'd have to go to them, whoever they were. He reached inside his jacket and took out his gun.

Bellman walked through the Torture Room, the Execution Room, the Black Magic Room, and the Human Sacrifice Room. He was amazed at how phony it all looked in the darkness—he would have supposed it would be spookier. He kept walking in the direction opposite the one indicated by the arrows, figuring that would take him back to the entrance. There would be maps there, and his search would be a lot easier. It would be easier still if he'd thought to bring a flashlight.

The flashlight question soon became irrelevant. Bellman heard the voices while he was still in the Human Sacrifice Room. Leo Calvin's voice. And Bulanin's. Bingo.

Still, he couldn't just run in there and tell them they were under arrest. He couldn't jump in guns blazing, either. Cold War politics aside, he had no way of knowing if they'd be close enough together for him to shoot both before one of them got him.

He walked carefully across the room, keeping well to the side to avoid being seen through the open door to the entrance foyer. He avoided the splash of light that fanned out on the stone floor as if it were a pool of acid. He dodged iron pots (South Seas) and stone altars (Druids). He made it at last to the doorway, got down low to the floor, and took a peek.

Leo Calvin, all right. And Bulanin. And two others, who weren't speaking at the moment. One was a black man in a pirate outfit. Bellman recognized him as the skater from the Kensington Gardens. A closer friend of Leo's than he'd let on, it seemed. Bellman remembered with anger that he'd given the bastard five pounds.

The other silent one was, unless Bellman was horribly mistaken, the elusive Sir Lewis Alfot. He was shabbily dressed, and he wore different spectacles from the ones Bellman had seen in the hotel corridor in Brighton. The remaining wisps of a fake beard hung from his chin.

If the old man hadn't been standing upright, and passing a furtive tongue over his lips every once in a while, Bellman might have taken him for a corpse. Except for the tongue, his face was motionless. His eyes were wide and unblinking. He might have been drugged, but if you were going to drug a man in a situation like that, you might as well put him out and have done with it. And if you were going to drug someone, you should at least give him something reliable enough so that you don't have to cuff his hands together behind his back.

And, as long as he was asking questions, how the hell had Sir Lewis come to be back in Leo's custody in the first place? No wonder there had been no ad in *The Times* addressed to The Captain.

Bellman stopped thinking of questions. He could get his answers once he had this all straightened out.

As soon as he figured out how it was going to *get* straightened out. It was going to be a little complicated.

As he'd feared, he couldn't do all the shooting he needed to do with any assurance of success—the men were scattered across

too wide a range. Bellman had to figure that everybody but Sir
Lewis had a gun. He could see the black man's. And there was
no way he could shoot anybody without making himself a
perfect target in the doorway.

He'd have to shoot the black man first, since he had his gun
out, but in order to do that, he'd have to make the best target of
himself. . . .

He ran through all his possible first moves as he watched Leo
Calvin take money from a large valise chained to Bulanin's wrist
and stuff it into a canvas suitcase. Bellman knew that when the
money was done changing hands, the party was over, and he
would have to act. All he had to do was decide which way gave
him the least chance of dying before he accomplished anything.

Going back to the window, he decided, was out. Not only
would it take too long to get there (an ambush was no good if
you set it up just two steps ahead of the arrival of the person you
wanted to ambush), but there was no guarantee that that was the
only way Leo had prepared to get out. He might even decide to
walk out the front door, arm-in-arm with his pal the Agricultural Attaché.

So he'd have to do something. Now. He decided he'd shoot
Leo and take his chances with Bulanin and the black man. If you
were going to get killed in the line of duty, you might as well get
a little personal satisfaction out of it.

Bellman fixed his eyes on Leo, in case he moved before the big
jump. The idea was to spring into the opening, set, fire, hit the
ground, roll, and come up shooting again. Bellman released the
safety of his gun, easing it off so it wouldn't click. He took a
deep, silent breath, got quietly into a crouch, and tensed his leg
muscles under him.

Then there was a sharp, booming sound as the door knocker
crashed into the heavy oaken door.

5

Bellman froze in his crouch. This could change everything. He held his breath and listened.

"What the hell is that?" the black man demanded.

"A signal," Bulanin said. "There is trouble for my men in the neighborhood. Have you betrayed me again, Calvin?"

"You don't think that yourself," Leo said. "You're not going for your gun."

"And have your friend here shoot me? I know I've given you evidence to the contrary, but I am not a total fool."

Leo smiled. "Just because I've had you going, it doesn't mean you're a fool. You didn't even flinch."

"I suggest we finish and get moving," Bulanin said. "Someone is out there. I presume there are other ways to leave here."

"Several," Leo said. He stuffed the last of the money into his suitcase and zipped it closed. "I'll show you out. Pleasure doing business with you. I assume you have a car planted nearby so that you can get away with our friend here."

Bulanin smiled. "Several," he said. "Shall we go? There is a disguise expert at the Embassy waiting for Sir Lewis, and an official plane ready to bring us back to Moscow."

"I'm traveling, too. Benton, if anyone comes in here, police, or whoever, you don't know anything, you were just closing up and going home."

"That's just what I was doing, mon," the Jamaican said, and he grinned.

"Good. You've got your money; spend it in good health." Leo picked up the suitcase and shook his head. "It was tough, but it was worth it. If only I had Driscoll in front of me now, this night would be perfect."

Bellman heard his old name, the name Leo had first heard of

him under, and watched Leo head straight for the door of the Human Sacrifice Room, where Bellman waited for him.

Now Bellman smiled.

It was the door again that upset the plan. This time there was a roar and a crash, and that heavy oak door splintered like a strawberry box. Through the opening Bellman saw DI Maurice Stingley wielding power jaws like a lumberjack. Behind him was Mr. Robert Tipton. And shining above both of them was the copper-colored hair of Miss Felicity Grace, her eye blazing with blue sparks as she waited for action.

And what the hell is she doing here? Bellman thought, then realized the question was silly. This was the cavalry arriving, British-style.

And all hell broke loose.

6

The first thing Felicity saw when the door gave way was a black man with a gun, who promptly shot Tipton, who had dashed past Stingley, in the stomach. As the Acting Director went down, Stingley and Felicity dove in opposite directions into the snow to get out of the line of fire.

Felicity drew her gun and waited; Stingley, in the fine tradition of the British police, was unarmed. The black man stuck his head out through the hole in the door, but pulled it back, turtlelike, when Felicity snapped off a quick round at him.

Felicity counted to ten, then edged along the door to the opening. She waited there, listening. Hearing nothing.

A voice croaked, "All clear. Felicity. All clear."

She didn't see how it could be a trap (who but Tipton would know her name?) but she had her gun ready as she jumped into the opening. She kept it ready as she knelt beside the Acting Director.

"Alfot is here," Tipton said. "I saw him. He ran off . . . ran off when the door splintered. Other two chased him. That's"—he coughed—"that's all I saw before he fired. Blacked out for a second."

Tipton tried to grin. "First bloody field operation I've been on in twenty-eight years, and I get shot like a bloody amateur. Maybe the Americans are right."

"How are you?" Felicity asked.

"Shot in the bloody stomach. I could be dead in five . . . five minutes. Or it may be nothing. But sod that. The black went through that door." He tried to raise a hand to point, and failed. He grinned again, and indicated the direction with his eyes. Felicity followed the gaze to another oaken door, normal-sized this time, that opened into a room shaped like a boot box nestled against the front wall of the Tombs.

"Why did he go in there?" Felicity asked. "There are no windows, no way out."

"It's some sort of control room. I don't know what he's doing in there." Tipton moved his head, groaned, spoke. "Stingley."

"Yes?"

"There's a gun in my right coat pocket. I—I'm lying on it, and it's quite uncomfortable. Would you take it out, please?"

"It would be a pleasure, guv," Stingley said. He removed the gun, gave it a quick, expert examination.

"Guard the door," Felicity told the policeman. "Shoot anybody that comes this way but Bellman."

Stingley raised his eyebrows. "And Alfot. Tipton said Alfot was here. This is Sir Lewis Alfot, right? I've been looking for him for weeks; I'm not going to shoot him. You just forgot about him, right?"

Felicity looked at him.

Stingley said, "Right?"

Felicity said, "Ask him." She pointed to Tipton and walked off toward the door of the control room. She stayed well to the side.

"Open the door," she said. "Gun out first, then you. You've got one chance. Twenty seconds." Felicity began to count silently.

Benton should have run. He knew he should have run. But how could he leave that money, all that beautiful money? It was his ticket home, where it was warm, even the rain was warm. And he was a man there, not a bloody nig-nog. With the money, he would be a *big* man. He could buy what he wanted when he wanted. He could make a woman happy out of bed as well as in.

All he had to do was get there with the money. And here he was, trapped like a bird in a box. Stupid, Benton, stupid.

Then it came to him. He was thinking like a poor man, but he was rich now. The money Leo had given him, that he had locked up safe here in the control room. It was here now. It was his. He would do what a rich man would do—he would *buy* his way out of trouble.

He had to decide how much to offer. A fifth of what he had? A third? Half?

He would offer a third, and go to half if he had to. He could still live like a king on half. He couldn't spend half of what he had in his whole life.

"Hey, wait!" he yelled through the door. "I've got money! A lot of mon—"

There was a crack and a zip and the bag of money sprung a leak. Benton held it close to him to protect it. More noise, another hole in the door, then another, then more. Benton tried to shout, but he was too busy dodging. Or rather, trying to dodge. In the small room there was really nowhere to go.

Felicity used the second to last bullet on the door lock. A glance inside the control room showed her she wouldn't need the last one. She reached inside and pulled the bag of money out of the man's arms and placed it on a desk.

She thought she heard Stingley's voice somewhere behind her saying Jesus Bloody Christ, but she paid no attention. This was nightmare day. She'd killed three men so far, and might have to kill more. If she took the time to be horrified about it, she'd end up dead, too.

She called back to Stingley to ask how Tipton was.

"Still conscious. He says you're a cold-blooded bitch and good show." Stingley swallowed.

Felicity began to reload. "This is where we see how honest you are, Stingley," she said.

"What do you mean by that?"

"There's a fortune in American dollars in here. What he came back for."

She finished reloading; she didn't wait for a reply. She stepped back into the control room, studied a panel for a few moments, then started pulling switches. If she were heading off on a one-eyed search for a terrorist, two spies, and a maniac, she would bloody well do it in the light.

7

Now things were getting spooky. Someone had put the lights on a few seconds ago, and Bellman was seeing the waxwork the way it was meant to be seen. The dim, yellow-tinted light raked the displays, so that things that had looked phony before were now hidden in ominous shadows, and the things that looked real were highlighted.

Bellman had heard gunfire behind him as he'd sprinted from the foyer. Undoubtedly the cavalry shooting it out with Benton. The reason he hadn't stayed where he was and caught the man in a crossfire was that the minute the door had started to crack, Sir Lewis Alfot had taken off on a sprint down another wing. Since (Bellman was almost proud of himself for remembering this) the original object of the exercise had been to retrieve Sir Lewis, Bellman had cut across and taken off after him.

He hadn't cut across fast enough, it seemed. Leo Calvin said, "Bellman," and, disregarding Bulanin's rapid demands for explanation, had taken off in pursuit.

Bellman wasn't going to make it easy for him. He kept pulling things over behind him, blocking the path as he ran by.

It was easy enough to follow Sir Lewis by sound. An old man runs, if he can run at all, heavily. An old man with his hands cuffed behind his back runs very heavily. Bellman followed through the Witch-Burning Room (upsetting a cauldron into the path) and through the Spanish Inquisition Room, where he pulled over a rack.

Then the lights went on. And everything else. Bellman had been running too close to an animated headsman when the power cut on; he almost lost his nose to the upswing of an executioner's ax. Bellman jumped away, but he managed to stop himself from crying out. He looked behind him. He saw nothing, but heard the metallic clang and the curse as someone tripped over the cauldron. That gave him some idea of how far behind him the pursuit was. Unfortunately, it was the last time it was likely to happen. The lights were dim, and brought no comfort—the opposite of comfort. But they gave enough light for a man to avoid an obstacle in his path.

The place was haunted with sound, now, too. Groans and screams and demonic laughter. Angry questions in Spanish about renouncing heresies. Too much noise, too loud for him to hear Sir Lewis anymore.

Bellman fought panic, forced himself to think. Leo Calvin and Bulanin were getting closer and closer, and he was accomplishing nothing. He thought of laying an ambush, and looked around for a good place, but found nothing. Nothing he could climb on, or under, or hide behind.

He decided to press on. He'd seen lots of good places before; there had to be something farther along.

And there was. Not an ambuscade, but a signpost, a little more elaborate than the usual arrows. This one offered a choice—THE WORLD OF FAERIE OR MODERN WARFARE.

It was to easy to guess the choice of the man who'd kept that little silver cup. Bellman headed toward Modern Warfare on the run. He might catch up to Sir Lewis yet.

8

Sir Lewis Alfot had known it was going to come to this. He must have known. Why else, in what he thought was his moment of triumph, would he have kept the foolish spectacles when he'd shed the false beard? Why had he even prepared the spectacles in the first place? True, he had been about to use them on the enquiry agent, but when an alternative had presented itself, he had used it gladly. It was almost as if he had been *saving* them for something.

He knew why, now. The Sussex Cyclops had been born to show the nation they had lost their vision, that they had turned a blind eye to the real cause of their problems. And the spectacles were symbolic of that. But why, then hadn't he used them?

And why, he told himself angrily, now that he *had* decided to use them, didn't he bloody well get on with it? Why did he keep lumbering down this bloody waxwork, with the yellow lights leering at him, and the moans chasing him?

Because he was looking for the right place.

And all at once he found it. He found it by sound, a sound anyone who'd been in London toward the end of the war knew, a rude, buzzing noise. A doodlebug. A buzz bomb. German V-1. His father had died under one. As long as the buzzing went on, you were all right. When it stopped—

It stopped now, and Sir Lewis nearly dove for cover. It was another noise that stopped him, a whistling sound, the stereotypical falling bomb. They hadn't sounded like that. There was the buzzing, then an ominous, horrid silence, then the explosion. There it was now, the blast, and a lighting effect of smoke and flame that was quite good. But they'd tried to be dramatic, with that whistling sound, and had ruined it.

Sir Lewis looked around him. It was familiar, and well done (a

258

shame about that bloody whistling). There was the rubble, and the distant flames. People, weary after five years of war and more, going about their business with a grim determination. The sirens. The buzzing.

A placard placed unobtrusively in a corner told him where and when this was supposed to be, but Sir Lewis didn't need to be told. He knew. He knew firsthand.

Then, as if in mockery of the thought, he saw the hand. A waxwork hand, crusted in artificial grime, sticking out palm up from a pile of fake rubble. And Sir Lewis started to weep.

"I'm sorry," he said. "I'm sorry." He was not apologizing to a wax hand, but to the people it represented. A people who stood alone against Hitler for a long, tough time. Who persevered. Who *won*—and knew they would. He apologized to them on behalf of a people who now lived in the ruins of a broken Empire and a decaying Welfare State, who felt—and acted—second-best. Who killed each other over played-out coal mines.

Sir Lewis wept because he knew now he had somehow passed from membership in the first group to the second. He had tried to awaken something in his countrymen, and had failed. Then he had tried to take symbolic revenge on the jackals that fed on his country's misery, the buzzards that flew about, pecking at the Lion's eyes. And he had failed.

There was only one thing left he could do—sacrifice himself to the Spirit of the Nation. Here, in front of a tawdry tribute to it, he could give the last thing he had to give. Because the spirit still lived. He knew it did. It had to. The reason he had failed to fan it in the people was that he no longer had it himself. He could be of no more help in the necessary—the *inevitable* rebuilding of the nation. After a lifetime of serving his country, the only thing he had left to do was to get out of the way.

Sir Lewis knelt near the wax hand. He bent as far forward as he could without being able to use his hands for balance, and shook his head. The spectacles came loose and skittered along the false paving. Sir Lewis made his way over to them on his knees. He bent over once more, and took the glasses in his mouth by the end of the mended sidebar. A few more shakes of the head, and the mend came apart. Sir Lewis spat out the useless earpiece, and made his way again toward the spectacles. It hurt his knees, but the pain would be only temporary.

Sir Lewis was glad to see that the spectacles had landed lenses down, with the sidebars unfolded. The point gleamed in the dull light, the point he had carefully made himself with a penknife and piece of sandpaper. It was sharp enough to have drawn blood from an experimental fingertip. It was plenty sharp enough to do the job now.

All it took was the courage. Which, he found to his shock, he seemed to lack.

He had never hated himself so much as he did in that moment. He had done it to others, now he was too much a coward to do it to himself. Coward, he told himself. Hypocrite. And still, he looked at the point as if it were the fang of a snake. And he would not embrace it.

Then the American came in. Sir Lewis looked up and saw him. What is he doing here? Sir Lewis thought irrelevantly.

The American said his name.

Lewis Alfot was damned if some bloody American would see him in his shame. That would not be allowed to happen. The old man managed a smile, looked the American in the eye, said, "Thank you, Yank," and threw himself forward.

At the end, Lewis Alfot's aim was true.

9

It was over before Bellman could stop it, before he even knew there was anything *to* stop. The old man lay twitching for a few seconds, then he lay still.

"Son of a bitch," Bellman said. He wasted a few seconds thinking. "Son of a bitch," he said again.

This was probably the best solution as far as the Section was concerned. And it also opened up some interesting possibilities in regard to the Russian, and the other American. Especially the other American.

First, though, he had to keep them from killing him. He turned his back on the fallen knight, and started back toward his pursuers.

Leo Calvin shot him.

Triumph. At times like this, it was hard for Leo to remember he had ever been afraid of anything. It was going his way, now. He hadn't even wanted to shoot from this distance; he never had been a very good shot. But Bellman probably was, and Bellman was turning; he'd see Leo in a second, better shoot now, if only to keep him from getting off a shot at you.

And to Leo's amazement and delight Bellman had grabbed at his thigh and gone down, and, under buzzes, whistles, and explosions, there had been the clatter of a gun skittering across the floor. Of course, the femoral artery is in the thigh, and if Leo had hit that, there was nothing more to worry about. If he hadn't, though, there was no time to waste. He hurried toward the spot where the American had fallen. Even if he *had* hit the artery, he wanted to hurry. He wanted to be there in time to see Bellman—or Driscoll—bleed to death.

When he got there, Leo was glad he'd hurried. The blood was oozing from his leg, not spurting, which meant that so far as that particular wound was concerned, Bellman might live for years.

Bellman was, in fact, dragging himself across the floor toward the gun. Leo ran to it, kicked it away. He could feel the smile on his face.

He raised his own gun, pointed it at Bellman's head.

"Beg, Driscoll," Leo said. "Come on, beg."

Bellman said nothing.

It was foolish, Leo knew. He was never emotional about his work before. But he was proud of it, and Driscoll had been the only one who'd ever thwarted him. Leo tightened his grip on the gun. That close, he couldn't miss.

"No!" Bulanin said. He fired a shot to make sure he had Leo's attention. He wanted to see how far this terrorist maniac would go, or, rather, he didn't want to interrupt him if he was going in the right direction.

But he was not, and Bulanin, who had arrived just as Leo was kicking away Bellman's gun, had decided to intervene.

Leo Calvin looked at Bulanin. Bulanin leveled his gun at the terrorist.

"I'm going to kill him," Leo said.

"Of course," Bulanin said. His irritation showed in his voice. He had had quite enough of Leo Calvin by now. "But I do not propose to have run all the risks I have run for nothing. That knock on the door means nothing. Men from Alfot's Section have apparently arrived already. To say nothing of the Special Branch, or even the CIA for all I know."

"Then I'll kill him, and show you the way out of here. Right away."

"I said no. We will make him tell us where Alfot is, or make sure he doesn't know. *Then* we will kill him. Then you will show me *and Alfot* a safe way out of here."

Bulanin spoke to the figure on the floor, who had lain silent through all this, except for an occasional grunt of pain. "There will be much more pain before it's over, Mr. Bellman. Unless you talk. Then it will be painless, I promise." Bulanin looked at his watch. An American-made watch. "You have ten seconds before we begin."

Bulanin listened. He heard a buzz. Then a whistle. Then an explosion. Then laughter.

Bellman laughed while he got himself propped up on one elbow. The situation was such that he would have laughed anyway, but it turned out to be the right move. It unsettled Bulanin and Calvin. It gained him an extra seven or eight seconds. And during those seconds, two important things happened—Felicity Grace showed up, and Bellman figured out what he was supposed to do.

Felicity stood in the doorway. She looked beautiful—a wild, one-eyed warrior princess. She had her gun up, leveled at the back of Bulanin's head.

Bellman was the only one in the room who could see her. He looked at her significantly, chuckled, and slowly shook his head.

"It's all right," he said. "No need to get nasty. I'll tell you where Alfot is."

"Tell me, then," Bulanin said.

"Over there." Bellman gestured with his head toward the pile of rubble farther into the room. "That's no wax dummy. Not a victim of the blitz."

Buzz. Whistle. Explosion. "There it is again," Bellman said. "If Hitler could have brought them over this fast, he would have won. Anyway, that's the mortal remains of Sir Lewis Alfot. He's the last victim of the Sussex Cyclops."

Leo said it was a lie, and began to elaborate, but Bulanin told him to shut up. He walked over to the body, his gun trained on Leo the whole time. It was like a broken daisy chain. Leo covered Bellman, Bulanin covered Leo, Felicity covered Bulanin. He still hadn't seen her. From the corner of his eye Bellman could see Felicity's arms swing to keep the gun centered on the Russian.

Bulanin turned the body over with his toe. He grimaced as he saw the eyeglasses sticking out from the man's eye, like a surrealist joke.

"He is dead," Bulanin said.

Bellman nodded. He tried to ignore how much his leg hurt.

"Changes everything, doesn't it?" Bellman said.

Indeed it did, and Bulanin knew it. He had to think. He thought for the space of two buzz bombs. The noise didn't bother him. Leo Calvin's screaming that it was all Bellman's fault didn't bother him. He simply filtered it out. Besides, it didn't matter whose fault it was. All that mattered was what Bulanin was going to do now.

He couldn't filter Bellman out, somehow, but that didn't matter, because Bellman only echoed Bulanin's own thoughts.

"Sure, you could kill me," Bellman said. "And diplomatic immunity might get you out of it. But you'll never escape detection. Too many people know you were here, and more will be told before you can get away. The folks back home might throw you to the dogs, turn you over to British Justice, just to avoid an international mess. That wouldn't be the worst thing that could happen. You might be sent home to Moscow. Want to bet what will happen then?"

Bulanin did not need to bet what would happen then. He would be brought to Borzov. Borzov would not be pleased. He would, in fact, be disappointed. Even angry.

Bulanin wished he had a cigarette.

Bellman spoke again, again echoing Bulanin's own thoughts. "But it doesn't have to be that way. *You can be the man who caught the Sussex Cyclops.* Tragically, too late to prevent the murder of the beloved Sir Lewis, but . . ."

Bulanin knew nothing of the Sussex Cyclops aside from what he read in the newspapers, but the rest of what Bellman said made undeniable sense.

"You have a candidate perhaps?"

Bellman raised himself up a little higher, wincing with pain as he did so. "Well, the Sussex cops are already looking for a certain American—not me—in connection with a murder . . ."

Leo Calvin made his way back into Bulanin's consciousness by the very volume and desperation of his screams. "*No!*" he screamed. "*No, you slippery bastard! Not again!*"

Calvin's finger began to tighten on the trigger. Bulanin wasn't through thinking yet; he was quite through with Mr. Calvin. He fired.

Calvin stayed on his feet a remarkably long time. Bulanin, preoccupied as he was with casting a whole new plan for his future, facing the fact that he would now never be Chairman, would never, in fact, see his homeland again, was impressed. He fired four times before Calvin fell, and even after he fell, the terrorist was still making noises. Bulanin walked over and planted one more in his head.

Part of Bellman wanted to be elated that Leo Calvin was out of his hair for good, but there were still too many things to worry about. He thought of reaching for the gun in Leo's hand, but decided Bulanin was likely to take it the wrong way. The Russian was dazed, acting on instinct.

Bellman said, "Again."

Bulanin blinked. "I beg your pardon?"

"Shoot him again."

"Oh," Bulanin said, and obliged. Leo's body jumped. "I don't think that last one was really necessary."

"I do," Bellman said. "It's empty now. Felicity, come in here and tie him up, in case he gets second thoughts."

Felicity sprinted over and went to work on the Russian. As she searched him, she looked at Bellman. "You're bloody amazing," she said.

Bulanin asked her for a cigarette.

10

Felicity talked to Stingley while Bellman, listening to no counsel but his own, limped off into the control room to use the telephone. Bulanin, who had apparently said all he'd had to say in a whispered conversation while he helped Bellman back to the foyer, stood silent beside her while she explained to Stingley that for the record, he had worked with Bulanin and had cracked the Sussex Cyclops case. He was to tell the Special Branch as much when they arrived.

"Right," Stingley said. "I don't know what any of this is about—"

Felicity said, "The Cyclops was Leo Calvin, the international terrorist. He was in the pay of an as yet unknown terrorist group. The Soviets learned about his activities, but for reasons of their own, decided not to tell us—

"But Mr. Bulanin here had his conscience bother him, and came to me, and we tracked him here and found him with this Benton, who was also a member of the terrorist group, and together we fought them. Bulanin shot Calvin, but not before he did for Sir Lewis Alfot. Though why *he* was here, *nobody* knows. Right so far?"

Bulanin offered a smile. "Perfect," he said.

"Bulanin has now gone off with a high government official, and more will be expected later. All right. I've given more reports than you've had hot dinners, my girl."

Felicity was tired, and her head hurt. "Then what is it you don't understand?" she asked.

"Why we're cooking up this pack of lies."

"National security," Felicity said. Stingley grunted.

Felicity went on, "And, you get to give the Yard, from the Special Branch on down, a kick in the arse. And you get the credit for cracking the case."

"You've talked me into it."

Robert Tipton groaned. He was unconscious now, his head pillowed by Stingley's jacket. His lips were pale, and despite the cold, a thin film of sweat shone on his forehead.

"That's shock," Stingley said. "He lost consciousness just before you got back here. What's taking Bellman so long about that bloody ambulance? How difficult is it to dial 999?"

Felicity was beginning to wonder herself, but it was only a few seconds before Bellman dragged his leg over to them.

"Ambulance should be here in a few minutes, and the Special Branch should make it sooner than that. Let's go."

Stingley looked at him, then at Felicity. "Ridiculous," he said. "You should go with Tipton to hospital, both of you. You've had your head knocked around by some thug, and you've got a bullet in your leg."

"Fortunately not," Bellman said. "Two holes. Went right through."

"It'll turn septic," Stingley said ominously. Felicity was sure he'd heard his mother say it just that way.

"Well, get going then. You're crazy, the lot of you."

Bellman insisted on driving the car. He said driving one-legged was something he did all the time, whereas she wasn't yet used to driving one-eyed. Once again, Felicity gave in.

Felicity sat in the back seat with Bulanin. She kept him covered while the Russian sat with his back in the corner, to avoid crushing his hands, which were now manacled behind him with the handcuffs he had used on Sir Lewis.

266

Bulanin wanted to talk. "It has stopped snowing, I see. That's good. The sky is very clear."

Bellman said the snow on the roads still made it hard to drive. Felicity ignored them both. She was busy wondering how she felt about Sir Lewis. She had seen him lying there with the spectacles sticking out of his eye, and for the first time, she could form a clear picture of what she must have looked like when Sir Lewis had attacked her. She had honored Sir Lewis, respected him. And he turned out to have been a monster.

Or at least partly a monster. Dr. Jekyll and Mr. Hyde sprang to mind. The truth would be easy to deal with, she decided. Sir Lewis had split in two, and the maniac had destroyed the great man.

Bellman drove around for a long time. "This isn't the way to the Tournament Press," she said at one point.

"I know what I'm doing," Bellman said. Then, softening, he said, "Stingley was right, you know. We both should have some medical attention."

"Especially you," Felicity said.

"Especially me. Before it turns septic." For some reason they smiled together, and Bellman drove on. He got no closer to the Tournament Press, and he didn't seem interested in stopping at any hospitals either.

"Where are we going?" Felicity demanded. "Don't go onto the bridge—dammit, you've taken us back to the South Bank of the Thames again."

"That's easily fixed," Bellman said.

"I want to get Bulanin back to headquarters and start his processing."

"I haven't said I'm defecting, you know," Bulanin put in.

"You have no choice," Felicity told him. "After Stingley speaks to the press, you'd be a dead man if you tried to go back."

"Perhaps you're right," Bulanin said. "Incidentally, I must tell you I find your natural hair color much more appealing."

How about my eyes? Felicity thought. Instead, she said, "You know I'm right."

Bellman suddenly turned off onto a drive, said a few words to an attendant at a gate, and drove through.

Felicity wanted to know what he was doing. This was the Westland Heliport, for God's sake. What could he possibly . . . ?

The question was answered by a flutter of rotor blades as a helicopter descended out of the cold, clear night sky and toward the landing pad. The machine was silver, and it bore the words UNITED STATES ARMY.

Felicity said, "No, you don't."

"Yes, I do," Bellman said. "I'm sorry, Felicity."

"You can't!"

"I have to." He opened the door and struggled to his feet. He limped around the side of the car to let Bulanin out. Bellman kept marking his path through the snow with red spots as blood dripped from his leg.

"I won't allow it," Felicity insisted. "He's ours!"

"Then, goddammit, *shoot* me and take him!" He spread his arms. "Come on. It would be a favor to me. Come *on*, do it!"

For a split-second, Felicity was going to do it. In the next, she knew she never could, and in the one after that came the knowledge that he'd known all along she wouldn't be able to.

"You *bastard*," she said.

Bellman helped the Russian out of the car. He kept talking as he did so.

"I'm sorry, Felicity, really. I hate this job, and I'd give anything to be able to stop doing it, but when I'm stuck with it, I have to do it right."

Felicity was silent. All she had in her mind was *you bastard*, and she didn't like to repeat herself.

"What's inside Bulanin's head is priceless. As valuable to our side as what Sir Lewis knew would have been to the Russians. I can't afford to—"

"Can't afford to *what*?" Felicity spat. "Trust him to a bunch of incompetents like us?"

"I didn't say that."

Bulanin spoke up. "*I* wanted it this way, Miss Grace. I feel much safer in the hands of the Americans. I know the sources my people—my former people—can reach in London. I, too, am sorry."

Felicity told them both to go to hell.

The helicopter was down, now. Felicity, almost in spite of

herself, got out of the car and followed them toward it. As they approached, a door slid open, and a white-haired, rugged-faced old man smiled out at them.

"I'll be a son of a bitch," the old man yelled against the roar of the engine. "I didn't believe you when I got your call, but here he is, by God."

So that's what took him so long to get an ambulance for Tipton, Felicity thought. He had to call his people first. It occurred to Felicity she might actually be setting eyes on the legendary Congressman. She did not feel especially privileged.

Then she got a surprise. "This is Miss Grace, of the Section. She's been instrumental in this whole operation, and she's here to insist that British interests be taken care of."

The old man looked at the young man, and Felicity could see quite a bit of similarity between them.

Strong American hands were pulling Bulanin into the helicopter. Before he disappeared, the Russian nodded at Felicity, then at Bellman, and said perhaps he would see them again.

The old man, meanwhile, had stopped grinning. "She's here to insist, is she?"

"That's right," Bellman said.

"And she's in a position to, ain't she? I mean, now that you let her get a good look at my face, so she can blow my cover if she feels she has to."

"Sorry, sir," Bellman deadpanned. "It never crossed my mind."

"I'll bet," the Congressman drawled. He turned to Felicity. "Well, don't you worry, miss. I'll see that British interests are protected. You'll have a representative there at any debriefing we do with him, provided it's you."

"Me?"

"You. Your friend here just staked his life on you, and he knows it. If he trusts you that much, you are the one. I'll be in touch with Tipton." Felicity started to tell him about Tipton's condition, but the old man spoke to Bellman. "What happened to your leg, boy?"

"Bullet," Bellman said.

"Get it attended to. It might get infected."

Bellman said, "Yes, sir. Right away." Felicity watched the

helicopter take off in a new mini-blizzard of blown snow, and tried to stop her head from whirling enough for her to make some sense of any of it.

Bellman stood beside her, laughing. That made the least sense of all.

EPILOGUE

In the midst of the word he was trying to say,
In the midst of his laughter and glee,
He had softly and suddenly vanished away—
For the Snark *was* a Boojum, you see.

—*The Hunting of the Snark*
Fit the Eighth

Bellman took a ride on the moving sidewalk at the airport. He noticed they'd filled in the bullet holes in the list of the cities.

He was walking with a cane now. Felicity had told him he looked ridiculously distinguished. He had to take antibiotics, and his leg had turned a lovely shade of purple around the wound, especially the exit wound, but he'd be all right.

It had been a strange operation. Crazy. Double-crosses, cross-purposes, purposeful doubling-back. A daisy chain of violence and death, the first link being formed in the brilliant mind of an old man who'd been disappointed about the way his countrymen had been behaving.

Bellman had been sent in to stir things up. Which he had. Had he ever. And Felicity had lost an eye, and Tipton had been shot in the stomach, and he'd been shot in the leg, and he'd lost count of how many had died. In a horrible way, it was all kind of funny.

The funniest thing about it was that it had been a big success. The whole operation had been a big success. The object of the exercise, way back in the dawn of time when he'd first arrived in England, had been to make sure Sir Lewis's report got delivered, to give clout to the effort to purge the moles from British Intelligence. The report was delivered. On schedule. Robert Tipton had spent his stay in the hospital putting it into palatable, but still hard-hitting form, and the report went out.

And looked likely to sweep all before it. After all, the beloved Sir Lewis himself had been murdered by the Sussex Cyclops, who now turned out to have been a terrorist working for some

273

enemy of the Realm. The old man tried to work things out, and they got him for it. Sir Lewis must not have died in vain!

Bulanin got to live. That was a lot less than he'd wanted, but a lot more than he deserved, considering the bullshit he'd let Leo Calvin get away with. They were setting him up in Washington, itching to ask him questions, but bound by the Congressman's promise to let him be until Felicity got there. That should be in about two weeks, when Tipton went back to work.

Dave Hamilton got to live, too. He was being groomed now as a conduit for false information to the Russians. His brother had a new, expensive doctor; Dave himself was going to start some important and exciting work. Considering he'd been expecting to be ground up for cattle feed or something, he couldn't believe his luck. Bellman knew that the day would come when Dave Hamilton would wish he *had* been ground up for cattle feed, but what the hell, let him enjoy it for now.

Bellman, meanwhile, was getting used to the idea that Leo Calvin was gone, that at this moment, there was no one in the world actively trying to hunt him down or kill him. He should feel great about it. Instead, he felt empty. It was stupid, and it made him angry, but that was the way he felt.

And there was Felicity. She hadn't actually forgiven him for spiriting Bulanin from under her nose. If she'd known he'd been in the control room at the Tombs calling his father at NATO headquarters in Belgium, she might have taken steps to prevent him. With Stingley there (Deputy Chief Inspector Stingley, he was now), she might have *had* to shoot him, to save face. Now only the two of them and Bulanin knew that she hadn't been ruthless enough to stop him.

They'd made love this morning, in the Tournament Press flat. The first time since Felicity'd lost her eye. It pained his leg, but it was worth it. Felicity was beautiful and tender and fierce. She kissed him, cursed him, cried. When it was over, she clung to him as if reluctant to let him go.

"If we were any other kind of people . . ." she said. It hadn't been necessary to finish. Bellman kissed her again.

"I get my false eye next week. I'll have it when I'm in Washington. They tell me they've matched the color perfectly."

"You're beautiful with it or without it," Bellman said.

274

"Spies are good liars. Will you be working on Bulanin?"

"No," Bellman said.

"Will I see you in Washington at all?"

"Maybe," he said. He didn't think he would; he didn't even think it was a good idea, but this wasn't the time to say so.

He kissed her instead, and kept kissing her until they were ready. This time when they were done, he held her until she went to sleep. Then he got dressed and went to the airport.

In the cab, he'd begun a mental draft of his report. The Congressman would examine his report; after that, he'd examine his head. It had been lunacy, first to last; madmen hunting madmen, using madmen as their tools.

Maybe it fit. Maybe the whole espionage world was like this, and since this operation was strictly an intramural Espionage Community affair, by spies, for spies, the essential madness of the enterprise stood out in stark relief.

The Snark Hunt. Well, Bellman had caught his Snark (though he wasn't entirely sure exactly who the Snark had been), but not before the Snark (or was it a Boojum?) had bitten everyone in sight. It was time for the Bellman to fade away. Time for the Congressman's son to find a new name, a new identity. A new life, or reasonable facsimile thereof.

The escalator dumped him out near the departure board. He'd already checked his bag. He read the gate number for his flight, and limped away toward the other moving sidewalk, the one that would take him there.

He'd strap himself in, and lean back. He wouldn't sleep— never when there was someone else around—but he would dream. And he'd let the plane take him back to whatever he could scrape up this time that might pass for home.

London–Paris, 1984